LAWMAN

DIANA PALMER

LAWMAN

HQN™

HQN™

ISBN-13: 978-0-373-77238-4
ISBN-10: 0-373-77238-6

LAWMAN

This edition published by arrangement with Harlequin Books S.A.

www.HQNBooks.com

Printed in U.S.A.

In memoriam

To Gene Burton,
Our neighbor, our friend.

1

THE OLD JACOBS PLACE was in disrepair. The last owner hadn't been big on maintenance, and now there was a leak in Garon's study. Right over his damned computer, in fact.

He glared at it from the doorway, elegantly dressed in a gray suit. He'd just arrived in Jacobsville from Washington, D.C., where he'd been taking a course at Quantico on homicide investigation. It was his new specialty, that area of law enforcement. Garon Grier was a career FBI man. He worked out of the San Antonio office, but he'd recently moved from an apartment there to this huge ranch in Jacobsville. His brother Cash was the Jacobsville police chief. The brothers had been alienated for some time. Cash had disowned his family over his father's remarriage just days after his beloved mother's death from cancer. That long feud had only just ended. Cash was newly, happily, married to Tippy Moore, the "Georgia Firefly" of modeling and motion picture fame. She had just had their first child, a little girl.

Cash thought the child was the crown jewels. To Garon, she looked more like a little red prune with flailing fists. But as the days passed, she did seem to grow prettier. Garon loved children. No one would ever have guessed it. He had a demeanor that was blunt and confrontational. He rarely smiled, and he was usually all business, even with women. Especially with women. He'd lost his one true love to cancer. It had eaten the heart out of him. Now, at thirty-six, he was resigned to being alone for the rest of his life. It was just as well, he decided, because he had nothing to give to a woman. He lived for his job. He would have liked a child of his own, though. A little boy would be nice. But he had no desire to risk his heart in pursuit of one.

Miss Jane Turner, the housekeeper he'd hired, came into the room behind him, her thin face resigned. "There aren't any construction people available until next week, Mr. Garon," she said in her Texas drawl. "We'd best put a bucket under it for now, I reckon, unless you want to climb up on the roof with a hammer and nails."

He gave her a superior look. "I don't climb up on roofs," he said flatly.

She looked him over in the suit. "That doesn't surprise me," she muttered, turning to go.

He gave her a shocked look. She must think he never wore anything but suits, when he'd grown up on a sprawling west Texas ranch. He could ride anything with four legs, and he'd won prizes in rodeo competitions in his teens. Now, he knew more about guns and investigation than he did about rodeo, but he could still run a ranch. In fact, he was stocking purebred black Angus cattle here, and he planned to give his father and brothers a run for their money in cattle shows. He had in mind founding his own champion herd sires here. If he could lick the problem of getting qualified cowboys to work for an outsider, that was. Small towns seemed to draw into themselves when people from other places moved in. Jacobsville had less than two thousand people living in it, and most of them seemed to watch Garon from behind curtained windows every time he walked around town. He was surveyed, measured up and kept carefully at a distance for the time being. People in Jacobsville were particular about letting strangers join the family, because that was what they considered themselves—a family of two thousand souls.

He glanced at his watch. He was already late for a meeting with his squad of agents at the San Antonio FBI office, but last night his flight had been unexpectedly delayed in D.C. by a security hitch. It was early morning before the plane landed in San Antonio. He'd had to drive down to Jacobsville, and he'd barely slept. He walked out onto the wide, concrete front porch with its gray floor and white porch swing and white wicker furniture and cushions. Those were new. It was late February, and his housekeeper said they needed someplace for his company to sit when it came. He told her he wasn't expecting to have any. She snorted and ordered the furniture anyway. She was an authority on everybody who lived around here. She'd probably become an authority on him in short time, but he'd told her graphically what would happen if she dared to pass on any personal gossip about his life. She'd just smiled. He hated that damned smile. If he could have gotten any other spinster lady with her cooking skills to work for him…

He glanced at an old, black car of unknown vintage coughing smoke as it went slowly down the road. That would be the next-door neighbor, whose little green-trimmed white clapboard house was barely visible through the pecan and mesquite trees that separated his big property from her small one. Her name was Grace Carver. She took care of her elderly grandmother, who had a serious heart condition. The granddaughter wasn't much to look at. She wore her blond hair in a long pigtail, and went around mostly in loose jeans and a sweatshirt. She was shy around Garon. In fact, she seemed to be afraid of him, which was curious. Maybe his reputation had gotten around.

He'd met her when her old German shepherd dog trespassed into his yard. He'd escaped his fenced pen and she came looking for him, apologizing profusely the whole time. She had green eyes, very pale, and an oval face. She was plain, except for her pretty mouth and exquisite complexion. She'd only stayed long enough to make her apologies and introduce herself. She hadn't come close enough to shake hands, and she'd left as soon as she could, almost dragging the delinquent dog behind her. She hadn't been back since. Miss Jane had mentioned a week or so later that the old dog had died. Old Mrs. Collier, Grace's grandmother, didn't like dogs anyway. Garon remarked that Miss Carver had been nervous around him. Miss Turner told him that Grace was "peculiar" about men. God knew what that meant.

Miss Jane also said that Grace didn't get out much. She didn't elaborate. He didn't ask anything else about her. He wasn't interested. He liked an occasional night out with an attractive woman, preferably a modern, educated one. Miss Carver was the sort of woman he'd never found interesting.

He checked his watch, closed the front door and climbed into his black Bucar for the drive to San Antonio. He was entitled to use a Bucar—the FBI's term for a bureau conveyance—even though a new black Jaguar sat in the garage next to his big Ford Expedition. He carried all his gear and accessories in the Bucar. So he drove it to work. It was going to be something of a commute, but no more than twenty minutes either way. Besides, he was tired of apartment living. Miss Turner was astringent, but she was a hell of a good cook, and she kept house without talking his ear off. He considered himself fortunate.

He set off down the driveway, casting a curious glance after Grace's choking engine. He wondered if she knew that her car had a mechanical problem, and reasoned that she probably didn't. He glimpsed her from time to time mulching and pruning her roses. She had several bushes of them. That was one thing they did have in common. He loved roses, and during his brief marriage, he'd grown several varieties. It was a hobby he enjoyed, and he had plenty of room to practice it again here at the ranch. Of course, it was February. Not many roses would bloom this time of year.

THE OFFICE WAS BUZZING when he got there. A local homicide detective with San Antonio P.D. was waiting for him, in his office.

"I haven't even had time to brief the SAC about the workshop, yet," Garon muttered to the secretary he shared with another agent. "What's he want?" he added, nodding toward the tall, dark-headed man standing at the window with his hands in his pockets and his black hair in a long ponytail, even longer than the one Garon's brother Cash, wore. It designated a renegade.

"Something about an abducted child case he's working on."

"I don't do missing person cases unless they end as homicides," he reminded her.

She gave him a knowing look. "I work here," she pointed out. "I know what you do."

He glared at her. "Don't get smart."

"Don't get snippy," she shot back. "I could be making twenty dollars an hour as a plumber."

"Joceline, you can't even put a washer in a faucet," he replied patiently. "Or don't you remember what happened when you tried to fix the leaky one in the women's restroom?"

She pushed back her short, dark hair. "The floor needed mopping anyway," she told him haughtily. "Now, if you want to know what Detective Marquez wants, why don't you go and ask him?"

He sighed irritably. "Okay. How about a cup of coffee?"

"Already had one, thanks," she said. She gave him a smile.

"I hate liberated women," he grumbled.

"Gee, can't you lift a coffee cup all by yourself?" she asked with mock surprise.

"When you come asking for a raise, see what happens," he said.

"When you want a case report typed, see what happens," was the smug reply.

He muttered in gutter Spanish all the way into his office. He hoped Joceline understood every single nasty word. But if she did, she didn't let on.

The detective heard his footsteps and turned. He had black eyes and an olive complexion, and a worried expression.

"I'm Marquez," he introduced himself, shaking hands. "You'd be Special Agent Grier, I assume?"

"If I'm not, I don't have to look at all that paperwork piled on my desk," Garon replied dryly. "Have a seat. Like a cup of coffee?" he added, then grimaced. "We'll have to go get it ourselves, of course, because my secretary is a *liberated woman!*" he raised his voice as she went past the door.

"The computer is about to eat your six-page letter to the attorney general about your proposed new legislation," she called merrily. "Sorry, but I'm sure you can draft a new one..."

"If you ever get married, I'll give you away!"

"If I ever get married, I'll give *you* away," she retorted and kept walking.

He sat down behind his desk with a rough sound in his throat. "She and my housekeeper must be sisters," he told the visitor. "I hired them and they tell me what to do."

Marquez only smiled. "I was told that you head a squad that deals with violent crimes against children," he said.

Garon leaned back in his chair, and all the humor went out of his face. "Technically I head a squad that deals with violent crime, up to and including serial murder. I've never worked child murders."

Marquez frowned. "Then who does?"

"Special Agent Trent Jones was our crimes against children specialist," he replied. "But he just got transferred back to Quantico to work on a high profile case. We haven't had time to replace him." He frowned. "I thought Joceline said you had a missing person case?"

Marquez nodded. He looked as solemn as Garon did. "It started out as a missing person case. Now it's a homicide; a ten-year-old girl," he said quietly. "We've checked out everyone close to her, including both parents, and we can't turn a perpetrator. Now we think it might have been a stranger."

This was serious business. The news had been full of abducted children who were murdered by convicted sex offenders, all over the country. The case was, sadly, not that unique.

"Do you have any leads?"

Marquez shook his head. "We only found the body yesterday. That's why I'm here. I found a similar case. I think it's a serial crime. That means I can ask you for help."

Garon leaned back in his chair. "When was she abducted?"

"Three days ago," Marquez said quietly.

"Any latents at the scene?" Garon asked.

"No, and we had the criminologists on their hands and knees all over her bedroom with blue lights. Nothing. Not a single latent fingerprint."

"He took her out of her bedroom?" he asked, surprised.

"In the middle of the night, and nobody heard anything," Marquez replied.

"Footprints, tire tracks…?"

Marquez shook his head. "Either this guy is very lucky, or…"

"…or he's done this before," Garon finished for him.

Marquez drew in a long breath. "Exactly. Of course, my lieutenant doesn't buy that. He thinks we've got a pedophile who carried the kid away and killed her. I told him that this is the second case of bedroom abduction we've seen in the past two years. The last one was over in Palo Verde, and the child was murdered in a similar manner. I found it listed on VICAP, the FBI's violent criminal apprehension program. I showed it to the lieutenant. He told me I was chasing ghosts."

Garon's eyebrow lifted. "Did you check for other unsolved child homicides?"

"I did," Marquez said somberly. "I found two in Oklahoma eight years ago. They happened about a year apart, and the children were abducted from their homes, but in daylight. I showed the cases to my lieutenant. He said it was coincidence, that there were no real similarities except the kids were strangled and stabbed."

"The victims," Garon replied. "How old were they?"

Marquez pulled out a BlackBerry and brought up a screen. "Between ten and twelve years of age. They were raped, strangled and then stabbed."

"God!" Garon burst out. "What kind of animal would do that to a child?"

"A really nasty one."

"I'd hoped that the red ribbon would show up in those VICAP postings that matched this homicide. But I had no luck." Marquez looked up from the BlackBerry. He reached into his pocket and pulled out an evidence bag. He handed it to Garon.

Garon opened it and looked inside. "A red silk ribbon?"

"The murder weapon," Marquez said. "The first officers on the scene were San Antonio P.D. They found it tied tight around the neck of the ten-year-old girl. Her body was found in behind a little country church north of here yesterday. We transported the body here to our medical examiner for processing. We haven't released that bit about the red ribbon to the press."

Garon could guess why. All homicide detectives tried to hold back one or two pieces of evidence so that they could weed out potential suspects who were lying about their involvement in the mur-

der. Every police department had at least one mental case who tried
to confess to any violent crime, for reasons best left to a psychiatrist.

He touched the ribbon. "It might have something to do with his
fantasy," Garon mused, having participated in seminars by the FBI's
behavioral science department, observing profilers at work. Modus
operandi was the method used to kill. Signature was a feature link-
ing all victims of a serial killer in a way that was important only to
the killer, and it never changed. Some left victims posed in obscene
ways, some used a particular marking of victims, but a number of
serial killers left something that identified them as the suspect.

Garon glanced at the detective. "Have you checked the database
for similar ribbons at other crime scenes?"

"First thing I did, when I saw the ribbon," he replied. "But no luck.
If there was such a ribbon, maybe it was overlooked or held back
from the file. I've tried to contact the police department in West
Texas, at Palo Verde, where the last homicide occurred, but they
don't answer phone calls or e-mails. It's a tiny little jurisdiction."

"Good idea. What do you want from us?"

"A profile would be a good start," he said. "My lieutenant won't
like it, but I'll talk to our captain and see if he'll make a formal re-
quest for assistance. He mentioned the profiling to me himself."

Garon smiled. "I'll fill in one of our ASACs, so that he'll expect it."

"Not the SAC?"

"Our special agent in charge is in Washington, trying to appropri-
ate funds for a new project we're trying to get started, partnering
with the local middle schools to discourage kids from using drugs."

"He might need to ask somebody with more money than our gov-
ernment seems to have," came the dry reply. "On a local level, our

own budget is cut to the bone already. I had to buy a digital camera out of my pocket so that I could get my own crime scene photos."

Garon laughed shortly. "I know that feeling."

"Is it true, that a lot of cases never get listed on VICAP?" Marquez said.

"Yes. The forms are shorter than they once were, but it takes about an hour to fill them out. Some police departments just don't have the time. If you could find a second case with a red ribbon involved, I might be able to help you convince your lieutenant that there's a serial killer loose. Before he kills again," he added somberly.

"Can you spare us an agent, if we put together a task force to hunt this guy?"

"We can spare me. The rest of my squad is trying to run down a mob of bank robbers who use automatic weapons in holdups. I'm not essential personnel to them. My assistant can run the squad in my absence. I've worked serial murder cases, and I know agents in the Behavioral Science Unit I can call on for help. I'll be glad to work with you."

"Thanks."

"No sweat. We're all on the same team."

"Do you have a business card?"

Garon took out his wallet and pulled out a simple white business card with black lettering. "My home phone is at the bottom, along with my cell phone number and my e-mail."

Marquez's eyebrows lifted. "You live in Jacobsville?"

"Yes. I bought a ranch there." He laughed. "We're not supposed to be involved in any business outside the job, but I pulled strings. I live on the ranch. The manager takes care of the day-to-day operation, so I have no conflicts."

"I was born in Jacobsville," Marquez said, smiling. "My mother still lives there. She runs a café in town."

There was only one café in town. Garon had eaten there. "Barbara's Café?" Garon asked.

"The same."

He frowned. He didn't want to step on the man's toes, but Barbara was a blonde.

"You're thinking I don't look like a man with a blond mother, right?" Marquez smiled. "My parents died in a botched robbery. They owned a small pawn shop in town. I was just six at the time. Barbara never married and had no family. I used to take mom and dad food from the café. After the funeral, Barbara came and got me out of state custody and adopted me. Quite a lady, Barbara."

"I've heard that."

Marquez checked his watch. "I have to run. I'll phone you when I've talked to my captain."

"Better make it an e-mail," Garon replied. "I expect to be in meetings for most of today. I've got a lot of catching up to do."

"Okay. See you."

"Sure."

IT WAS A GOOD DAY, Garon thought as he drove himself back to Jacobsville. The squad was working witnesses at the last big bank robbery to find any information that would further the investigation. Men armed with automatic weapons were a danger to the entire community of San Antonio. He'd talked to the senior ASAC about setting up a task force in concert with San Antonio homicide detectives to work on the child murder. He had a green light. The ASAC had a friend in the Texas Rangers. He gave Garon his number. They were going to need all the help they could get.

He glanced toward the Carver place as he drove by. Her car was still sitting in the driveway. He wondered if she could start it again. It was a miracle the piece of junk ran at all.

He pulled into his driveway and almost ran into the back of a silver Mercedes convertible. A familiar brunette with dark eyes got out, dressed in a black power suit with a skirt halfway up her thighs that showed off her pretty legs. He knew her. She was the realtor who'd just gone to work for Andy Webb, the man who'd sold him this ranch. Her aunt was rich; old lady Talbot, who lived in a mansion on Main Street in town.

What was her name? Jaqui. Jaqui Jones. Easy to remember, and her figure was more than enough to make her memorable in addition to her job.

"Hi," she said, almost purring as he climbed out of the Jaguar. "I just thought I'd stop by and make sure you were still happy with your ranch."

"Happy enough," he said, smiling.

"Great!" She moved closer. She was only a little shorter than he was, and he was over six feet tall. "I'm hosting a party at my aunt's a week from Friday night," she said. "I'd love to have you join us. It would be a nice way to meet Jacobsville's upper social strata."

"Where and what time?" he asked.

She grinned. "I'll write down the address. Just a sec." She went back to her car and bent over to give him a good view of her body as she retrieved a pen and pad. It didn't take second sight to know that she was available and interested. So was he. It had been a long, dry spell.

She wrote down the address and handed it to him. "About six," she said. "That's early, but we can have highballs while we wait for the others to show up."

"I don't drink," he said.

She looked startled. He was obviously not joking. "Well, then, we can have coffee while we wait," she amended, smiling so that he could see her perfectly capped teeth.

"Suits me. I'll see you then."

She hesitated, as if she wanted to stay.

"I'm just in from D.C. very early this morning," he said. "And it's been a full day at the office. I'm tired."

"Then I'll go, and let you get comfortable," she said immediately, smiling again. "Don't forget."

"I won't."

He'd gone around her car to put the Bucar in front of the house, on the semicircular driveway, so she simply pulled around him to shoot out the driveway, waving a hand out the window as she passed him.

He went inside, almost colliding with Miss Jane. "That fancy woman parked herself in the driveway and said she'd wait for you. I didn't invite her in," she added with a faint belligerence. "She's only been in town two months and she's already got a reputation. Put her hand down Ben Smith's pants right in his own office!"

Apparently this was akin to blasphemy, he reasoned, waiting for the rest.

"He jerked her hand right back out, opened his office door, and put her right out on the sidewalk. His wife works in the office with him, you know, and when he told her what happened, she walked into Andy Webb's office and told him what he could do with the property they'd planned to buy from him, and how far!"

He pursed his lips. "Fast worker, is she?"

"Tramp, more like," Miss Jane said coldly. "No decent woman behaves like that!"

"It's the twenty-first century," he began.

"Would your mother ever have done that?" she asked shortly.

He actually caught his breath. His little mother had been a saint. No, he couldn't have pictured her being available to any man except his father—until his father had cheated on her and hastened her death.

Miss Jane read his reply on his face and her head jerked up and down. "Neither would my mother," she continued. "A woman who's that easy with men she doesn't even know will be that way all her life, and even if she's married she won't be able to settle. It's the same with men who treat women like disposable toys."

"So everybody in town is celibate?" he queried.

She glared up at him. It was a long way. "People in small towns mostly get married and have children and raise them. We don't look at life the way people in cities do. Down here, honor and self-respect are a lot more important than closing a business deal and having a martini lunch. We're just simple people, Mr. Grier. But we look deeper than outsiders do. And we judge by what we see."

"Isn't there a passage about judging?" he retorted.

"There are several about right and wrong as well," she informed him. "Civilizations fall when the arts and religion become superfluous."

His eyebrows went up.

"Oh, did you think I was stupid because I keep house for you?" she asked blithely. "I have a Master's Degree in History," she added with a sweet smile. "I taught school in the big city until one of my students beat me almost to death in front of the class. When I got out of the hospital, I was too shaken to go back to teaching. So now I keep house for people. It's safer. Especially when the people I keep house for work in law enforcement," she added. "Your supper's on the table."

"Thanks."

She was gone before he could say anything else. He was still reeling from her confession. Come to think of it, the Jacobs County Sheriff, Hayes Carson, had recommended Miss Jane. She'd worked for him temporarily until he could get the part-time housekeeper he wanted. No wonder she was afraid of her old job. He shook his head. In his day, teachers ran the classrooms. Apparently a lot of things had changed in the two or so decades since he graduated from high school and went off to college.

He was lying awake, looking at the ceiling, when there was a frantic pounding at the front door.

He got up and threw on a robe, tramping downstairs in his bare feet. Miss Jane was there ahead of him, turning on the porch light before she started to open the door.

"Don't open it until you know who it is!" he shouted at her. His hand was on the .40 caliber Glock that he'd stuffed into his pocket as he joined her.

"I know who it is," she replied, and opened the door quickly.

Their next-door neighbor, Grace Carver, was standing there in a ratty old bathrobe and tattered shoes, her long blond hair in a frizzed ponytail, her gray eyes wide and frantic.

"Please, may I use your phone?" she panted. "Granny's gasping for breath and her chest hurts. I'm afraid it's a heart attack. My phone won't work and I can't start the car!" Tears of impotent fury were rolling down her cheeks. "She'll die!"

Before she got the words completely out, Garon had dialed 911 and given the dispatcher the address and condition of the old woman.

"Wait for me," he told Grace firmly. "I'll be right back."

He ran up the stairs, threw on jeans and a shirt and dragged on his boots without socks. He grabbed a denim jacket, because it was cold, and was downstairs in less than five minutes.

"You're quick," Grace managed.

"I get called out at all hours," he said, taking her elbow. "Jane, I don't know when I'll be back. I've got my keys. Lock up and go to bed."

"Yes, sir. Grace, I'll keep her in my prayers. You, too."

"Thank you, Miss Jane," she said in her soft voice. She had a faint south Texas drawl, but it was smooth and sweet to the ear.

Garon bypassed the Bucar, unlocked the black Jaguar and put her inside. She felt uncomfortable, not only because she was in her night-clothes, but because she wasn't accustomed to being alone with men.

He didn't say anything. He drove to her grandmother's house, pulled up in the driveway and cut the engine. Grace was up the steps like a flash, with Garon on her heels.

The old lady, Mrs. Jessie Collier, was sitting up on her bed in a thick blue gown that looked as if it had been handed down from the 1920s. She was a big woman, with white hair coiled on her head and watery green eyes. She was gasping for breath.

"Grace, for God's sake," she panted, "go find my bathrobe!"

"Yes, ma'am." Grace went to the closet and started rummaging.

"Stupid girl, never can do anything right." She looked at Garon angrily. "Who are you?"

"Your next door neighbor," he replied. "The ambulance is on the way."

"An ambulance!" She glared at Grace, who'd returned with a thick white chenille robe. "I told you…we'd go in the…car! Ambulances cost money!"

Grace grimaced. "The car won't start, Granny."

"You broke it, did you?" she raged. "You stupid…" She groaned and held her chest.

Grace looked anguished. "Granny, please don't get upset," she pleaded. "You'll make it worse!"

"It would suit you if I died, wouldn't it, young miss?" she chided. "You'd have this whole house to yourself and no old lady to wait on."

"Don't talk like that," the younger woman said softly. "You know I love you."

"Hmmmf," came the snorted reply. "Well, I don't love you," she returned. "You cost me my daughter, held me up to public disgrace, made me ashamed to go to town…!"

"Granny," Grace ground out, her face contorting with pain.

"Wish I could die," the old woman raged, panting. "And be rid of you!"

The ambulance came tearing up the dirt road, its sirens blazing, its lights flashing. Grace gave a sigh of relief. She hadn't wanted their neighbor to hear any of this. It was none of his business. She was too embarrassed even to look at him.

"I'll go and bring them up here," she said, anxious to escape.

"Fool girl, ruined my life," the old woman grumbled.

Garon felt a ripple of pure disgust as he watched the elderly woman clutching her chest. The girl was doing all she could for her grandmother, who seemed about as loving as a python. Maybe it was her illness that made her so nasty. The woman in his life had died expressing apologies to the nurses for having to lift her onto bedpans.

That kind, loving, sweet woman had been an angel even in her final hours. What a contrast.

The paramedics came up the steps behind Grace, carrying a gurney. With a nod to Garon, they went to work on old Mrs. Collier.

"Is it a heart attack?" Grace asked worriedly. "Will she be all right?"

One of the paramedics glanced at her. "Are you her daughter?"

"Granddaughter."

"Has she had spells like this before?"

"Yes. Dr. Coltrain gives her nitroglycerin tablets, but she won't use them. He gives her blood pressure medicine, but she won't take that, either."

"Medicine costs money!" the old lady snarled at them. "All I have is my social security. Couldn't feed a mouse on what *she* makes, working part-time at that flower shop and cooking…"

"I can't leave you alone all day, and I'd have to if I worked full-time," Grace said in a subdued tone. She didn't add that she'd have to pay someone to stay with her grandmother, also, and there was no way anybody who knew her would take the job.

"Good excuse, isn't it?" Mrs. Collier grumbled. She cried out, suddenly, clutching her chest. "Oh!"

"Where are her nitroglycerin tablets?" one of the medics asked quickly.

Grace ran around the bed to the side table, and handed them to him.

Mrs. Collier protested, but he got it under her tongue anyway.

She shivered as it took effect, but the medic who was monitoring her vitals gave the other one a speaking glance.

"We're going to have to transport her," he told his colleague. "Can you come with her?" he asked Grace.

"Yes. Just…just let me get dressed. I won't be a minute."

She went out without a backward glance, dashed into her room, threw on jeans and a sweatshirt and her old sneakers and rushed right back to her grandmother. She didn't bother with makeup or even comb her hair. She wasn't going to a social event, after all.

Garon glanced at her. She wouldn't win a beauty contest, but she was a fast dresser, he thought with admiration. Most women he knew took hours dressing and making up.

"I'll follow you in the Jag and bring you home," he told her.

She started to protest, but one of the attendants shook his head. "We'll probably have to keep her overnight at least," he said.

"I won't stay!" Mrs. Collier raged, but she was still gasping and clutching her chest.

"She'll stay," the older paramedic said with a deliberate smile. "Let's load her up, Jake."

"You bet."

Grace stood back beside Garon as they wheeled Mrs. Collier out, still muttering angrily.

Garon didn't say anything. He escorted Grace down to the Jag and helped her into the passenger seat.

"You'll need your purse, won't you?" he asked.

She indicated the fanny pack around her waist. "I've got Granny's cards to check her in," she said dully. "She can't die," she added in a hollow tone. "She's all I've got in the world."

Which wasn't a hell of a lot, Garon was thinking. But he didn't say it. He was resigned to losing most of the night's sleep he'd been hoping for.

2

IT WAS MIDNIGHT before they had Mrs. Collier through the battery of tests that had been ordered. It had been a heart attack, fairly severe. Dr. Jeb "Copper" Coltrain came out into the waiting room to talk to Grace after he'd seen the results of the tests.

"She's bad, Grace," Copper told her. "I'm sorry, but it can't come as much of a surprise. I told you this would happen eventually."

"But there are medicines, and they have these new surgical procedures that I saw on the news," she argued.

He started to put a hand on her shoulder but immediately drew it back before it could make contact. She'd stiffened, something Garon noted with idle curiosity.

"Most of those procedures are experimental, Grace," he said gently. "And the drugs still haven't been approved by the FDA."

Grace bit her lower lip. She had a beautiful bow of a mouth with a natural pink tint, Garon noticed without wanting to, and a peaches and cream complexion that he'd rarely seen on a woman once she took her makeup off. Her hair was a soft, golden-blond. She had it in a ponytail, but when unfettered, it must reach halfway down her back, and it had just a faint wave. She had small, pert breasts and a small waistline. She was perfectly proportioned, in fact. Looking at her long legs and rounded hips in those tight jeans made him uncomfortable and he averted his gaze back to Coltrain.

"Maybe it was just a little attack," she persisted.

"There will be a bigger one, and soon," he replied grimly. "She won't take her medicine, she won't give up salty potato chips and brine-soaked pickles—even if you stop buying them for her, she'll have them delivered. Face it, Grace, she's not trying to help herself. You can't force her to live if she doesn't want to!"

"But I want her to!" she sobbed.

Coltrain drew a long breath, his gaze drawn to Garon, who hadn't said a word. He frowned. "Aren't you Cash's brother?"

Garon nodded.

"The FBI agent?"

He nodded again.

"I couldn't get the car to start and the phone didn't work," Grace told Coltrain before he could interrogate Garon any further. The red-headed doctor was abrupt and antagonistic to people he didn't know. And Mr. Grier here looked like a man who wouldn't take much prodding before he exploded. "I had to ask him for help," she concluded.

"I see." Coltrain was still staring at Garon.

"I could stay with Granny tonight," she offered.

"No, you couldn't," Coltrain said shortly. "Go home and get some sleep. You'll need it if she gets to come home."

Her face fell tragically. "What do you mean, 'if'?"

"When," he corrected irritably. "I meant, when."

"You'll have them call me, if I'm needed?" she persisted.

"Yes, I'll have them call you. Go to the office and do the paper-work," he ordered. She hesitated for a minute, glancing at Garon. "He'll wait," Coltrain assured her. "Git!"

She went.

Coltrain stared at the taller man through dark-circled eyes. "How well do you know the family?"

"We've spoken once until tonight," he replied. "They live next door to me."

"I know where they live. What do you know about Grace?"

Garon's dark eyes began to take on a glitter. "Nothing. And that's all I want to know. I did her a favor tonight, but I am not in the mood to take on dependents. Especially spinsters who look like juvenile bag ladies."

Coltrain was indignant. "That attitude won't get you far in Jacobs-ville. Grace is special."

"If you say so." Garon didn't blink.

Coltrain drew in a long breath and cursed under it. He stared after Grace. "She'll go to pieces if the old lady dies. And she's going to," he added coldly. "Along with the other tests I ordered, I had them run an echocardiogram. Half her heart muscle's dead already, and she'll finish off the rest of it the minute I let her out—if she even lives that long. Grace thinks I sedated her. I didn't. She's in a coma. I didn't have the heart to tell her. That's why I can't let her see Mrs. Collier—she's in ICU. I don't think she'll come out of it. And Grace has nobody."

Garon frowned. "Everybody has relatives."

Coltrain glanced at him. "Her mother and father divorced when Grace was ten. Mrs. Collier had to take Grace," he added without explanation, "and never let the girl forget what a favor she did her. Her mother was living out of town when she died of a drug overdose, when Grace was twelve," he said. "Her father had been killed in a light plane crash two years before that. There are no uncles or aunts, nobody except a distant cousin in Victoria who's elderly and disabled."

"Why does she need anyone? She's a grown woman."

Coltrain looked as if he was biting his tongue. "Grace is an innocent. She's younger than she seems," he said enigmatically. He sighed. "Well, if you can drive her home, I'll be grateful. Maybe Lou and I can manage something, if we have to."

Lou was his wife, another doctor. They were in practice together with Dr. Drew Morris.

Garon scowled. He felt as if he was being put in charge, and he didn't like it. But he couldn't just walk off and leave Grace, he supposed. Then he had an inspiration. Someone had to be sacrificed, but it didn't necessarily have to be himself. "Miss Turner works for me. She knows Miss Carver," he began.

"Yes," he replied. "Jane was her teacher once. She's the closest thing Grace has to family in Jacobsville, even though there's no blood relationship."

So that was it. He shrugged. "I can spare Miss Turner to help out. She can stay with Miss Carver tonight."

"Kind of you." It was said with faint sarcasm.

Garon didn't even blink. His dark eyes were glittering. He didn't give an inch.

Coltrain, having met his match, drew in a slow breath. "All right. But I'm going to sedate Grace before I send her home. If Miss Turner can stay with her tonight, I'll appreciate it."

"No problem," Garon returned.

COLTRAIN DREW GRACE into the emergency room, into a cubicle, and listened to her heart.

"I'm okay," she fussed.

"Sure you are," he agreed as he turned to pick up a syringe that he'd already filled. He swabbed Grace's arm and shot the needle in. "Go home. You'll sleep."

"I didn't call Judy at the florist to tell her I couldn't make it in the morning," she said dully. "She'll fire me."

"Not likely. She'll understand. Besides, Jill, who works in the ER, is Judy's cousin. She'll tell her what happened long before you can call her," he added with a kind smile.

"Thanks, Dr. Coltrain," she said, standing.

"Your neighbor is going to loan Miss Turner to you. She'll stay with you tonight," he added.

"That's nice of him," she said. She made a face. "He's uncomfortable to be around."

He frowned slightly. "He's in law enforcement. In fact, from what his brother, Cash, told me, he's good at homicide detection…"

"I have to go," she broke in, avoiding his eyes.

"You don't have to like him, Grace," Coltrain reminded her. "But you need someone to help you through this."

"Miss Turner will do that." She turned toward the door of the cubicle. "Thanks."

"You'll get through this, Grace," he said quietly. "We all have to face the loss of people we care about. It's a natural part of life. After all," he added, joining her in the hallway, "nobody gets out of the world alive."

She smiled softly. "It's good to remember that."

"Yes. It is."

GARON WAS WAITING, his hands in the pockets of his jeans, pacing. He glanced up as she and Coltrain reappeared. He looked tired as well as irritated.

"I'm ready," she said without meeting his dark eyes. "Thanks for waiting."

He nodded curtly.

"I'll call you if there's a change," Coltrain assured her. "Honest."

"Okay. Thanks, Dr. Coltrain."

"You're welcome. Get some rest."

She started toward the door without another word. She'd forgotten that her phone didn't work, so how could Coltrain call her?

Garon followed behind her, his hands still in his pockets. He hadn't said another word to Coltrain, who glared after him until a nurse caught his attention.

GARON OPENED THE DOOR for Grace and settled her into the passenger seat. By the time they pulled out of the parking lot, she still hadn't spoken a word.

He glanced at her as he drove. "You know the doctor well, do you?"

She nodded without looking at him.

"He's abrasive."

Pot calling the kettle black, she thought amusedly, but she was too shy to say it. She nodded again.

His eyebrow jerked. It was like talking to himself. He wondered why Coltrain had given her a shot instead of something to take by mouth. Hell, he wondered why the doctor was so concerned about her that he wanted someone with her at night. A lot of people had serious illness in their families. Most people got through it without tranquilizers. Especially women as young as this one looked.

Well, it was none of his business, he thought. He pulled out his cell phone and called Miss Turner. She answered at once, obviously still up.

"Can you go home with Miss Carver for the night?" he asked her.

"Of course," she replied without a second's hesitation. "I'll be ready when you get here." She hung up.

He flipped the cell phone shut and laid it in the empty cup holder. "We'll pick Miss Turner up at the house and I'll drive you both over there. Tomorrow, Miss Turner can use the Expedition and drive you to work and then to the hospital. I'll have one of the boys run it over first thing tomorrow and leave the keys with Miss Turner." The SUV was his second vehicle, which he used primarily around the ranch. His foreman and the rest of his cowboys had their own transportation. He didn't tell Grace, but he was going to have one of his mechanics overhaul her car as well. He didn't like having her as a responsibility longer than he had to.

He didn't mind helping out this neighbor, as long as it didn't require any personal involvement with her beyond the minimum. Still, he did feel sorry for her. She seemed to be a misfit in this small town. Obviously she wasn't overly interested in him. She was as far over in her seat as she could get, and she did nothing to try and attract his attention. He hadn't missed the way she flinched when Coltrain had started to lay a compassionate hand on her shoulder. It raised a red flag in his mind, but he was too worn-out from the travel and the interrupted sleep to pursue it. The sooner he had her settled, the sooner he could go back to bed.

They pulled up at the front door of the ranch house and Miss Turner came out with a small satchel and her purse. She got into the back seat.

"I locked up," she told him. "You'll have your house key with you, of course."

"Of course," he drawled.

"Grace, are you all right? How's your grandmother?"

"She's not well, Miss Turner," Grace replied drowsily. "Dr. Coltrain thinks it's a heart attack. He won't give me a lot of hope."

"Never you mind. He's the best we have. He'll do whatever he can, you know that."

"Yes, I do. Thank you for coming home with me," she added. "It's a big house."

"It is," Miss Turner agreed.

He pulled up at the front door of the rickety old white Victorian house, making a face at the lack of fresh paint. Presumably there wasn't any spare cash for upkeep. Pity. It was a pretty house.

"Thank you for all you've done," Grace said formally, "and for letting Miss Turner stay with me."

She looked as if it were like pulling teeth to say that. She had a fiercely independent stubborn streak that he was just meeting. His estimation of her changed a little.

"Lock the doors," Garon cautioned Miss Turner after she'd exited the car and was helping Grace toward the front porch.

"We will. I'll get up early and come over to fix breakfast, as soon as the Expedition gets here."

"Okay. Good night."

He drove off, already going over the next day's routine in his mind. He didn't give Grace a second thought.

BUT THE NEXT MORNING, awake and rested, he felt badly about the way he'd treated Grace the night before. He remembered how he'd felt when his mother had died; but especially, when the woman he loved had died. He remembered how sad and depressed those events had made him. At the time, he'd had no one to help him get through it. His family was back in Texas, and he'd been living in Georgia, working out of Atlanta, when it happened. He should have remembered how alone he'd felt. He'd been less than sympathetic with Grace.

So he got up earlier than usual, made biscuits, fried bacon and scrambled eggs. He phoned the Collier house and only then recalled that the phone was out of order. He climbed into the car, dressed in city clothes and drove over to get Grace and Miss Turner.

They were dressed, just coming down the steps. Grace was wearing jeans and the floppy sweatshirt again, with her hair in a bun. They both looked surprised to see him.

"I made breakfast," he said without preamble. "Let's go."

"But you didn't have to do that," Grace protested.

He started to take her arm, to herd her out the door, but she stepped back in an instant, her eyes wide, her cheeks rosy.

He glowered at her. "It's only breakfast. I'm not proposing," he added sarcastically.

Her eyebrows went up. "Well, thank God for that," she replied carelessly. "I'll consider it a lucky escape." She hesitated when he gave her a blank stare. "Or shouldn't I have said that until *after* breakfast?"

He didn't smile, but his eyes did. He made a rough sound in his throat, avoided Miss Turner's amused gaze and led the way out to the car.

Grace ate with apparent enjoyment, but she was wary of her big, taciturn neighbor. She'd never met anyone quite like him. If he had a sense of humor, it must be very deeply hidden.

"It was very nice," she said when she finished the last strip of bacon. "Do you mind if I use your phone to call the hospital?"

"Help yourself," he said. "There's an extension in the hall."

She got up, wiping her mouth gently, and went to find the phone.

"How's she doing?" Garon asked Miss Turner.

"She's going to take it badly," she replied. "Mrs. Collier is a nightmare of a mother substitute, but Grace has lived with her so long that I think she just overlooks the bad attitude."

"I noticed that the old lady seems to dislike her."

Miss Turner grimaced. "It's even worse than it seems. Mrs. Collier failed Grace at a time when she needed her most. I think it's guilt that makes the old woman treat her so hatefully."

"What happened?" he asked curiously.

"It's not my business to talk about Grace's business," came the terse reply.

He sighed and finished his coffee. Apparently secrets were part of small town life.

Grace came back subdued. "She's in ICU," she said as she sat back down at the table. "He didn't tell me that last night."

"I'm sure he had his reasons. Are you going to work?"

"I have to," Grace said baldly. "Granny's social security check barely pays for the utilities. I have to get in as many hours as I can."

"No ambition to go to college or learn a profession?" Garon asked.

Grace gave him a bald stare. "And where would I get the money to do that, even if I didn't have to take care of Granny? She's been an invalid since I graduated from high school, and I'm all she has." She scowled. "You know, for a man who wants everybody else to mind their own business, you sure spend a lot of time prying into other people's."

His eyebrows arched. "See here, I'm loaning you my housekeeper..."

"Miss Turner doesn't have to be loaned," Grace replied. "*She* has a heart."

He glowered. "So do I."

"You must keep it put up in a safe place, so that it doesn't get used much," she returned. She got up. "Thanks for breakfast. You're not a very pleasant person, but you are a good cook."

"Thank you the hell for small favors," he gritted.

"You're nasty, I'm nasty," she returned. "If you ever develop a pleasant personality, I'll even smile at you."

Miss Turner was trying very hard not to smile. She did like this job, despite the odd behavior of her boss.

"I won't hold my breath," Garon assured her. "I have to go. I'm up to my neck in meetings today. The keys to the Expedition are on the key rack by the front door," he told Miss Turner. "Use it as much as you need to." He hesitated. "Try not to run over her with it unless you absolutely have to," he added, nodding toward Grace. "She'd probably puncture a tire with her attitude."

"It's no surprise to me that you're not married," Grace observed. "But thank you for the use of your vehicle. I'll see about getting mine fixed."

"Most mechanics won't work for free," he pointed out.

She glared at him. Her eyes sparkled when she was mad, and her soft complexion took on a pretty blush. "I can trade eggs and cakes for a tune-up with Jerry down at the filling station," she told him.

"Bartering?" he said, astonished. "What century are you people living in ?"

"A better one than yours, I guarantee," she replied. "Around here, we're people, not numbers in a case book."

"I'm amazed you're not a number in a home for the unbalanced," he said under his breath.

"We'll go when you're ready, Grace," Miss Turner interrupted, sensing an explosion.

"I'm ready now, Miss Turner."

Garon glanced at her disapprovingly. "You go to a job looking like that?" he exclaimed.

She frowned, glancing down at her neat, clean jeans and spotless white sweatshirt. "What should I wear to work in the back of a florist's shop, a ball gown?" she asked.

He shook his head. "The women in my office wear pantsuits and makeup."

"That's probably because they think you're eligible, and they want to impress you," she retorted. "My boss is a woman and she dresses the same way I do."

His eyebrow jerked. "To each his own. I'll be home late tonight, Miss Turner. Just put some cold cuts in the fridge for me."

"I'll do that, boss," she replied.

He turned at the front door. "I hope your grandmother improves," he told Grace quietly.

"Coals of fire?" she muttered.

"Glad you noticed." He went out and closed the door.

Grace felt an odd sensation in the pit of her stomach. She hoped she wouldn't have too much more contact with her taciturn neighbor. And she really hoped that Granny would get better as the day wore on.

Judy, in the florist shop, was all kindness and compassion. She offered to let Grace off, with pay, to stay with her grandmother.

Grace shook her head. "Thanks, but Dr. Coltrain would have a cow," she murmured as she constructed a wreath for a funeral. "He doesn't want me hanging around ICU. I can't go in, you know, except for a few minutes three times a day. She's really bad, Judy. I'm afraid."

"She's been your family for a long time," Judy agreed. "But there's a whole world out there that you've never seen, Grace. You have to think ahead."

She moved restlessly. "I don't know what I'd do, if she…well, I mean, Cousin Bob in Victoria would let me come and visit, but he's in bad shape himself and he has a nurse who stays with him. I'd be alone, here in Jacobsville."

Judy reached over, patted her hand, and smiled. "You'll never be alone in Jacobsville. We're your family, Grace. All of us."

She managed a smile through a mist of quick tears. "Thanks."

Judy shrugged. "You'll get by. We'll all look out for you. Not that you need it anymore," she added. "You've become very independent over the years. I'm proud of the way you've handled yourself. You're an inspiration."

"Not me."

"You." Judy smiled. "Not many people could come back so well from what happened. You've got guts, girl."

Grace didn't like to talk about the past. She moved some more red roses closer to where she was working and started Judy talking about the new water rates. That was good for an hour.

MRS. COLLIER was still in the coma when Grace left her about dark. Miss Turner had come in the Expedition, probably at Coltrain's urging, and insisted that Grace come home.

"You can't work and stay at the hospital all hours," Miss Turner said firmly. "Besides, Jolie will call you if you're needed. We've gotten your phone fixed. Right?" she asked the pretty nurse on night duty.

"You bet I will," Jolie assured her with a smile.

"All right, I'll go home. Thanks," she added, and followed Miss Turner out to the Expedition.

GARON HAD COME HOME a little later than his usual time and had still gone out to help his boys with some heifers who were calving for the first time. Late February was just right for new calves, with the first green grass cautiously poking its head up out of the cold ground. His black Angus cattle were pretty, and he bred for specific traits, since he ran beef cattle. It was something of a blessing that the former owners, the Jacobs family, had been horse ranchers, because the barn was well-kept and the fences had been built to last almost new. It had been a simple matter to string electric wire around the existing pastures to ensure that his animals didn't wander.

He came up onto the porch just as Miss Turner drove up at the steps.

"How's her grandmother?" he asked when she joined him.

"No change," she replied. She shook her head. "She's holding up well, but I think she'll go to pieces if the old lady dies. She's not used to having to live alone."

"Don't tell me she's afraid of the dark," he laughed.

She looked up at him and she didn't smile. "If Mrs. Collier dies, I'll have to find someone to stay with Grace for a while, just until she gets used to the idea. Or maybe she might go up to Victoria and stay with her cousin Bob for a few days," she added, thinking aloud.

"Take it one day at a time," he said. "It's not wise to borrow trouble."

"I suppose so." She hesitated. "Her car is missing," she said suddenly.

"I know. I had Brady bring it over here and overhaul it," he replied. "I was tempted to send it to the junkyard instead, but I guess it's got two or three miles left in it..."

The phone rang insistently. He reached for it before Miss Turner did. "Grier," he said shortly.

"You stole my car!" Grace Carver accused.

3

"I DO NOT STEAL CARS," he replied indignantly. "I work for the FBI."

"They wouldn't have hired you in the first place if they knew you stole cars," she replied, ignoring his defense. "Where's my car? It's no use saying you don't know, because the mailman saw one of your cowboys driving it off this morning after I went to work."

He didn't deny it. "It's a death trap. I'm having it overhauled by my mechanic," he said. "Then you can drive yourself."

There was a brief pause. "I see."

He bit his tongue. "I didn't mean that I mind you and Miss Turner using the Expedition," he said irritably. "Stop putting words in my mouth!"

"I didn't say anything!"

"You were thinking it!"

She blinked. "It must be a handy sort of gift, reading minds, considering your line of work," she said too sweetly.

His eyes darkened angrily.

She hesitated, but only for a moment. "Sorry, that slipped out. Just pretend you never heard it."

"There's a saying," he began slowly, "about biting the hand that feeds you…"

"I wouldn't bite yours," she replied. "No telling *where* they've been!" Before he could react to that she thanked him again for helping with the car, and hung up quickly.

He slammed the freedom phone down into its cradle and muttered something under his breath.

Miss Turner's eyes widened. She'd never seen evidence of a temper in her taciturn new boss. Well, she thought as she walked toward the kitchen, at least he seemed more alive than he usually did. She wondered what in the world Grace had said to him to provoke that response.

GRACE, MEANWHILE, was feeling mean. Her neighbor had taken her car out of good intentions, so that he could fix it for her. She knew he wouldn't charge her for it, either. She grimaced. She needed to stop taking out her frustration on him. Just because she was frantic about Granny was no reason to hurt other people. Not that he seemed the sort of person you could hurt…

She wasn't working today, except on her own little project that consumed much of her free time and what little of her income she could spare. So when she got to a stopping point, she went into the kitchen and started cooking. She'd heard Miss Turner say that Garon was partial to an apple cake, and she was famous for hers. She used dried apples, which gave the dessert a taste all its own.

That afternoon, when Garon's foreman, Clay Davis, brought the car back, she went out to thank him with the cake in a carrier.

He was headed toward a pickup truck driven by one of his men, but he stopped when he saw Grace coming and smiled, doffing his wide-brimmed hat.

"Miss Grace," he said respectfully.

She grinned. "Hi, Clay. Would you do me a favor and take this to your boss?"

He looked at the cake in its carrier. "Hemlock or deadly nightshade?" he asked wickedly.

She gaped at him.

He shrugged. "Well, we've sort of heard that the two of you don't get along."

"It's just a nice apple cake," she defended herself. "I felt guilty for saying unkind things to him. It's sort of a peace offering."

"I'll tell him." He took the cake.

She smiled. "Thanks for fixing my car."

"Key's in it," he said. "And you need to watch that oil gauge," he added. "We patched the leak, but just in case, don't set off anywhere until you're sure it's got oil in it. If you notice a leak, let us know. We'll fix that."

"Thanks a lot, Clay."

He shrugged. "Neighbors help each other out."

"Yes, but there's not a lot I could do for your boss. He's already got all the help he needs."

He smiled. "He does have a sweet tooth," he confided, "although Miss Turner isn't much of a hand at cakes or pies. Don't tell her I said that," he added. "She's a great cook."

"She just doesn't do pastries," Grace finished for him, smiling back. "That's okay. I can't fry chicken or make biscuits."

"We all have our gifts," he agreed.

"Thanks again."

"No problem."

He drove away with the cake beside him on the truck seat.

THAT NIGHT, Grace drove herself to the hospital. She sat outside the intensive care unit, in the waiting room, until very late. Coltrain found her there, alone, when he made his last rounds.

He ground his teeth together. "Grace, you can't work all day and sit here all night," he grumbled, standing over her.

She smiled. "If it were your grandmother, you'd be sitting here."

He sighed. "Yes, I would. But I'm in better health than you are..."

"Don't start," she said curtly. "I take very good care of myself and I have a terrific doctor."

"Flattery doesn't work on me," he replied. "Ask Lou," he added. Lou was his wife.

She shrugged. "It was worth a try." Her eyes became solemn. "The nurse said there's no change."

He sat down beside her, looking worn. "Grace, you know that heart tissue doesn't regenerate, don't you?"

She grimaced. "Miracles still happen," she said stubbornly.

"Yes, I know, I've seen them. But it's a very long shot, in this case," he added. "You have to get used to the idea that your grandmother may not come home."

Tears pricked her eyes. She clasped her hands together, very tightly, in her lap. "She's all I've got, Copper."

He bit his tongue trying not to say what he was thinking. "Don't make her into a saint," he said curtly.

"She was sorry about it all," she reminded him with big, wet eyes. "She didn't mean to get drunk that night. I know she didn't. It hurt her that Mama went off without a word and dumped me in her lap."

"Is that what she said?" he fished.

Her face closed up. "She wasn't a motherly sort of woman, I suppose," she had to admit. "She didn't really like kids, and I was a lot of trouble."

"Grace," he said gently, "you were never a lot of trouble to anyone. You were always the one doing the work at your house. Your grandmother sat and watched soap operas all day and drank straight gin while you did everything else. The gin is why her heart gave out."

She bit her lower lip. "At least she was there," she said harshly. "My father didn't want kids, so when I came along, he ran off with some minor beauty queen and never looked back. My mother hated me because I was the reason my father left. And no other man wanted her with a ready-made family, so she left, too."

"You looked like your father," he recalled.

"Yes, and that's why she hated me most." She looked at her clasped hands. "I never thought she cared about me at all. It was a shock, what she did."

"It was guilt, I imagine," he replied. "Like your grandmother, she had a high opinion of her family name. She expected what happened to be in all the newspapers. And it would have been, except for your grandmother playing on Chet Blake's soft heart and begging him to bury the case so nobody knew exactly what happened. But it was too late to save your mother by then."

She swallowed, hard. "They never caught him."

"Maybe he died," Coltrain replied curtly. "Or maybe he went to prison for some other crime."

She looked up at him. "Or maybe he did it to some other little girl," she said curtly.

"Your grandmother didn't care. She only wanted it hushed up."

"Chief Blake was sorry because of what happened to my mother," she said absently. "Otherwise, I expect he would have pursued the case. He was a good policeman."

"It was more than that," he said, his expression solemn. "The perpetrator thought you were dead. Chet thought you were safer if he kept thinking it. He didn't mean for you to live and testify against him, Grace."

Her skin crawled at just the memory. She wrapped her arms around herself. "Do you suppose he kept the file?"

"I'm sure he did, but it's probably well hidden," he told her. "I doubt Cash Grier will accidentally turn it up, if that's what's worrying you," he added gently.

She grimaced. "It was. Garon has been very kind to me," she told him, "in a sore-paw, irritated sort of way. I don't want him to know about me."

"It was never your fault, Grace," he said, his voice soft and kind, as if he were talking to a small child. In fact, it had been Copper who treated her when the policemen brought her to the emergency room. He'd been a resident then.

"Some people say I asked for it," she bit off.

"Hell!"

"He lived close by and I used to wear shorts," she began.

"Don't ever make excuses for a creature like that," he lectured. "No normal man is going to leer at a twelve-year-old child!"

She managed a smile for him. "You're very good to me."

"I wish I was good for your social life," he replied. "You don't even date, Grace. You're twenty-four years old. You should have had therapy and learned to get on with your life. I blame your grandmother for that. She wouldn't have a relative of hers connected in any way with a psychologist."

"She's very old-fashioned."

"She's an ostrich," he corrected hotly. "Protecting the family name by pretending nothing happened."

"Everybody knows what happened," she reminded him.

"Not really. They only know the bare bones."

"They all look out for me, just the same," she said, feeling warm and protected. "We're all family in Jacobsville," she added thoughtfully. "Like old Mr. Jameson who was in prison for bank robbery and came home when he was released. He's paid his debt to society. He's sorry. Now he's just accepted."

He smiled. "It's one of the nicer things about little towns," he had to agree.

"You don't think anybody would tell Garon...?"

"Nobody gossips about you," he said. "Not even Miss Turner."

One thin shoulder lifted. "He's a stranger here, even if his brother is our police chief," she said. "I don't suppose people would rush to air the dirty linen."

"You're not dirty linen," he said firmly.

She smiled. "You're a nice doctor." She hesitated. "Can't I see Granny, just for a minute?"

He made a face. "If you'll promise to go home afterward."

She was reluctant, but she did want to see Mrs. Collier. "Okay."

"Come on, then."

He led her into the unit, spoke briefly to the nurse and escorted Grace into a small cubicle where her grandmother, white as a sheet and unaware of anyone around her, lay quiet on the bed.

Grace had to bite her tongue to keep from crying out. The old lady already looked dead. She was breathing in a way that Grace remembered vividly from her early childhood. Her grandfather had breathed like that the day he died. It was a rasping sort of sound. It was frightening.

Coltrain moved to her side. "Grace, it helps to remember that this is something all of us will face one day. It isn't an end. It's a beginning. Like the cocoon that produces a butterfly."

She looked up at him with eyes that were far too bright. "My whole family is dead."

"You still have a cousin up in Victoria, and he likes you."

She had to admit that he was right. Although the cousin was in his late seventies and a semi-invalid. She moved to the bedside and slowly, hesitantly, touched her grandmother's broad shoulder.

"I love you, Granny," she said softly. "I'm sorry...I've been such a burden to you—" Her voice broke. Tears poured down her cheeks.

Her grandmother moved jerkily, as if she heard, but her eyes didn't open. After a minute, she was still again, and the raspy breathing worsened.

Coltrain, who knew what it meant all too well, drew Grace out of the cubicle and back into the waiting room.

She pulled a handkerchief from her purse and dabbed at her eyes. "I'm sorry."

"There's no need to be. Damn, Grace, you shouldn't be here alone!"

Just as he said it, the door opened automatically and Garon Grier, in a three-piece gray suit, walked into the waiting room.

Coltrain stared at him blankly. Grier was the last person in the world he'd expected to see, especially after the man had been so cool with Grace when her grandmother was brought in.

Garon joined them, his dark eyes on Grace's ravaged face. "Miss Turner said you'd probably be here," he said curtly. "I went by to thank you for the apple cake, and your car was gone."

"You baked him an apple cake?" Coltrain asked, surprised.

Grace moved restlessly. "I was rude to him and I felt guilty," she explained. "He had one of his men fix my car."

"Which she accused me of stealing," Garon added. One dark eyebrow lifted. "But the cake did make up for the insult. It's a damned good cake."

She smiled through her tears. "I'm glad you liked it."

He glanced at Coltrain. "I thought I'd follow you home," he told her. "Clay said the car may still leak oil. You live on a lonely stretch of road."

Coltrain liked the man's concern, but he wasn't showing it. "Let him follow you home, and stay there," he told her. "You can't do any good here, Grace."

She drew in a long breath. "I guess not." She turned to Garon. "I have to stop by the lady's room for a minute, then I'll be ready to leave."

"I'll wait," he assured her.

She walked down the hall. When she was out of earshot, Coltrain turned his attention to Garon.

"Mrs. Collier won't last more than a few hours," he said bluntly. "I think Grace knows, but she's going to take it hard."

Garon nodded. "I'll make sure she's not alone over there. When her grandmother is gone, she can stay at the ranch with us for a week or two, until she gets her bearings. Miss Turner will treat her like a long lost daughter."

"Isn't that something of a turnabout for you?" Coltrain asked warily. "Just recently, you didn't even want to be bothered with Grace's transportation."

Garon avoided his eyes. "She's got a good heart."

Coltrain hesitated. "She's a good person," he amended. He frowned. "Aren't you working late?"

He nodded. "We have a murdered child north of here," he replied. "Homicide is my specialty, so I was assigned to the case." His expression tautened. "I've been in law enforcement most of my life. Usually, not much shocks me. This case..." He shook his head. "The perp took the child right out her bedroom window. We found evidence of a violent encounter in the room." His eyes flashed angrily. "This man is an animal. He has to be caught."

"Have you found any clues?"

He shook his head. "Not yet. But I'm like a snapping turtle. I won't stop until I've found him."

Coltrain smiled. "You're like your brother in that I gather."

"Back when he was a Texas Ranger," he confided, "Cash chased a robbery suspect all the way to Alabama."

Coltrain chuckled. "That, I'd believe."

He shook his head. "If anyone had told me that he'd settle down in a small town and have kids, I'd have laughed my head off. Since his daughter was born, earlier this month, he's become a committed family man."

Before Coltrain could reply, Grace came back down the hall, looking morose and lonely.

Garon felt her pain keenly. He was no stranger to loss.

"Come on," he said gently. "I'll follow you home."

Grace hesitated. She looked up at Coltrain. "You'll call me...?"

He nodded. "I'll call you, Grace."

Above her head, Garon's eyes met Coltrain's and a silent message passed between them. Coltrain would call Garon as well. He told him, without saying a single word.

GRACE PULLED UP at her front steps with Garon right behind her. She got out of the car hesitantly. It had been a very long time since she'd been alone with a man at night. She didn't trust men.

She hesitated at her steps, turning on the gravel path to watch Garon get out of his car and join her. She was stiff as a poker, something he must have recognized.

His dark eyes narrowed. "Do you want me to send Miss Turner over to spend the night with you?" he asked.

"No. I'll be fine. Thank you," she added jerkily.

He scowled. She'd been relaxed at the hospital, with Coltrain nearby. But on her own like this, with him, she seemed to grow thorns and barbed wire. It didn't take rocket science to know that she was uncomfortable. He wondered if she was that way with other men.

"You've got our number," he reminded her. "If you need us, just call."

"Thank you. It's very kind," she said.

He drew in a long breath. "I have a hard time with relationships of any sort," he said out of the blue. "My line of work puts off any number of people, especially when they realize that I carry a gun all the time, even off duty. I make them uncomfortable."

She bit her lower lip. "I'm not used to people, either," she confessed. "Granny and I keep to ourselves. I have little jobs that I go to," she added, "and I have just a handful of casual friends. But nobody close."

He cocked his head. "Is there a reason for that?"

"Yes," she said simply. "But I don't talk about it."

She made him curious. He noticed that she was still wearing jeans and a sweatshirt, with a jacket. None of her clothing was new, and her loafers had torn places and scuff marks. She must budget like crazy, he thought.

"You like roses?" he asked, noticing the pruned bushes near the front porch.

"I love them," she replied, smiling. "I'm especially fond of my Audrey Hepburn and my Chrysler Imperial."

"A pink and a red," he mused.

"Why, yes!" she burst out, surprised.

"I haven't had much opportunity to plant bushes in recent years," he said. "I might get back to it, now that I've got the ranch. It used to be a hobby."

"I've babied these rosebushes since I was a little girl," she recalled warmly. "My grandfather—he's dead now—loved to grow them. He knew all the varieties, and he taught me. We were best friends. He died when I was nine."

"I never knew any of my grandparents," Garon replied. "They all died before we were born."

"We?" she asked. "You and Cash?"

"There are four brothers," he replied. "Cort and Parker are the other two. Cort runs our West Texas ranch with our father. Parker's in law enforcement."

"Was your dad a lawman?" she wondered.

"No. But our grandfather was a U.S. Marshal," he said proudly. "I've still got his gunbelt and his old Colt .45."

"My granddad was a horse wrangler," she said. "But he got kicked by a bull and crippled. He retired and moved here with Granny when my mother was a little girl."

"Your roots go back a ways here," he said.

"Yes. It's nice to have some."

He checked his watch. "I'd better get home. I've got some paperwork to do before I can go to bed. Call if you need us."

"I will. Thanks," she added.

He shrugged. "It was a good cake."

She smiled. "I'm glad you liked it."

"Lock your doors," he called as he got into his car.

"I will. Good night."

He waved and drove off, but she saw him hesitate at the end of her driveway until he saw lights go on in her house. It was rather comforting.

SHE LOCKED THE DOORS and checked them twice. She checked the broom handles placed crosswise in all the long, old-fashioned windows to keep anyone from opening them. She checked her bedroom window four times. It was a ritual that she never skipped.

Her neighbor had surprised her by showing up at the hospital. He was a loner, as she was. She hadn't liked him at first, but he did seem to have a few saving graces.

She put on her long white gown and brushed out her hair so that it swirled around her shoulders like a sheet of gold. She didn't look into the mirror while she did it. She didn't like looking at herself.

It was almost dawn when she heard someone knocking like crazy at the front door. She was sleeping in a downstairs room, rather than the old bedroom she'd had on the second floor of the house. It wasn't far down the hall. She threw on a thick robe and paused to look out the small square windowpanes after she turned on the porch light.

She frowned. It was her neighbor, dressed and solemn. Her heart ran away with her. She could only think of one reason he might be here.

She opened the door with a little sob in her voice. "No," she said huskily. "Please, no...!"

"I'm sorry," he said quietly.

"She's...gone?"

He nodded.

Tears ran down her cheeks. She didn't make a sound. She just looked up at him with her tragic face, crying helplessly.

He moved forward to take her by the shoulders. It was an invasion of her personal space that shocked, frightened her. She jerked nervously, but when his hands loosened and were barely resting on her, she relaxed suddenly and moved into his arms. She couldn't remember a time in her young life when anyone had held her while she cried.

He smoothed her long, tousled hair with a big, gentle hand. "People die, Grace," he said gently, using her name for the first time. "It's something we all have to go through."

"You lost your mother," she recalled, sobbing.

"Yes." He didn't add that she wasn't the only person close to him that he'd lost. He didn't know her well enough to confide in her.

"Was it quick?" she wanted to know.

"Coltrain said she just took a little breath and relaxed," he replied. "It was quick and painless. She never regained consciousness."

She bit her lower lip. "Heavens," she choked, "I don't know anything about her burial policy. She went to the funeral home herself and filled out all the papers. She had a little policy…I don't know where it is." She wept again, liking the feeling it gave her to lean on him. She hadn't ever been the sort to lean. He was warm and strong and right now, he wasn't threatening.

"I'll help you with that," he said. "But you're coming home with me now. Go upstairs and change, Grace. We'll worry about the arrangements tomorrow. Which funeral home?"

"Jackson and Williams," she recalled.

"I'll phone them while you're getting dressed. I'll phone the hospital, too," he added before she could ask.

"I don't know how to thank you…" she began, lifting a face torn with grief to his eyes.

"I don't want thanks," he returned. "Go on."

"Okay."

She turned and went to her room.

Garon watched her go with narrowed eyes. Coltrain had been emphatic about keeping an eye on Grace. He said that she was going to take it hard, and she'd need someone to watch her. The redheaded doctor had known her for many years. Maybe he just cared more than most other people did.

Garon pulled out his cell phone and dialed information.

4

GRACE SAT WITH GARON in the office of the funeral home, while Henry Jackson went over the arrangements for Mrs. Collier's funeral with her. Garon had taken a vacation day so that he could help. He didn't tell her that he hardly ever took time off, but she guessed it.

There weren't a lot of arrangements to make. Mrs. Collier had laid out her desires, and even paid for her casket, a simple pine one. She was to be buried in a local Baptist church cemetery, next to her late husband. Her insurance would cover the costs of the service, so that Grace had nothing to worry about.

The next stop was Blake Kemp's office, where Grace learned that she'd been left the house and land. It was a little surprising, because she'd expected her grandmother wouldn't leave her anything at all.

Garon was sitting in the waiting room while Grace spoke to her grandmother's attorney.

"I didn't think she'd leave me anything," she began.

Blake leaned forward. "She had a guilty conscience, Grace," he said gently. "She failed you the one time she shouldn't have. I know she wasn't kind to you. Maybe that was just an involuntary response to her own behavior."

"She blamed me for Mama," she replied.

"She shouldn't have," he said with the ease of someone who'd known the family for many years. "Nothing that happened was your fault."

"That's what Dr. Coltrain said."

"And he's right. We'll go ahead and file the papers, making you executrix of her estate." He held up a big hand when she started to speak. "You don't have to do a thing. I'll handle it. Now, about the funeral," he began.

"Mr. Grier is helping with that," she said.

"Cash?" he exclaimed.

"No, his brother Garon. He lives next door to our place," she said.

His eyebrows arched. He wasn't expecting that. From what he'd heard of Cash's brother, he didn't go out of his way to help people.

"He's very nice," she continued. "He had his men fix my car. And I baked him an apple cake."

He smiled gently. "It's about time you started noticing bachelors, Grace."

She closed up at once. "It's not like that," she assured him. "He's only being kind. Miss Turner probably had something to do with it."

"She might have," he conceded. "Well, if you need anything, you know where I am."

"Yes. Thank you."

He smiled. "It's no trouble. When we get the papers drawn up, you can swing by and sign them. I'll do the rest."

She started back out of the office, smiling at the receptionist, a new girl who'd replaced Violet Hardy, who was now Kemp's wife. Garon got up from the comfortable sofa and went with her. The receptionist's eyebrows arched and she grinned at Garon. He scowled.

"It's the thing about small towns," Grace said uneasily when they were out on the sidewalk. "If you're seen with anybody, people gossip. It's not malicious."

He didn't reply, but he didn't like it, and made it obvious.

"Thank you for taking time off to help me do these things," she said when they were on the way back to her house. "I really appreciate it."

"I didn't mind." He checked his watch. "But I have to go back to my office. We're working on a murder. A child. I have some more calls to make."

She stiffened. "Do you have any leads?"

He shook his head. "It's early times. She was apparently taken right out of her bedroom, with her parents asleep next door and kept for several days. A hiker tripped over her body behind a church." His face hardened. "She was ten years old, and all her immediate family members have alibis. She was assaulted. What the hell kind of human being feels attracted to little girls?"

She was breathing uneasily, her arms folded tight over her chest. "Inadequate men," she bit off, "who want control."

Her reply surprised him. He glanced at her. "Excuse me?"

"Men who can't make it with grown-up women," she said tautly. "And they hate women because of it. So they victimize the most helpless sort of females."

"You're good," he murmured with a faint smile. "Yes, that's my take on the case, too." His eyes were still on the road. "You've got potential. Ever think of law enforcement for a career?"

"I hate guns."

He laughed. "You don't have to have a gun. We employ civilians at the Bureau," he added. "Information specialists, engineers, linguists..."

"Linguists?"

He nodded. "In the old days, you had to be an agent to work for the Bureau. But now we're more laid-back."

She smiled in spite of herself. "You're not laid-back, Mr. Grier," she returned.

He glanced at her curiously. "How old are you?"

Her eyebrows lifted.

"Tell me," he persisted.

"Twenty-four."

He smiled. "I'm thirty-six. That doesn't qualify me for a rocking chair. You can call me Garon."

She gave him a long look. "That's a name I've never heard before."

"My mother had four children, all boys. My father says she used to sit on the porch and go through baby name books for hours. At that, my name isn't quite as bad as Cash's."

"Cash isn't all that unusual," she pointed out.

"His real name is Cassius," he replied with a smile.

"My gosh!"

"That's why he uses 'Cash,'" he chuckled.

"Are the two of you close?"

He shook his head. "We've had some family problems since my mother's death. We're in the process of getting to know each other.

Cash went off to military school when he was about eight or nine years old. Until this past year, we didn't really speak."

"That's sad, to have a family and not speak."

He wondered about her parents, but it was too soon to start asking personal questions. He didn't want any more contact with her than necessary. He was married to his job. On the other hand, he'd just talked to her about his work, and that was something he'd never done before. She had an empathy about her that was hard to resist. He felt at home with her. That was dangerous, and he wasn't going to let anything develop between them.

GARON DROPPED GRACE OFF and went back to work. Marquez's captain had called and the senior ASAC called Garon into his office and authorized the Bureau's assistance. Garon would head up the task force as they searched for a murderer who killed little girls. Nobody was saying it out loud, but it was very possible that they had a serial killer on their hands. At least four cases shared the same basic pattern of death.

"I'll get started, then," Garon told him.

"Marquez's captain said the case needs to be solved as soon as possible," ASAC Bentley remarked. He was older than Grier, near retirement and had asked for assignment to San Antonio, where he had relatives. He was a kindly man, with a good heart, and he was a superior agent. Garon respected him. "The captain has an open mind, but Marquez's lieutenant doesn't. He thinks it's all coincidence."

"I don't. The cases are too similar," Garon said doggedly.

The ASAC smiled. He'd known Garon a long time. He knew how

determined the agent could be. "That would be my gut feeling, too. Stay out of trouble."

"I'll try," he replied. The grin gave him away.

HE PHONED MARQUEZ and they met at a local diner. Marquez looked tired. There were dark circles under his eyes.

"You look like you've been burning the midnight oil," Garon remarked.

He laughed, a little hollowly. "I take these homicides seriously. I phoned the Oklahoma P.D. where the other red ribbon murder occurred. That was an eleven-year-old girl. They found her facedown in a patch of brown-eyed Susans near a cemetery."

"Assaulted?" Garon asked.

Marquez nodded curtly. "Yes. Strangled, as well. And then stabbed about twenty-five times. Just like this one we're working on. Too similar to be unrelated."

Garon's lips made a thin line. "A very personal attack."

"Exactly my feeling. The perp hated the child, or what she represented. It was overkill, plain and simple. Something else—there was another victim, same basic MO, over near Del Rio, about ten years ago, killed with a knife and left in a field. I was looking for similar cases and happened to run into one of our older investigators who remembered it. It wasn't even fed into a database, it was so old. I e-mailed the police department over there and asked them to fax me the details." He ran a hand through his thick, straight black hair. "Little girls. Innocent little girls. And this monster may have been doing it since the nineties, at intervals, without getting caught. I'd give blood to get this guy," Marquez added. He paused long enough to give the waitress his order and wait until she could pour coffee in his cup before he spoke again. "He's got to be a repeat sex offender. He's too good at what he does for a sloppy amateur. It takes a wily so-and-so to take a child right out of her own bedroom with her family in the house. And he does it over a period of years, if the cases do match, without getting caught or even seen."

"That piece of red ribbon?" Garon murmured, sipping coffee, "must have something to do with a fantasy he's acting out."

"That's what I thought," the younger man said. "The detective who told me about the Del Rio case also remembered hearing of a similar cold case, from twelve or more years back, but he couldn't recall where it happened. He thinks it happened in south Texas."

"Did you look in the database for that case?"

"Yes, but the Del Rio case wasn't there. God knows how many others aren't, either, especially if they happened in small, rural towns." He smiled. "I told my lieutenant about that Del Rio cold case, and about the other two children in Oklahoma who were taken from their homes and found dead. I said we needed to get the FBI involved so you guys could do a profile of the killer for us, and he laughed. He said the deaths had no connection. So I went to the captain, and he called your ASAC. Thanks."

"No problem," Garon mused. "Most veteran cops hate paperwork and complications. Nobody wants to be looking for a serial killer. But we might catch this one, if we're stubborn enough."

Marquez pursed his lips. "I asked one of your squad members about you," he said. "He says that you'll chase people to the gates of hell."

Garon shrugged. "I don't like letting criminals get away."

"Neither do I. This guy's a serial killer. I need you to help me prove it."

Garon paused while their steaks were served. "What sort of similarities are we talking about, with that cold case in Del Rio?"

"All I have is sketchy information," came the reply, "but the manner of abduction was the same, and they narrowed the suspects down to a stranger. The victim was assaulted and stabbed. I don't know about red ribbons. I filled out our case on the form for VICAP and I did turn up several child murders in other states. But none of the children were strangled and stabbed, which may signify some other perp."

"Or he might have changed his habits. Maybe a gun gave him more power in an abduction." As they both knew, a murderer might change the way he killed, but if the crime had a signature, it usually wouldn't vary from crime scene to crime scene.

"Any red ribbons in those other cold cases?" he asked, because the ribbon did seem to serve as a signature in at least one case.

"No. At least," he added, "there were none in the information I accessed. As I said earlier, we always hold back one or two details that we don't feed to the media. Maybe those detectives did, too."

"Did you try calling the detectives who worked the Oklahoma cases?"

"I did. The first Oklahoma one was sure I was actually a reporter trying to dig out unknown facts in the case. I gave him my captain's phone number, and he hung up on me. He said anybody could look that information up online. Nobody at the second police department knew anything about a cold case."

"How about the other Texas case?"

"That's a doozy of a story," Marquez told him with pure disgust in his tone. "It's in Palo Verde, a little town up near Austin. I couldn't get their single policeman on the phone at all. I tried e-mailing him, along with my phone number. That was week before last, and I'm still waiting for an answer."

"We get a lot of kooks e-mailing us for various reasons," Garon told him. "And we get about two hundred spam messages a day. The captions are so misleading that you occasionally open one without meaning to. It's always a scam or a link to a porno Web site. Even with filters, they get through. Maybe your message ended up in the deleted files."

"I hate spammers," the younger man muttered.

"We have a cyber crime division that spends hours a day looking for scams and shutting them down."

"Good for you, but that still doesn't solve my problem."

"You can fly to Oklahoma and show your credentials in person, can't you?"

"I can barely pay my rent," Marquez said miserably as he finished his steak. "I can't afford the airfare."

"Your department would pay for the tickets," Garon said.

Marquez's eyebrows met his hairline. "Like hell it would," he shot back. "Didn't I tell you that I had to buy my own damned digital camera because my lieutenant wouldn't authorize the expenditure? He likes his job and the city manager goes over departmental budgets with a microscope."

"I know how that feels."

"No, you don't," the younger man assured him. "Unless you've had to bring in a receipt for a cup of ice water you bought from a convenience store to back up claiming it on your expense account!"

"You have got to be kidding!" Garon exclaimed.

"I wish I were," the other man said sadly, shaking his head. "I guess they'd lock me up for a whole giant Coke."

Garon chuckled helplessly. "You need to come and work for us," he told Marquez. "You could even have a Bucar."

"A what?"

"A bureau car," Garon told him. "I get to drive mine home at night. It's like moving storage for all my equipment, including my guns."

"Guns, plural?" the detective exclaimed. "You have more than one?"

He gave the detective a wry look. "Surely you have access to body armor and stop sticks and a riot gun…?"

"Of course I do," he muttered, "but it's not my own. As for stop sticks, I pull my service weapon and try to blow out tires as long as the suspect isn't near anything I might conceivably hit by mistake. As for a riot gun…" He pushed back his jacket to display his shoulder holster. "This is it. I hate shotguns."

"They let you wear a shoulder holster?" Grier asked. "We aren't allowed to."

"I don't know if I want to apply to the Bureau if I can't wear a shoulder holster. Besides, they move you guys around too much. I like being near home."

"To each his own."

"Who else is going to be on this task force you're setting up?" Marquez asked.

"We've got the sheriff's department, because the murder took place out of town in the county, along with a K-9 unit, a Texas Ranger…"

"A Ranger? Wow," the other man said with a wistful sigh. "I tried to get in, five years ago. I passed everything except the marksmanship test, but two other guys had higher scores than I did. That's quite an outfit."

"Yes, it is. My brother was a Ranger, before he came down to work in San Antonio. He was with the D.A.'s office as a cyber crime expert, then he moved to Jacobsville."

"He's chief of police there," Marquez nodded. "Quite a guy, your brother. He's making some major drug busts."

Garon felt a ripple of pride. He was proud of his brother.

"Who else?" Marquez persisted.

"We have an investigator from the D.A.'s office who specializes in crimes against children. We've volunteered our crime lab at Quantico for trace evidence."

"We have one of the best forensic units in the country."

Garon smiled. "I know. I don't have a problem with letting them process data."

"When do we meet?"

"Tomorrow afternoon, at El Chico's. About one o'clock. I found one policeman who knows the family of the victim and used to live in the neighborhood. He'll meet us there."

"I'll have the Texas Ranger on hand and the D.A.'s investigator," Garon told him. "I hope we can get this guy."

"No argument there." He glanced at his watch. "I've got a couple of hours off after this, but I should be back in my office before quitting time, if you need to contact me. I forgot to give my numbers. If you can't reach me at the office," he added, pulling out a business card, "my cell phone number is on this."

"Thanks. I'll be in touch."

Marquez reached for his wallet when they were finished and the waitress had produced the bill, but Garon waved him away and passed his credit card to the woman.

"My treat," he told Marquez with a smile. "It was a business lunch."

"Thanks. I wish I could reciprocate, but my lieutenant would send me out to solve stolen gas station drive-off cases if I presented him with a lunch bill."

Garon just laughed.

THE LAUGHTER FADED when he got home. Miss Turner was looking worried and standing by the telephone.

"What's going on?" Garon asked her.

"Nothing, I hope," she replied. "It's just that I can't get Grace on the telephone. I'm sure she's all right. Maybe she's just not answering her phone."

"I'll drive over and see," he replied, and was out the door before Miss Turner could ask to go with him.

He pulled up in the front yard of the old Victorian house, noting again how little maintenance had been done on it. He took the steps two at a time and rapped hard on the door. He did it three times, but there was no answer.

He started around the side of the house. And there she was. In the rose garden, with pruning shears, cutting back her rosebushes. She was talking to them, as well. Obviously she hadn't heard him drive up.

"I know she never liked you," she was telling the roses. "But I love you. I'll make sure you get all the fertilizer and fungicides you need to make you beautiful again, the way you were when Grandaddy was still alive." She sniffed and wiped her wet eyes on the sleeve of the flannel shirt she was wearing. "I don't know why I'm crying for her," she went on after a minute. "She hated me. No matter what I did for her, she never wanted me in her life. But now she's gone and it's just you and me and this enormous house…"

"Are the roses going to live in it with you, then?" he asked curiously.

She turned so fast that she almost fell over. Her hand went to her chest. She was almost gasping for breath. "You move like the wind," she choked. "What are you doing here?"

"Miss Turner couldn't raise you on the phone. She was worried."

"Oh." She went back to trimming the rosebushes. "That was kind of her."

He glanced around at the bare landscape. There was a garden spot behind the house that looked as if it had just been plowed. He wondered if she kept the garden, or if her grandmother had grown vegetables.

"Did you find the man who killed that little child?" she asked.

He shook his head. "It's not that simple to solve a murder. This is one of several similar crimes, some from years ago. It takes time. We're forming a task force to investigate it."

"My father used to work for the sheriff's department here as a deputy, just like Grandaddy did. That was a long time ago," she added. "He quit when he married my mother because she didn't like him taking risks."

"What did he do afterward?"

"He got a job as a limousine driver in San Antonio," she replied. "He made good money at it, too. Then he met a pretty, rich woman that he'd been hired to drive around, and he went head over heels for her. He left my mother and filed for divorce. She never got over it. The other woman was ten years older than she was, and she owned a boutique."

"Is your father still living?" he asked.

She shook her head. "He and his new wife were driving to Las Vegas when a drunk driver ran into them head-on. They both died."

"You said your mother disliked you?"

She nodded. "I look like my father. She hated me for that."

"What happened to your mother?"

"She…died about twelve years ago," she said. "Just two years after Daddy did."

"What did she do for a living?"

"She was a nurse," Grace said quietly.

"You're going to kill those bushes if you keep snipping," he pointed out. "And the temperature's dropping."

She shivered a little as she stood up. "I suppose so. I just wanted something to do. I can't bear to sit in that house alone."

"You don't need to. Pack a small bag. I'll take you home with me. You and Miss Turner can watch movies on the pay per view channel."

She looked up at him, frowning. "That's not necessary…"

"Yes, it is," he said gently, studying her face. It was wet with tears. "You need a little time to get adjusted to life without your grandmother. No strings. Just company."

She gnawed on her lower lip. She didn't understand his motives, and it showed.

"I'd do it for anybody," he continued. "Think of it as one neighbor helping another out."

She shifted in place. "If I wouldn't be in the way…" she began.

"I work in the study all hours trying to get herd records up-to-date," he said simply. "You won't bother me. I'll give you the guest room next to Miss Turner's. If you get scared in the night, she'll be around."

She still hesitated. It was hard for her, trusting a man. Any man.

"If you stay over here talking to rosebushes, somebody's going to notice," he pointed out. "Think of the scandal."

She smiled despite herself. "All right, then. Thank you," she added a little awkwardly.

"You'd do it for me, I'm sure."

And she would have.

Miss Turner was surprised and delighted at the unexpected company. "He hates having people here," she told Grace as she poured her some tea in the kitchen of the long, single level house.

"It's only because I was talking to the roses," Grace faltered.

Miss Turner stared at her.

Grace flushed. "Well, I'm not exactly overcome with visitors these days."

"You can talk to me," she told her. "At least, I can answer you back."

LATER, MISS TURNER showed her to the guest room and pointed out the quilt at the foot of the bed in case Grace got too cool.

"He says he can't sleep in a warm house, so he keeps it like a deep freeze," Miss Turner muttered. "Likely you'll get frostbite, but at least you won't be lonely. Got your medications?"

Grace nodded.

"Good. There's water in the carafe by the bed. Sleep well."

"You, too."

The door closed and Grace sat down on the bed. It was a pretty room, done in cool blues and beiges. She was amazed at her host for the invitation, and grateful as well. She'd dreaded spending the night alone.

For a man with no social skills to speak of, she thought, he was surprisingly kindhearted.

SHE SETTLED UNDER the comforter and closed her eyes. But the events of the day had damaged her, and not only her grandmother's death. She kept seeing little girls lying in beds of roses, wearing red ribbons around their necks...

When the screams started, she didn't even realize that they were coming from her own lips.

5

"GOD ALMIGHTY!" CAME A deep voice from somewhere nearby. "Grace. Grace!"

She was dying. Blood was seeping out all around her, and it was red, as red as her grandmother's roses. She was lying in a patch of sunflowers, looking up at the sky. There was pain. So much pain! She could almost feel merciless hands on her shoulders, shaking her, shaking her...!

She gasped and her eyes flew open. Garon Grier was sitting on the side of her bed in a bathrobe, his blond-streaked brown hair mussed, his dark eyes narrow and concerned. Behind him stood Miss Turner with her hair down, gray and thin, wrapped in a thick bathrobe, chewing her lower lip nervously.

Grace took a long breath and another one. She was shaking. "S...sorry," she stammered. "I'm sorry!"

The big hands holding her shoulders relented, pulling her into a sitting position. Her long blond hair had come undone from its cloth tie and draped around her shoulders like a fall of silk. She was wearing a thick cotton gown that covered her from throat to heels. Only her face and hands peered out from its whiteness.

"What happened?" Garon asked.

She swallowed hard, looking around her in relief. She wasn't lying in a field. She was in a bed, in a house. Safe. She swallowed again, aware that her eyes and cheeks were wet.

"What was it?" he persisted. "A nightmare?"

She only nodded, still shaken. It had seemed very real.

"How about some warm milk, Grace?" Miss Turner asked. "It might help you sleep."

"Milk, hell," Garon said curtly. "Bring her a tot of Crown Royal."

"I hate spirits," Grace began.

"Now," he added, fixing Miss Turner with a level stare that didn't invite defiance.

"Back in a jiffy," Miss Turner said.

Garon let go of Grace's shoulders. His eyes were like lasers, probing, inquiring. "This isn't a new thing, is it?" he asked suddenly.

"The nightmare? No." She leaned forward, drawing her knees up under the cover to rest her forehead on. Her heart was skipping madly. She could barely get her breath at all. "I've had them for a long time."

He wanted to ask questions, demand answers. But she was a guest in his house. He didn't want to invade her privacy. He didn't want to know intimate things about her, either. He only felt sorry for her. This was just a brief interlude in his life, and hers. She needed help that he could give. But he didn't want to let her too close.

She took one last deep breath and grimaced when she saw the look on his face. He was hating this. She didn't even have to ask.

She pushed back her unruly hair. "I'll be all right now," she said without meeting his eyes. "Thanks for checking on me. It's just an old bad dream. I have them once in a while when I'm really stressed. Losing granny has been...difficult."

He couldn't imagine why. The old lady had been constantly critical of Grace. But if the old woman was all she had left, it was understandable that she was grieving for her. He knew grief intimately. It was still too fresh in his mind. He'd never shared it, with anyone. Not even with his father and brothers.

Grace was painfully aware that he was only wearing pajama bottoms under the black robe. It was open in front, and his broad, muscular, hair-roughened chest was too close for comfort. She glanced at it nervously, her body tensing with nervous discomfort. Her hands tightened around her knees.

Garon saw that reaction and was irritated by it. She'd been screaming her head off, so why was she acting as if he were trying to attack her? He got to his feet will ill-concealed impatience, glaring down at her.

She couldn't meet his eyes or explain or apologize. He didn't understand. He was a handsome, sensual man who never lacked female attention. It made him angry that this frumpy little woman looked at him as if he were a rapist.

The silence that grew between them was dark and explosive. Miss Turner broke it finally with her return. She had a whiskey jigger full of amber liquid. "Here you go, boss," she said, handing it to Garon.

He put it in Grace's hand. "Drink it," he said impatiently.

She grimaced as she sniffed it. "I've never had spirits," she tried to explain.

"You're having this, or Miss Turner will hold you down while I pour it in," he said curtly, stung by her attitude when the two of them were alone together.

She looked at him aghast. "You wouldn't dare," she challenged.

"Come here, Miss Turner," he beckoned the housekeeper. "I'll show you a half nelson to use on her."

He meant business. Grace grimaced again, but she held her breath and tossed the liquor down. It burned her throat and almost came up again. She gagged.

"Here," Miss Turner said quickly, pouring her a glass of water.

"Gasoline would taste better!" Grace raged, glaring at him.

"Bite your tongue, woman," he shot back, offended. "That's Crown Royal!"

"Diesel fuel," she muttered.

He threw up his hands and got to his feet. "You can't share precious things with peasants," he muttered.

"I am not a peasant."

"Or lunatics," he persisted.

"I am not a…!"

"You talk to rosebushes," he pointed out.

While she simmered, Miss Turner grinned. "Actually he does talk to tractors that won't start. I heard him use some Spanish slang that he could be arrested for in Del Rio."

He glared at her, narrowing one eye. "Some profanity is occasionally necessary to teach the stupid machine that you mean business. It's lucky it didn't get shot, at that."

"If you shoot the tractor, the foreman will bury you with it," Miss

Turner replied. "He says it's barely usable as it is, and he's trying to get the soil ready to plant."

"It's February," he exclaimed.

"In February we plant potatoes," she said shortly.

"I hate potatoes."

"We also plant forage grasses for the cattle," she amended.

He sighed. "I suppose he might need the tractor, at that." He glanced at Grace with his hands in his pockets. "If you think you can sleep, we might all try to get back to bed. I've got to drive up to Lytle first thing for a meeting."

"I'll be all right," she assured him. She recalled that the next day was visitation at the funeral home, and she shuddered.

He remembered that. Reluctant sympathy pushed his wounded ego aside. "I'll be home by five. You aren't having visitation until six, are you?"

She shook her head, surprised at his sudden knowledge of what was wrong with her.

"I'll drive you. Miss Turner can come, too."

"But you don't have to do that," she protested weakly.

"There isn't anybody else to do it," he said without rancor.

She bit her lower lip. "Thank you."

Her appreciation made him uncomfortable. "You're welcome. Let's go, Miss Turner."

"Sleep well, Grace," the housekeeper said gently.

"You, too. I'm sorry I woke you all up."

"I'm used to it," Garon said easily. "I work homicide. It isn't exactly a nine-to-five job."

Her eyebrows arched. "You mean you get called out at night?"

"Night, holidays, weekends," he agreed. "It's my job. In fact, it's my life. I like catching crooks."

She managed a wan smile. "It must be challenging."

He nodded, but he wasn't inclined to linger. She'd made her opinion of him as a man blatantly clear. "Sleep well."

She watched him go, followed by Miss Turner, with vague regret. He'd only been trying to comfort her, and she'd offended him. She was sorry about it. Her whole adult life had been one lonely ordeal as she met any masculine attention with rigid coldness. She wished she could sleep and escape the memories. That wasn't possible right now. She was too wired to rest. So she didn't lie down right away. She couldn't bear to have the nightmare come back. She propped up in bed and found a paperback to read. Once she was really sleepy, she'd try again.

HE WAS ALREADY GONE when she got up the next morning. She and Miss Turner had a small breakfast and then Miss Turner drove Grace home.

"I don't like leaving you here alone," the older woman said.

"I'm not, really," Grace told her with a smile. "The house is warm and kind. Three generations of my family lived and died here." She looked around, her eyes lingering on the huge maple tree in the front yard, bare now because it was still winter. In the autumn it was glorious, a symphony in red and gold. Cold winds made it shed its leaves in what Grace always called a rain of leaves. She loved to run through it, with her arms outstretched, and feel the nip of the first cold air on her face.

"That tree is going to come down one day and crush the house," Miss Turner mentioned.

"No, it won't," Grace assured her. "It's sturdy, and very long lived. It's the most beautiful tree in this area, in autumn."

"I'll reserve judgment until I see it," Miss Turner chuckled. "I'll come back for you about six. Okay?"

"If you're sure," Grace replied.

"I am."

She watched the older woman drive away and wondered again at the closeness she felt to Garon Grier and his housekeeper. They were all three misfits, in a way. She didn't know Garon very well, but she knew that he didn't socialize much and that he was a worka-holic. So was Miss Turner, apparently. Grace had to admit that she did her own share of work, at two jobs plus her after hours project that never seemed to get finished.

She went through the closet, hoping for one decent black dress. Her spare cash for months had gone to augment her grandmother's social security and pay for medicines that the old lady needed. Mrs. Collier didn't have much of a drug benefit, certainly not enough to cover drugs that cost over a hundred dollars a bottle. Often, Grace did without her own full prescription to cover her grandmother's. Coltrain said that was risky, but Grace figured what he didn't know wouldn't worry him.

"Wilbur!" she called loudly. There was a muffled answer as her old cat came out from under a discarded window box that was propped on a step. "What are you doing there?" she asked, bending to pet him. "Something scare you, baby?"

He only meowed. She didn't see anything near the house, but she'd heard one of Garon's men mention they'd seen coyotes in the area. She hoped none of them showed up at her house. She'd heard they killed cats and dogs. She was fond of Wilbur. He was twelve now, and the two of them had shared some traumatic times. Old Mrs. Collier hadn't tolerated Wilbur in the house, although Grace had sneaked him in during bouts of bad weather without the old lady knowing. Now, it didn't matter anymore. Grace decided that he was going to live inside now and keep her company. It would make her solitude less lonely.

That afternoon, the community came to her door with bowls of salad and platters of meat and cakes and pies. Someone even brought her four pounds of coffee, which she wasn't allowed to drink. But she made a pot, for the visitors.

It was the custom in small towns, bringing food for the family when there was a death. It was a way of showing sympathy. This way, the bereaved wouldn't have to prepare meals while they were going back and forth to the funeral home. Of course, there was only Grace in the family locally. But that didn't stop people from bringing food. Barbara, who owned the local café, brought meats and vegetables. Two sheriff's deputies and their wives came along with cakes and pies. The Ballenger brothers sent two of their sons along with homemade bread, and Leo Hart's wife Tess brought a Crock-Pot full of chicken and dumplings. It fascinated her that some of the town's leading lights thought so much of old Mrs. Collier, and she mentioned it to Barbara.

"Don't be silly," she chuckled. "It's you they're fond of, Grace," she added. "You used to baby-sit Calhoun Ballenger's kids, something Abby's never forgotten, and you helped Tess Hart with her rose garden. You should remember that you've always been one of the first to take food to other families, and none of the new rich families in town are snobs—unlike some of the older monied generation."

"I suppose so," Grace replied with a smile. She'd noticed that Mrs. Tabor, a leading light of the old money crowd, had actually sent a tray of finger foods, although she didn't mix much with common people. Her niece, who worked at Andy Webb's realty company, had already made a reputation as the worst of the local wild women. In fact, it was she who brought the tray.

"Thank you," Grace had told her, uneasy at the older woman's piercing scrutiny as she put the food on the dining room table alongside all the other platters.

"I just wanted a look at you," the woman chided. She was wearing jeans that must have been sprayed on, with a deeply low cut red blouse and sweater. She gave Grace's loose jeans and pink sweatshirt a mocking glance. "Well, it can't be your looks that fascinate Garon. I wondered why he'd be helping you out. I suppose it really is a case of just being neighborly." She laughed coldly. "I can't believe I was worried about the competition," she added carelessly, and walked out without another word.

Grace stared after her, speechless. She couldn't imagine her taciturn neighbor being interested in herself, of course, but she could see why he might go after Mrs. Tabor's niece. Oddly the thought hurt. Garon had never mentioned the flashy woman. Was he seeing her? She shouldn't care. She couldn't care. But it hurt to think of him with someone like that, who was self-centered and cruel. It seemed to Grace, without knowing why, that life had been cruel enough to Garon already.

SHE INVITED MISS TURNER and Garon over to eat with her that evening before they went to the funeral home. They protested, but she reasoned with them that she wasn't going to be able to eat it all herself. It would only go to waste.

She had paper plates and napkins ready when they drove up. It was a short, silent meal, but very enjoyable. Jacobsville boasted some of the best cooks in the county. There were homemade rolls, spice breads, baked ham and broiled chicken and all sorts of salads and side dishes.

"I know who made this chocolate cake," Miss Turner murmured with a smile as she savored her slice. "Barbara did this."

Grace laughed. "It's the only thing she can cook," she confided.

"Well, it's a good thing she doesn't have to depend on her skills to keep the café afloat, I suppose," came the reply. "Although she could certainly fill the tables with people eating chocolate cake. This is wonderful."

"I'll pack some for you to take home, when we get back from the funeral home," Grace said. "I hate to waste food."

"So do I," Miss Turner agreed.

"Mrs. Tabor's niece brought the snack platter," Grace told Miss Turner without looking at Garon.

Miss Turner didn't say anything, but her glance was eloquent.

Garon heard the comment. It surprised him. He hadn't spoken to the woman since she'd turned up in his driveway. He'd better call her about that party she'd invited him to, he supposed. She wasn't bad looking, and he was feeling his job lately.

He didn't say it aloud, but his face mirrored it. He and his task force had spent the morning looking over crime scene photos. He couldn't get them out of his mind. No homicides were pleasant to look at, but those with children were particularly disturbing.

"You're very quiet," Miss Turner remarked when Garon was pushing apple pie around on a saucer and sipping coffee.

"It was a long day," he said, without elaborating.

But Grace recalled that he'd been working on a task force, and she knew what it was about. She glanced at his set features with sympathy.

"You really don't have to go with us tonight," Grace began.

He looked up. "I don't mind."

"There will be a lot of people there," she continued without looking at him. "There might be some gossip…"

"I'm not worried about it," he said nonchalantly. He checked his watch. "We need to get moving pretty soon."

Grace got up. "I'll cover everything, and put the food in the refrigerator."

"I'll help," Miss Turner volunteered.

GRACE HAD KNOWN it would be an ordeal, but it wasn't as bad as she'd feared. Mrs. Collier was in a purple dress, her favorite church dress, and she looked very peaceful. Tears prickled at Grace's eyes and she dabbed them with a handkerchief. It would be lonely without the old lady, even with her constant criticism.

Grace's cousin, Bob Collier, came in a wheelchair, pushed by Tina, his caregiver. Tina was Miss Turner's age, dark haired and eyed, with a thick Spanish accent. She took good care of the elderly gentleman, and she was fond of Grace, as well.

Tina hugged her warmly. "You come see your cousin sometimes, huh?" she invited. "He gets lonely."

"I will." Grace bent and hugged Bob, who was dark-eyed with silver hair.

He chuckled. "You get prettier every year, girl," he teased. The smile faded. "I'm sorry about your grandmother. She and I didn't get along, but she was still family."

"That's what I always thought."

"Who's the man in the gray suit?" he added, nodding toward Garon.

"My next door neighbor," she said. "He's been very kind. So has his housekeeper, Miss Turner. She's standing next to him."

"You're lucky to have someone close to you," he said. "Tina and I are miles off the road. It gets lonely."

"I'll visit you more. I promise," she said gently.

He held her hand between both of his. "Had a hard life, haven't you, girl? You're due a little happiness. Maybe it's standing over there in a gray suit, huh?"

She laughed and flushed. "It's not like that. He's in law enforcement."

He raised his eyebrows. "Grace, have you been doing something illegal?" he asked with a twinkle in his eyes.

She laughed again. "I wouldn't know how."

Garon was watching her with the old man in the wheelchair. She had a caring nature, a nurturing personality that made him uncomfortable. He knew the old man was curious about his place in Grace's life. He was sure she'd tell him the truth. He wasn't interested in a relationship with his neighbor. He'd have to find a way to get that across, but not tonight. Grace needed a little support, to get her through this bad time.

Cash Grier, Jacobsville's police chief, walked into the funeral home and stopped to extend his sympathy to Grace. He noted his brother near the casket and joined him.

"I thought you didn't go to funerals," he mused.

Garon shrugged. "She was all alone. Miss Turner and I have been looking out for her."

"Uh-huh."

Garon glared at him. "I'm not in the market for a frumpy girlfriend."

Cash's smile faded and he gave his brother a hard glare. "That was uncalled for. Grace doesn't have the sort of money she'd need to dress for every occasion."

Garon shifted his weight, his eyes going reluctantly to Grace's trim figure in the slightly too large black dress she was wearing. It did nothing for her and looked as if it had come from a yard sale.

"You'd think the old lady could have afforded one good dress for her," Garon muttered.

Cash frowned. "You haven't got a clue, have you?" he asked. "Mrs. Collier had several prescriptions that she was required to take. She and Grace had to choose between medicine and food, never mind dressy clothing. I'd lay odds that dress is one of the old lady's. Until tonight, I've never even seen Grace Carver in a dress."

"You're kidding," Garon returned.

"I'm not," his brother said firmly. "Old people in this town sometimes do without groceries to pay drug bills. Health care is expensive. People living on social security don't have a lot of options. Grace worked two part-time jobs to help pay for the old lady's medicines. She may be poor, but she's proud."

Garon averted his eyes. "Now that the old woman's gone, maybe she can get a good paying job, or go back to school and finish her education."

Cash studied the other man quietly. "Not all women have a yen to start international corporations," he pointed out.

Garon had to admit that Cash was right. He couldn't see Grace in a power suit throwing out orders to a cadre of underlings.

"What's eating you?" Cash persisted, because the man he was beginning to know wasn't petty or critical.

Garon's mouth pulled down. "We're investigating a homicide. A ten-year-old girl."

"Ah. That one." Cash shifted his weight. "We've heard about the case, even down here. Brutal."

"Very. And it looks as if it might not be the only one," he added with a quick glance. "That's between you and me."

"Of course. Any leads?"

Garon shook his head. "It's early days."

"Some cases are harder than others to work," his brother agreed.

Garon was watching as Grace spoke to citizens who came by to offer their condolences. She was friendly, warm, welcoming, grateful. She was completely natural. He knew she must be cut up inside, but she wasn't letting it show.

"Do you know what happened to her mother?" Garon asked Cash.

He shook his head. "Only that she died some years ago, when Grace was still a child. The old lady had a vinegary personality, but she was respected around town. Her late husband had been a deputy sheriff. So was Grace's father, for a short time."

"That's what I heard."

"I suppose you know that being seen with Grace is going to start rumors flying," Cash pointed out.

"She said that," he replied. "The rumors will wind down when this is all over."

"You don't date at all, do you?" Cash asked.

"I've been asked to a cocktail party next Friday at the Tabors', by the niece. Grace said she brought food to the house this afternoon for the funeral."

Cash whistled through his pursed lips.

"What?" Garon asked.

Cash gave him a speaking glance. "Mrs. Tabor's niece is raising eyebrows locally, and she isn't well liked."

"Most of the founding families have been invited to the party, from what I've been told," Garon said defensively.

"Most of them have also sent their regrets," Cash interjected, "most prominently the Ballengers, the Harts and the Tremaynes. Without them, nobody else is going to show up, either."

"What have they got against the niece?" he wanted to know.

"Have you met her?" Cash murmured dryly.

"Sure. She came to the ranch and invited me to the party."

"Anything about her strike you as unusual?"

Garon thought for a minute. "She's rather forward, and she dresses in a seductive fashion."

"Exactly. And how well do you think that behavior is going to go over in a small conservative town?"

"She's out of place here," Garon said. "But so am I. I hate small town politics."

Cash smiled. "I love it, warts and all. It's the first place I've ever belonged."

"Your wife seems to like it here, too."

He nodded. "The baby has opened even more doors for us, locally," he said, smiling dreamily. "I never thought I'd end up a family man."

Garon took a step away. "I hope it's not contagious," he muttered darkly. "I'm married to my job."

"Where have I heard that before?" Cash wondered.

The Coltrains walked in with their son, Joshua. His father was carrying him, although he looked to be about two years old. Copper was tall and redheaded. His wife, Lou, was blond. Their little boy had blond hair with red lights, and he favored his father most.

They made a beeline for Grace. Lou hugged her warmly. So did Copper.

"What is it with Miss Carver and the Coltrains?" Garon asked curiously. "He takes an unusual interest in her well-being, although he seems to be in love with his wife."

"Copper has a special place for his long-time patients," Cash said. "I've heard that Grace was one of the first people who went to him when he opened his practice here. She was just a kid at the time."

"Oh."

"Do you automatically put the worst possible interpretation on people's relationships?" Cash asked.

"I work in law enforcement."

"So do I," Cash reminded him, "but I try to give people the benefit of the doubt."

"Yes, I remember you giving it to our stepmother."

Cash closed up and his eyes glittered dangerously.

Garon let out a long breath. "Hell, I didn't mean that." He averted his face. "The little girl was ten. She was raped and sodomized and cut to pieces. Ten years old!"

Cash laid a big hand on the other man's shoulder. "Listen, I've seen my share of grisly murders, in the military and in police work. I know what it's like. But you have to keep some emotional distance. You know that."

Garon swallowed, hard. He had a history that he'd never shared with his family. He'd lived away from them back East for years, during which they'd all but lost touch. He was keeping secrets that were too painful to share, even now. The child's death had affected him in unexpected ways, and he wasn't coping well.

"I've never had to work a child killing before," Garon said shortly. "I've done hostage rescue and SWAT, I've even worked a serial murder. But I've never had to work a crime scene where a child was literally butchered. I wasn't prepared."

"Nobody's ever prepared," Cash replied. "I worked in covert areas for years. Some of the things I had to do involved children."

Garon glanced at him. "Children carrying AK-47s, if memory serves."

"Yeah," Cash replied. "That didn't make it any easier to pull the trigger."

"At least it was a clean kill. This is messy. It's messy and deliberate and depraved," he said harshly. "I don't like sharing the planet with a human being who could do something like that to a little girl."

"So catch him and make sure he gets Death Row," Cash replied.

Garon glanced at his brother and managed a smile. "You're an optimist. We don't even have a suspect yet."

"Ask enough people, and somebody will have seen something," came the reply. "I guarantee it."

Garon nodded. He stared at Grace without actually seeing her. "Thanks," he said curtly.

"What are brothers for?" Cash chuckled.

THE WAKE was only two hours, but Grace felt exhausted, physically and emotionally, when it was all over. She climbed into the car with Garon and Miss Turner without a word.

She went into her house to fix the cake and some of the food for Garon to take home with him while Miss Turner waited in the car.

"I really appreciate you and Miss Turner going with me tonight," she said in a subdued tone. "I didn't realize how lonely it would be."

"Lonely?" he murmured, watching her put food in sealed plastic containers. "Half the town was there."

She turned, staring at him. "You can be alone in a city."

"I suppose so. Save some of that for yourself," he told her.

"I'll still have plenty. I'll freeze what I don't eat right away."

"Don't bother with that apple pie," he stopped her when she began to unwrap it.

"But you like apple cake," she replied, perplexed.

"I like *your* apple cake," he corrected.

She flushed and laughed a little nervously. "Oh. Thanks."

"Compliments embarrass you," he noted.

She shrugged. "I'm not used to them."

But she should have been, he thought, watching her. From what he'd heard, she was a good little cook. And she seemed never to get tired of listening to other people talk. So few people could listen.

She put the plastic containers in a big plastic bag and handed them to him. "Thanks again," she said shyly.

"Thank you." He hesitated. "What time is the funeral tomorrow?"

"It's at eleven," she said. "But please don't feel obliged to—"

"I can't make it," he interrupted. "I have to help interview neighbors around the child's home. I'm sorry."

"You've done so much already," she began.

"Miss Turner will go with you," he continued. He held up a hand. "She volunteered."

"All right, then. Thank her for me."

He nodded. "She'll pick you up a few minutes past ten in the morning."

"All right."

She looked sad and lonely and lost. Impulsively he reached out and touched a lock of her blond hair that had escaped from its bun. She caught her breath and moved back a step instinctively.

That irritated him. His dark eyes flashed. "Good night, then," he said curtly, took the bag and turned to leave.

She bit her lower lip almost through. He was being kind, but she couldn't help her own reactions.

He paused at the front door. "Keep this locked," he told her as he opened it. "Even out here in the country, there are dangerous people."

"I will."

She was like a stick figure. Her posture spoke volumes. Her large gray eyes were glittery with fear. He turned and moved toward her, noticing how much more she tensed as he approached her. He scowled down at her. "Why are you afraid of me?" he asked very softly.

She stumbled for words and couldn't find any that would suit the occasion. She grimaced, avoiding his penetrating gaze. He saw too much.

"Never mind," he said when she didn't reply. "It isn't as if I'm interested in you that way," he added almost as an afterthought, and with a cold, faint smile. "Good night."

He walked down the steps as nonchalantly as if he'd forgotten her existence. She knew he'd been mentally comparing her with that flashy niece of Mrs. Tabor's and it made her furious. She wished that she were a whole woman, a beautiful woman, who could drive him mad with her good looks and make him forget that flashy newcomer. But it was a forlorn hope. She dressed as she lived—behind barriers of sexlessness. It was a prison from which there would never be an escape for her. Despite the attractions of her sexy next-door neighbor.

6

THE FUNERAL was brief, and only a few people attended it. Grace wept for her grandmother at the graveside service and then dried her eyes. She had to learn to take care of herself, to live alone and work alone, with nobody to talk to. It was going to be a hard existence, until she got the hang of it. She was aware, and surprised, that Garon had shown up just in time for the graveside service. He stood apart, frowning curiously at one of the other people attending the ceremony.

After the minister offered his condolences, she got up, turned and almost plowed right into Richard Marquez, standing beside Barbara.

"Thank you both for coming," she said, smiling. "I wasn't expecting you."

Barbara hugged her warmly. "You're family. Of course we came."

Marquez nodded, and smiled. Garon noticed that Marquez made no move to touch Grace or even approach her. Why was he here? How well did the man know his mysterious next-door neighbor? He hadn't mentioned Mrs. Collier's funeral to Garon when the task force met.

Grace looked toward Garon a little uneasily. He joined the small group, with Miss Turner beside him.

"I didn't know you'd be here," Marquez said, shaking hands. "Did you know Mrs. Collier?"

"He and Miss Turner have been kind enough to watch out for me in the past few days," Grace said without looking at Garon.

Marquez seemed curious, but he didn't press it. "I have to get back to work," he told Grace. "Mom wanted to come, and I didn't want her to have to come alone."

"Worrywart," Barbara chided the young man. "I'll outlive you."

"See you around," Marquez told Garon.

He nodded, including Barbara in the gesture. She smiled secretively at Grace and followed Marquez out of the cemetery.

"I didn't know you were acquainted with Marquez," Garon remarked as they walked back toward their cars with Miss Turner. Miss Turner had ridden in with Grace, and she went a little ahead of them to wait at the Expedition for her.

"We grew up together," she replied to Garon. "Sort of," she amended. "He was six years older than me."

He didn't say anything else, but he was curious.

GRACE WENT BACK HOME and started cleaning out her grandmother's bedroom. It gave her something to do, kept her busy. It was a sad task. In the closet, the old lady had kept some gowns that had belonged to Grace's mother. There were photographs, too, of her parents and both sets of her grandparents. She sat in her grandmother's chair, looking through the photo album, and crying a little as it grew later. Death wasn't exactly an option in life—everyone had to face it sooner or later. But she wasn't ready. As unpleasant as her grandmother could be, it was lonely without the old lady.

She didn't have to go to work the next morning, so she slept late. It was just as well; the nightmare had come back again in the early hours before dawn. She'd sat up in bed, sobbing wildly. She recalled Garon's strong hands on her shoulders, lifting her, the night when she'd been afraid. She felt drawn to him, but she had an irrational fear of men when they got too close. It was a shame that she was imprisoned in her own memory. He seemed a very decent sort of man, and he had a kind heart.

She had a light lunch and spent the afternoon hard at work on her project, in the sewing room that her grandmother had once used. She was pleased with her progress and hopeful that it might one day provide a new source of income, if she were lucky.

The afternoon was cold and the wind was blustery. It was slowly growing dark and her old tomcat, Wilbur, hadn't come up for his evening meal.

She walked out into the yard, looking for him. There was a faint cry on the wind. She heard it without realizing what it was until the pitch escalated. It was Wilbur, and he was squalling.

She turned and ran toward the sound, at the back of the house, calling him at the top of her lungs.

He squalled again. She ran faster, pausing just a minute to catch her breath before she forced her body back into speed. As she approached the beginning of the plowed field, she saw a flash of orange with a big, reddish brown form gaining on it.

Instinctively she picked up a fallen limb from the pecan tree and hefted it. "Wilbur!" she yelled.

The old cat veered, quickly for an animal of his years, and moved toward her. As the animal behind it came closer, she realized that it was a coyote. She'd heard neighbors talk about them eating cats and killing dogs. She got a firmer hold on the limb. He wasn't eating Wilbur!

She moved toward the animal, no thought of the danger she could be in, and slammed the limb down at his head. He stopped abruptly and let out a cry. Then he looked at her, crouched and growled.

"You get out of my yard! You're not hurting my cat!" she yelled, swinging the limb again. This time it connected with his hind quarters and he let out a yowl. She was too angry to feel fear. She went toward him again, yelling as she swung the limb. He started backing up, growling, but retreating.

"Git!" she yelled.

He shook himself, gave her a last indignant look and trotted back off into the field.

She leaned on the limb. Her ankle was throbbing. She'd run right over a bush chasing the coyote. She hadn't fallen, but she'd tripped uncomfortably hard. She groaned as she bent to wrap her fingers around it. "Wilbur?" she called.

The old cat came trotting up, looking as if he hadn't a care in the world. He rubbed up against her leg, twirling around it affectionately. She could hear him purring in the stillness of late afternoon.

"You horror," she muttered. "Look what you made me do!"

He purred louder.

She started to turn and fell heavily to the ground. Holding her ankle, with the cat now in her lap and rubbing against her furiously, she couldn't get up. This was a fine way to end the day, she thought miserably. She'd probably be out here all night, unless she could drag herself to the front porch. Well, at least the coyote was gone…

"Grace!"

She frowned. That deep voice sounded oddly familiar. It sounded like Garon. But surely he hadn't heard her?

"I'm here!" she called.

He came around the house, still dressed in his work clothes. "What the hell happened?"

"A coyote was chasing Wilbur. I ran him off with a stick, but I turned my ankle in the process," she said with a small laugh.

"I heard you yelling from the front porch. I thought you were being attacked," he muttered, bending. "Here, I'll carry you…!"

She froze, her eyes wide, her body rigid as he bent. She jerked back, clutching her sweater around her chest.

He swore fiercely, standing abruptly upright. "What the hell is the matter with you?" he demanded.

Tears stung her eyes. She hated the way she was with men. He didn't mean to hurt her. He was trying to help. But she couldn't bear a man's touch on her skin. How could she explain that to him?

"I…don't like…being touched," she whispered, not looking at him. She was too embarrassed.

It had been a long day, full of frustration, and he wasn't in a good mood. He almost stormed off and left her to it. Then he remembered the nightmare she'd had at his house. He remembered the shapeless clothing she wore, her lack of makeup, her uneasiness with men. He'd been in law enforcement long enough to recognize those signs. It hit him like a brick. He should have seen it sooner.

He knelt down in front of her, his eyes even with hers. "Grace," he said gently, "I won't hurt you. I promise I won't. But you can't walk, and you can't stay here all night."

She still had a stranglehold on her sweater, but his voice was calm and steady, and he didn't look angry anymore. He didn't even look threatening. She ground her teeth together.

"It isn't…personal," she gritted.

"Of course it isn't. Come on."

He held out his arm and she took it, pulling herself to her feet. She assumed that he would lend her some support on her way to the porch. But he suddenly bent and swung her up in his arms, carrying her toward the porch.

She made an odd, frightened little sound in her throat and stiffened.

He stopped, looking down into her eyes. "You don't like being carried," he murmured. "It frightens you."

She swallowed, hard, her eyes full of pain. He didn't know. She couldn't tell him. She drew in a long breath, and then another. He wasn't going to hurt her. He was a kind man.

She forced herself to relax. Her cold hands eased up around his neck as he shifted her weight. "S…sorry," she stammered.

He wondered what in the world could have happened to her, what had made her so jumpy and uneasy with men. An attack of some sort? A rape? He didn't know her well enough to ask questions. He wished he did.

"Taking on a coyote with a stick," he murmured as he carried her back to the house. "Now I've heard everything."

"He was trying to hurt Wilbur," she explained.

He smiled. "I see."

"He's just a helpless old cat," she said.

"No need to explain. I used to have a cat, myself."

"What happened to it?"

He didn't like the memory. "I had to give it away. I was transferred to another city and the apartment didn't allow cats."

"That's sad."

"There was a little girl next door who loved cats. I gave it to her."

She wanted to know about him, about his past. But she sensed that he was very much like her; he didn't talk about himself.

She was noticing other things. He smelled of a nicely masculine aftershave. He smelled of soap, too. He was a fastidious man. His shirts were always starched and pressed, his boots highly polished. His skin was olive tan, and his eyes were dark and mysterious. He had high cheekbones and a sensuous mouth.

The thought embarrassed her. She hadn't thought of a mouth being sensuous before. And she was having some odd sensations because of the way he was holding her, so that one of her breasts was almost flattened against his broad chest. Her heartbeat accelerated, and her breath came unsteadily past her lips.

He felt those reactions in her with an odd sense of pride. She was afraid of men but she was vulnerable with him.

He carried her into the house and put her down in an easy chair. "Do you have an Ace bandage?"

She gave him a wide-eyed look. "And what would I be doing with an Ace bandage?" she asked reasonably.

"Good question." He eyed her calmly. "We could manage with some gauze and adhesive tape, I suppose."

"Nobody normal uses that on cuts," she pointed out. "We have Band-Aids."

He pursed his lips. "We could use an old pair of panty hose."

"I don't wear…"

He held up a hand. "Please. I have problems discussing women's underthings."

At first she took it seriously, and then she saw the twinkle in his dark eyes and she started laughing.

The action made her face glow, emphasized the softness of her gray eyes and the beauty of her perfect skin and pretty mouth. He found himself staring down at her helplessly. Her hair was up in a high ponytail. He wanted to take it down and see if it felt as silky as it looked.

"Well, you're going to have to come home with me," he said. "I'm sure Miss Turner can find something to bind your ankle with."

"I've only just come back home," she pointed out. "And Wilbur has to be fed."

He shrugged. "I'll feed Wilbur."

"I suppose I could leave him inside," she began. "I just bought a litter box…"

He left her in midsentence to attend to the old tomcat, who came right in when he opened the front door and led him to the kitchen.

HE HELPED GRACE into his car, leaning over her to fasten her seat belt. He noticed her breathing changed as he came close, and his gaze suddenly dropped to meet hers in the glare of the top light. It was like lightning striking. His dark eyes narrowed and fell to her full mouth, lingering there until he heard a faint gasp come out of her throat.

He had to force himself to stand up. He closed her door and moved around the car, reciting silent multiplication tables to himself as he got in beside her and started the car. It really had been a long, dry spell, if this frumpy woman was arousing him, he told himself.

He carried her into the house, pausing to ring the doorbell and wait for Miss Turner to answer it. He looked down into Grace's face and felt his arms involuntarily drawing her closer. She shivered, once, and her hands stole up around his neck as she met the open curiosity of his gaze.

His chest rose and fell heavily. His jaw tautened. He looked at her mouth and felt an insane fever to take it under his and devour it.

Grace didn't understand much about men, but even in her innocence she felt the heat and sensuality of that look, and her body responded to it helplessly.

"Playing with fire, little girl," he whispered gruffly.

The tension in his deep, velvety voice rippled through her like liquid fire. Her hands tightened behind his neck. She actually lifted toward him in the few explosive seconds before the sound of the front door opening split them quickly apart.

"What in the world...!" Miss Turner exclaimed when she saw Grace being carried.

"She tripped while she was chasing a coyote with a stick," Garon muttered, brushing past her with Grace. "I need an Ace bandage."

"I'll go get one. I keep them for the men," she murmured, retreating as he headed for the living room. "Somebody's always spraining something. Chasing a coyote?!"

"He was trying to eat my cat," Grace called.

"He'd throw him right back up," Garon returned as he put her quickly down on the sofa. "Your cat looks like five miles of rough road, and he stinks."

"He does not!" she exclaimed.

"Well, you can take my word for it that nothing sane would try to eat him," he retorted.

He put his hands in his pockets and stared down at her with confusion. She was wearing baggy jeans and that same pink sweatshirt. He wondered what she'd look like in black lace and silk. He blinked, hard. Where had that odd curiosity come from?

Miss Turner was back in a flash with the bandage. She handed it to Garon. "Are you planning to repair her and take her home, or is she staying?"

Garon knelt at her feet, opening the elastic bandage. He looked up at Grace with a fever of hunger. He didn't understand it, but he couldn't fight it, either. "She's staying," he murmured, lifting her foot onto his thigh. "For a few days, at least."

"But, my job…"

"I'll phone Judy at the florist for you, Grace," Miss Turner said, delighted.

"You can't work if you can't walk," Garon agreed. "Just a couple of days off your feet should do the trick. Rest, ice packs, compression and elevation. RICE," he added, smiling. "We'll take good care of you."

She didn't even have the will to resist. She wanted to be with him. It was going to end in tragedy, she knew it. But she couldn't help herself. "Okay," she said.

He smiled to himself. Fevers were best allowed to burn themselves out, he thought, and refused to think any deeper than that.

HE WENT TO WORK the next day, leaving Grace propped up in bed with plenty of reading material and Miss Turner for company. The ice packs had reduced the swelling, and the rest was helping as well.

"I feel much better," Grace told the older woman.

"A couple more days and you'll be walking," was her reply. She smiled. "I think you're getting to the boss," she added on a chuckle. "Only a week ago, he'd have had Coltrain admit you to the hospital."

"He just feels sorry for me," Grace said, not getting her hopes up. "That niece of Mrs. Tabor's brought food to the house," she said. "She told me that she'd worried I was some sort of competition until she saw me. She was very insulting."

"You should tell the boss."

"No," Grace returned. "I couldn't. She must have something going with him."

"An invitation to a party," Miss Turner replied. "He may find her interesting, but she isn't the proper sort of companion for a man in his position. Law enforcement types tend to be extra conservative. She's being gossiped about all over town, and not in a good way. The woman's a nymphomaniac. She doesn't even stop at married men."

"What do you mean?"

"They say she made a play for Leo Hart, and Tess walked right up to her in Andy Webb's office and told her she'd tar and feather her if she ever made a move on her husband again. Andy's still laughing about it."

"What did she say?"

"There was nothing she could say. Tess was furious, and she didn't lower her voice any, either. I wouldn't say the woman was em-barrassed, exactly, but Calhoun Ballenger was walking past the office when Tess said it, and he gave the woman a look that meant trouble. She got out of Tess's way real fast."

Grace couldn't resist a smile. Redheaded Tess was a tiger when she lost her temper.

GARON AND MARQUEZ had gone together to the outskirts of the city to interview, among many others, a witness who said he saw a shadowy figure take the child out of her house late one night. Garon had a BlackBerry, like Marquez's. It came in handy here.

"Couldn't swear to it," the witness, Sheldon, told them. He lived next door to the child who had been abducted. "But he looked sort of like a drifter I saw near the computer shop in town. I write software," he added in a lazy tone. "The man was tall, thin, completely bald on top. Middle-aged. He looked dirty. And he limped."

"Could you see the child?" Garon asked.

He shrugged. "He was carrying something. It could have been a bundle of clothes for all I know. I was up late. I went to the kitchen for water, and there he was. It wasn't until the next morning that I heard the child was missing. I did tell the police."

"Yes, we had the patrolman's report," Marquez replied. He gave the man a long, steady scrutiny, noting his gloves. "Why do you wear gloves in the house?" he asked.

"I had an accident when I was a child," the man replied, his eyes growing cold. "I have scars on them. People stare."

"Sorry," Marquez said.

"Can you type like that?" Garon queried, noting how very white the wrists were above the gloves.

"Yes, they're kid leather, very thin."

"Well, thanks," Garon said, putting away his BlackBerry.

"Anytime," he replied, rising from his chair. He was a tall, timid sort of man who seemed to like the best computers money could buy. He had two, a base computer and an expensive laptop. He said he had a girlfriend, but he lived alone in the small apartment complex just inside the San Antonio city limits.

"How long have you lived here?" Marquez asked.

"About a year," he said. He smiled pleasantly. "I don't stay one place much. I get restless. And my job is portable. All I really need is a post office."

"Well, thanks again. If you think of anything else, give us a call," Marquez added, handing him a business card.

The man looked at it curiously. "Sure. Sure I will." He smiled oddly. "How's the case coming? Any leads?"

"We're hoping you might have given us one," Marquez said.

"I can see how you'd need help finding this guy," he remarked. "You cops aren't required to have much education, are you? I was invited to join MENSA."

MENSA, the organization for geniuses. Garon gave the man an odd look. "Were you?"

"Hey, I might only have two years of college, but the Fed here—" Marquez indicated Garon "—he's got a degree."

The man stared at Garon without blinking. It was disconcerting. "Fed?"

"Sure," Marquez said. "He's FBI."

"I...I didn't know they'd called the Bureau in on this case," the man stammered.

"We requested his help," Marquez said. He didn't say why.

The man looked less confident. "Well, of course, the FBI would have experts on serial murder," he murmured, almost to himself, "and you'd need one for this case."

Garon frowned. "Why do you think this case is a serial killing?"

The man laughed hollowly. "No reason. It's just, there was a very similar case in the papers last year sometime. That was a child, too. It was in Texas somewhere. Two of them would make it serial, wouldn't it?"

Garon stared at him. "We're not prepared to call it that just yet."

The man was all smiles as he walked them out. "Anything more I can do, I'll be here. Just ask."

Marquez and Garon left, walking slowly back to the Bureau car that Garon had driven here in. The man watched them leave, waving again as they got into the car and pulled away.

"I don't like him," Marquez said suddenly.

"Why not?"

Marquez shifted, adjusting his seat belt. "I don't know. There's something about him. Something not right."

Garon gave him a curious look. "How long have you worked homicide?"

"Four years. Why?"

Garon smiled to himself. "You carry a gun with you when you empty your trash can."

Marquez's eyes widened. "How the hell did you know that?"

"You keep one by the bed, one in the bathroom, one in the kitchen and you wear a spare in an ankle holster."

"Who's being investigated here?" the younger man demanded.

"I'm right. You know I am."

Marquez made a rough sound in his throat. "They aren't catching me off guard," he said firmly.

"You need to work in another area for a while," he commented. "Too many homicides will burn you out."

"And you'd know this, how?"

"I was in the FBI's Hostage Rescue Team, and then in SWAT," he said. "I wanted something to keep my mind busy. But I saw too many dead people. I woke up one night with a victim sitting in the chair beside my bed, asking why I didn't shoot before the kidnapper did. The victim had been a hostage." He shrugged. "You can work homicides too long."

Marquez laughed hollowly. "I guess so."

"But don't ask for a transfer until we solve this case," Garon added. "I think you're right about the murders being related. He's good. He's very good. He put the body in a field near the road, where it would be found easily. He wanted her found. If your crime scene investigator was right, she'd been tortured for some time. That means the killer has to have a place where he feels comfortable keeping a child bound, without fear of discovery. It also means he's cocky. He thinks he's smarter than we are."

"Did you ever do profiling?"

Garon shook his head. "We have professionals who do that. But I've read the crime scene report and talked to the parents. I've worked serial killings before. This guy is a sadistic killer. He likes to hurt children. He gets off on their pain."

"Organized or disorganized?"

"Organized, definitely," Garon replied, stopping at a red light. "He took time to dress the child and even put her shoes and socks back on. He posed her at the site where she was found. He tied a red ribbon around her neck. In fact," he added grimly, "she was likely strangled with the ribbon."

"You think there's a connection to the Palo Verde case?"

"Yes, and also to the Del Rio case two years ago."

"That would make three similar child murders in three years," Marquez said.

He nodded. "And that makes it serial murder. We're going to drive over to Del Rio right now," he added, making a turn. "If we can't get anybody to talk to us on the phone or via e-mail, we'll just drop in for coffee."

"I'll bet you they drink instant," Marquez muttered.

"I'll bet you're right."

In fact, they did. There was only one policeman on duty when they arrived, and he was responsible for every facet of policing.

He apologized for not answering their calls. "We've had a clown calling the office day and night to report ghostly apparitions," he muttered. "The guy's got two screws loose and every time we ignore him, he threatens us with his family's lawyers. They're rich, his family." He shook his head. "It was better when we had the voodoo guy, trying to put spells on us by sticking pins in a G.I. Joe doll."

Garon smiled despite himself. "We want to know what you've got on the child killing year before last."

He frowned. "Now that's a funny thing," he said. "No, I don't mean the killing was funny. There was this guy, said he was a reporter for one of the east Texas dailies. He asked to see the file on the murder. I figured it wouldn't hurt, to have a little publicity. Might turn up a suspect. I had a call, so I left the guy with the file and told him

I'd be right back. I had to work an accident, and wait for the state police because there were injuries. By the time I got back to the office, the reporter was gone. The phone started ringing. The file was on the desk, so I just stuck it back in the cabinet and answered the phone." He sipped coffee. "Next day, I wanted to take another look at the case, so I pulled out the file. It had ten sheets of blank paper in it. No evidence, no crime scene photos, no nothing."

"Damn!" Marquez grumbled.

"I know, it was naïve to leave the guy alone with the file. But I figured I could track him down. I phoned every daily in east Texas."

"He didn't work for any newspaper," Garon figured.

"Apparently not."

"What was in the file?" Marquez asked.

"Crime scene photos, trace evidence, swatches of the child's underwear."

Garon frowned. "Nothing else?"

"Not really."

"Did you have negatives of the photos?"

"No, but I figured the photographer would, so I phoned him." He shook his head. "He'd had a fire in his studio and all the negatives were gone."

Garon and Marquez looked at each other curiously. It was some coincidence, those two mishaps.

"You're sure there was no other evidence?" Marquez persisted.

The police officer pursed his lips. "Well, yes, there was the long piece of wide silk ribbon he used to strangle her…"

"Ribbon?" Garon asked quickly. "What color?"

"Why, it was red," the officer replied. "Blood-red."

7

GRACE WAS SITTING IN the living room watching the news when Garon came in, tired and hungry. It was obvious that he didn't work an average eight-hour day. In fact, FBI agents were expected to work ten-hour days, and they were paid accordingly.

He sat down in his big armchair. "What a day," he said heavily.

"You're still working on the little girl's murder?" she asked.

He nodded. "That's all I've done today. But my squad is trying to track down a team of bank robbers who carry automatic weapons. And on my desk, waiting, are a drive-by shooting, a gang murder, a supposed suicide and an attempted murder that the victim's spouse hired a hit man to commit." He glanced at her with a weary smile. "She had the bad luck to solicit an FBI agent to do the dirty deed."

"Entrapment," Grace chided.

He chuckled, leaned back and loosened his tie. "That's exactly what the perpetrator called it. You don't solicit hired killers in bars that law enforcement personnel are known to frequent. The man she asked came straight to us."

Miss Turner heard him come in and paused at the doorway. "You ready to eat?"

"Yes."

"Come on, then."

"Shall I bring Grace?"

"That would be nice."

He stood up and moved to where Grace was sitting. She colored prettily when he reached her, and those shy gray eyes made him feel odd inside.

He bent toward her. "Put your arms around me," he said in a low, soft tone.

She caught her breath. He did have the sexiest voice she'd ever heard. She lifted her arms around his neck and felt him pick her up as if she weighed no more than a feather. He looked down into her eyes at close range and then at her mouth.

"I could get used to this," he remarked.

Before she realized his intention, he brushed his hard mouth over her lips in a shiver of contact that made her heart jump.

He drew back, watching her reaction. She seemed nervous, but she wasn't trying to get away. He bent again. This time, he brushed her lips apart with slow, sensuous motions and caught her upper lip between both of his in a sensuous, nibbling motion. She trembled. Her lips followed his as she gave in to the first rush of desire she'd ever felt for a man.

He laughed softly, under his breath, and then he kissed her. He was no longer teasing. His mouth was demanding, masterful. He curled her into his body, crushing her soft breasts against his broad chest. He groaned faintly and pressed her lips apart with a hunger that was contagious.

Just as her arms tightened around his neck, Miss Turner called down the hall, "It's getting cold!"

His head jerked up. He stared at Grace with mingled desire and irritation. She was drawing him in, with her vulnerabilities and her sense of humor, and he didn't like it. He didn't want her in his life. But her eyes were soft and searching, and his heart was still racing from the heady contact with her lips. He shifted her and walked down the hall toward the dining room, mentally reciting square root solutions all the way.

He hardly knew what he was eating. Grace's sudden response had sent him spinning. He knew he should back off. But he wasn't certain that he could. She appealed to him strongly.

They stared at each other all through supper, with Miss Turner watching covertly and grinning.

After supper, Garon carried her back into the living room and put her down gently on the sofa. Despite her ardor earlier, she was jittery and inhibited with him. He sat down in his armchair across from her. He didn't turn on the television.

"Something happened to you," he began quietly, wanting to understand her. His eyes narrowed when she reacted suddenly to the words. He leaned forward. "Yes. When you were a child. Someone made advances to you, frightened you."

She bit her lower lip, hard, and averted her eyes. "How could you know that?" she asked, stiffening as she waited for the answer. He couldn't know...could he?

"I've worked in law enforcement all my adult life," he said simply. "I know the signs."

She relaxed, only a little. Then she frowned and glanced back at him when she realized what he was insinuating. "Signs?"

"Yes. You cover your body in every way possible. You don't wear makeup. You screw your hair up and keep your eyes down. You stiffen if a man comes too close." His dark eyes narrowed on her face. "Some man touched you inappropriately."

She swallowed, hard. "Yes," she bit off.

"Not a boyfriend."

Her face colored. "Definitely not."

"A relative?"

She shook her head. It was hard to talk about it. She couldn't, even now, tell him the truth. At least, not the whole truth. She couldn't bear to remember. "A stranger," she corrected.

"Did you tell someone?"

She had, eventually. At the hospital. "Yes."

He drew in a long breath. "Did they catch him?"

She smiled sadly. "No. He was gone when the police got there."

"I don't suppose your mother got you into therapy."

"She was long gone by then, like my father," she said simply. "My grandmother said we didn't talk about such things to strangers."

He wanted to curse roundly. No wonder she was messed up. Small towns and their secrets. "Were there any more cases like yours, at the time?"

"You mean, did they look for the man who did it," she interpreted. "Yes, they did. But he wasn't known locally. He didn't leave a trail that anyone could follow. Even if he had, my grandmother convinced the police chief at the time to bury the file."

"That was stupid."

"Yes, it was," she agreed. "He might still be doing it, somewhere."

"If he's still alive, he probably is," he agreed coldly. "Men who do inappropriate things to children don't ever stop."

It was worse than he knew, but she didn't talk about it to anyone outside her family. She felt dirty when she discussed it.

He saw her discomfort. "Grace, it wasn't your fault."

"Everybody says that," she bit off. "But he said it was! He said it was because I wore shorts and halter tops and...!"

"God in heaven, what sort of normal man is tempted by a child, whatever she wears?" he exploded.

That made her feel better. She searched his angry face. "I don't suppose normal men would be," she conceded.

He made an effort to calm his temper. It hurt him that a grown man could have approached a child that way, especially Grace. "Have you ever talked about it?"

"Only to Dr. Coltrain."

So that was it. That explained her relationship with the redheaded doctor. He'd been her confessor. "I'll bet he gave your grandmother hell about covering it up."

She managed a smile. "He did. But she gave it right back to him. She said it wasn't anything I couldn't get over." That was a joke, but he wouldn't know.

He nodded. "Most women come to terms with it, eventually. Counseling helps."

"So they say."

His eyes narrowed. "You don't go out much, do you?"

She shook her head. "I told you. I don't like being touched."

He pursed his lips, remembering the growing excitement of the kiss they'd shared earlier. "I'm working on that," he drawled.

She laughed, surprised, delighted, by his attitude. He accepted her limitations without anger, without question. It was the first time she'd felt she could trust a man closer than arm's length.

"You're a nice man," she commented.

His eyebrows arched. "Nice? I'm extraordinary!"

She laughed and started to reply when his pager sounded.

He pulled it from his belt and read it, grimacing. "Damn." He got up and went to the desk where he'd placed his cell phone. He punched a number into it and put it to his ear. "Grier," he said.

Someone spoke to him. He looked solemn. He nodded. "Yes, I can do that. When? All right. I'll meet you there. Better call Marquez. Fine."

He snapped the phone shut and glanced toward Grace. "I have to go. The medical examiner's starting the autopsy on the child. I need to be present. There'll be trace evidence to secure, in addition to the information the autopsy will give us."

She gasped. "You have to watch?!"

"It isn't something I look forward to, but yes, I do occasionally need to watch. We gather forensic evidence while it's going on. The chain of evidence is important. If we break one link, if we ever catch this SOB, we won't be able to convict him."

"Oh. I see." She was picturing the child's body, sliced and broken and beaten. She swallowed down a wave of nausea.

He bent and brushed his mouth gently over her soft lips. "At least you're still in one piece, Grace," he said quietly. "Improper touching is unpleasant, certainly. But what happened to this child was infinitely worse. You were lucky. You didn't die."

Lucky. She would have laughed, but he wouldn't have understood. She'd misled him. She had only herself to blame. "I suppose I was lucky," she agreed. She was still alive. That was lucky.

"Want me to carry you down the hall before I leave?" he asked. "I may be late."

She smiled. "It's okay. I have a cane that Miss Turner found for me. I'll be fine. I'm sorry you have to see that."

"I've seen worse," he said flatly, and he was remembering things he wished he could forget. "Sleep well."

"I could go home," she began.

He gave her a speaking glance. "You and the coyote don't get along. You'd better stay here for a day or two, until you're fit for battle." He grinned, and winked at her, as he went out.

She tingled all over. He wanted her in his house, in his life. They both knew she was perfectly capable of taking care of herself, but he liked her here. She could have floated. Life wasn't bad, all of a sudden. It was sweet and heady and full of hope.

THE MEDICAL EXAMINER, Jack Peters, was doing the autopsy. He was a forensic pathologist, and widely known in law enforcement circles for his attention to detail. His forensic investigator observed. The investigator was someone that Garon knew from another case, last year. Alice Mayfield Jones had worked as a crime scene technician for a long time before she took the courses that would allow her to work as an investigator for the medical examiner's office.

"Well, if it isn't one of the Grier boys," Alice murmured dryly.

Her short, dark hair was under a cap, and part of her face was covered by a mask, but her shimmery blue eyes were unforgettable.

"How many of the Grier boys do you know, Jones?" he chided.

"Your brother Cash worked out of the D.A.'s office here," she recalled. "He was a lot cooler than you are."

"I can see that he wears his heart on his sleeve," the M.E. replied dryly, giving Garon a wry look.

"No. Cooler!" Alice corrected. "His brother wore a ponytail and an earring."

"Hell will freeze over before you see me wearing an earring," Garon obliged.

Marquez disguised a chuckle as a cough.

Alice glanced at him over the autopsy table. "Do you wear an earring, Sergeant Marquez? It would go nicely with your hair. Something dangly and unobtrusive…"

"If you don't shush, Jones, you'll be wearing one through your lips," the M.E. told her firmly. "Shall we begin?"

He drew the sheet off the small body. Garon had to grit his teeth to keep from cursing. He noticed that his companions were feeling something similar. There were no more jokes. This was deadly serious.

The M.E. pulled down his microphone and began describing the patient, from her height and weight and age to the stark recital of her wounds and the damage they did. While he worked, Jones photographed the body in all stages of the autopsy. She'd already taken the sheet and body bag that had covered the victim downstairs to the crime lab.

With a slight movement of his hand, he covered the child's face with a cloth after Jones had photographed it. "It's easier like this," he said, faintly sheepish. He'd done so many autopsies that they hardly bothered him, but he had a daughter this age and this job was painful.

He made the initial "Y" incision and Jones handed him a pair of cutters to sever the rib cage with, so that he had access to the soft tissues inside the body.

Garon could see for himself what the knife the perpetrator used had done to her small, thin body. Her internal organs were destroyed, from her lungs to her liver and intestines. The cuts were done with some force, as if the attacker had been in a rage.

"Were these wounds pre or postmortem?" Garon asked quietly.

"Pre," the M.E. said curtly. "She was tortured. You can tell from the bleeding. If they were postmortem, they wouldn't have bled. The heart stops pumping at the moment of death."

"You should watch more television, Grier," Jones piped. "They show all this stuff on the forensic shows."

"Don't get me started," Peters snarled at her. "All that high tech gadgetry, millions of dollars worth of equipment, and look what I'm working with!" he exclaimed, nodding around him at aged gurneys and an old porcelain sink and a microscope that seemed to be patched with gray duct tape. "What I wouldn't give for just one of those computers...!"

"They did give you a super investigator, though," Jones reminded him. "And I'm much better looking than that woman on TV who plays the M.E.'s assistant..."

"Stop while you still have work," Peters muttered.

They cataloged the evidence, placing tissue from under her fingernails in one evidence bag, and swabs from her genital area into another.

"With any luck at all, DNA will catch him," Garon said tautly.

"Only if the perp's DNA is on file," Marquez interjected.

"It's amazing to me," the M.E. commented, "how many molesters aren't in any database. What gets reported is just the tip of the iceberg."

"That's often the case," Marquez agreed.

Finally the ordeal was over and the M.E. readied the body for pickup by the funeral home.

"Poor kid," the M.E. remarked. "And her poor parents. I hope the mortician's good at his job."

Jones rolled the victim away while Marquez and Garon spoke with the M.E.

"I'll send this downstairs to the crime lab," he told them, indicating the evidence bags. "Unless you want to do it?"

Garon shook his head. "I've initialed all the vials that have swabs. Marquez can pick them up when you finish and put them in his property room at San Antonio P.D. for safekeeping."

Marquez nodded. "We'll take good care of everything."

"Just make sure somebody signs for it."

"You'd better believe it," he said. "If we catch the miserable excuse for a human being who did this, I don't want him to walk on a breach of the chain of evidence."

"When will you know something about the DNA?" Garon asked the M.E.

"Get Jones to sweet talk the evidence technicians downstairs," the M.E. suggested. "She has pull."

"I bribe them," she remarked, overhearing them. "I can make éclairs. The head tech is crazy about them. I used to work with him. I know his weaknesses!"

They laughed. It was a nice break from the somber atmosphere of the autopsy. Humor was how they coped with the horrible sights they carried home with them. It kept them from giving in to the pain. They were the victims' advocates. They had to be able to do the job.

"I'll get this report written up sometime tomorrow," Peters told the men. "You can call and make sure it's ready. But I can tell you, based on what I've seen, that the child died of asphyxiation. The knife wounds would have been fatal, but they weren't the primary cause of death."

"You're sure she was asphyxiated?" Marquez asked.

The M.E. pulled away the cloth over the child's face and lifted one of her eyelids. The eye under it was blue. Probably it had been a soft blue, full of hope…

"See these little hemorrhages?" Peters asked, indicating the small red dots in the white of the eye. There were more in the skin of her face. "They're capillaries that ruptured due to sudden, drastic pressure on the neck. We call the condition petechial hemorrhages. They're a hallmark of strangulation. I'm guessing, due to the amount of skin tissue I found under her nails, that she fought for her life. Her attacker will have scratches all over his hands from her attempt to free herself."

Marquez nodded, knowing that it was unlikely they'd find a suspect before those scratches healed and faded away. "We use similar techniques in law enforcement to subdue dangerous perpetrators; the bar arm hold and the carotid hold."

"I know," the M.E. replied. "They depress the carotid artery and induce unconsciousness. I get a victim of it occasionally. Usually kids practicing wrestling moves on each other without supervision. If it isn't done right, it can be fatal."

"Don't remind me," Marquez sighed. "We try everything else first, to subdue a lawbreaker. But sometimes everything else doesn't work, and our own lives are in danger."

"I hope you can find the person who did this," Peters said, indicating the child.

"We've got to find him," Garon said simply. "He'll do it again."

GRACE INSISTED on going home the next morning. Thanks to the quick treatment Garon had given her sprain, she was walking with barely a limp. She had to go to work or she wouldn't be able to pay her bills. She didn't want to tell him that. He wouldn't understand her sort of poverty. From what she'd heard people say about his brother Cash, she knew the family was wealthy.

Garon looked oddly relieved when she asked him to drop her by her house. He was having second thoughts. He'd spent a long, sleepless night thinking about how sweet it was to kiss Grace, and it had left him irritable. He wasn't going to risk getting involved with her. Never again, he told himself.

She was oddly disappointed that he took it so easily, even smiling as they finished breakfast. Maybe he would have kissed any woman he'd brought home. Or maybe he just felt sorry for her. He'd guessed a little of her past. He probably thought he was helping her adjust to men.

Her own thoughts were confusing her. She got into the car with him without a word, waving at Miss Turner. All the way to her house, she stared out the window without speaking.

He let her out at her front door. "Don't chase coyotes," he said firmly through the window.

She gave him an indignant look. "Are you a wildlife advocate? I won't hurt him unless he hurts my cat."

He laughed in spite of himself. "If you need us, call."

"You can do the same," she told him pertly, and grinned.

That grin made him feel warm inside. He hated it. "That'll be the day," he muttered, throwing up a hand as he pulled out of the driveway.

She watched him drive off with a sinking feeling. Things would never be the same again. He shouldn't have touched her.

He was thinking the same thing. Which was why he phoned Jaqui Jones, Mrs. Tabor's niece, and told her he'd be at the party the next night, which was Friday.

As Cash had hinted, the founding families of Jacobsville weren't in attendance at the party. Only a few obvious outsiders turned up. Garon felt oddly out of place with these people. Especially with Jaqui, who rubbed against him at every opportunity, almost panting with desire. He didn't like public displays of affection, and it showed in his face.

She laughed breathily. "You're an odd one," she told him as they sipped cocktails beside the buffet table. "Don't you find me desirable?"

"You must know you're beautiful," he said easily. He smiled. "But I work at a conservative job, and I'm uncomfortable with blatant invitations."

Her eyebrows went up. "And I took you for an unconventional free spirit," she purred.

"Looks deceive," he said, lifting his glass to toast her.

"Yes, well, don't sell yourself short," she added. "And don't think I'll give up. I get what I want, eventually."

"Do you?" He smiled. "Why don't you introduce me to your aunt?"

He left early, despite Jaqui's protests. "Surely you don't work Saturdays?" she asked irritably.

"I run a ranch," he reminded her. "Weekends are the only time I can devote to it." He didn't add that his job required him to be on call seven days a week. He worked on the ranch in spurts, leaving the daily operation to his ranch foreman.

"As long as you aren't running after your little neighbor," she chided. "God, that frumpy woman! And you had her staying in your house, I hear!"

"Her grandmother died," he said tautly. "She's having a hard time."

"She's a loser, like most people around here," she said carelessly. "Pity has brought down many a man. Don't let it bring you down." She moved against him deliberately when they were on the front porch, alone. She reached up, dragged his head down and kissed him with her whole mouth.

He was vaguely aroused by her, but not enough to accept what was blatantly an invitation to ravish her in the shadows.

He pulled back. "I'll call you," he said.

"You'd better, lover," she purred. "Or I'll come looking for you! Good night."

"Good night."

He got back into his car, thinking that Grace's shy response was far more exciting than this wildcat's ardent aggression. He felt sorry for Jaqui's aunt. She was a sweet, kind-natured but shy little woman who seemed anxious to please people. Her niece's scandalous behavior had obviously cost her some friends. None of the local rich families had set foot in her house tonight. It was a visible snub, although Jaqui was too thick-skinned to notice. Well, it wasn't his problem.

HE WAS FILLING IN HERD records on the computer when Miss Turner came bursting into his study late on Saturday evening.

"I have to be away for a few days," she said. "My father lives in Austin. He's had a heart attack and is in the hospital. I must go to him."

"Of course, you must," he said at once. "Take the Expedition."

"Are you sure?"

"Yes, I'm sure. You know where the key is. Do you need an advance on your salary?" he added.

She was pleasantly surprised. "No. But thank you."

"Is there anything I can do?"

"No, nothing. Thanks, boss," she added. Her face was pinched with concern. "I'll be back as soon as I can."

"If you need anything, call me," he said firmly.

"What about your breakfast?" she wailed.

"I'll fix my own," he returned. "Now, go. And drive carefully."

She managed a smile. "Okay."

"Call me when you get there, and tell me how things are going," he added.

She was touched by his concern. "I'll do that."

HE WENT TO BED LATE and was groggy when he woke up the next morning. He got dressed and went downstairs. The house felt emptier than usual with Miss Turner gone. He found a message on the answering machine. It was her, telling him she'd arrived safely in Austin and that her father was holding his own.

He made himself two pieces of buttered toast and a pot of coffee and sat down to drink it. The weekend had gone by amazingly fast. He felt a little guilty that he hadn't phoned to see how Grace was doing. It had probably hurt her feelings that he'd dropped her off at her own house and not bothered to check on her, with her ankle hurting.

Guilt made him impatient with himself. He owed her nothing. But just the same, he drove past her house on his way to San Antonio. Odd, her car was gone. It was barely six o'clock in the morning. He wondered where she was. But everything looked fine, so he put it out of his mind and continued down the road.

GRACE DIDN'T SEE Wilbur when she got home. But she did see why. He'd managed to get out a slightly open window, ripping his way through the screen, while she was at Garon's ranch. She didn't have time to search for him the morning she'd come home because she was already overdue at the florist shop. Saturday was one of their busiest days.

When she got home again, after a day of hobbling and mostly sitting to do flower arrangements, she got the cane Miss Turner had loaned her and hobbled around the property looking for Wilbur.

She found him in a terrible condition, already dead. It looked as if the coyote had gotten him after all. Raging at the top of her lungs, she promised the varmint that she'd even the score one day if it took the rest of her life. Tears rolled down her cheeks as she imagined the poor old cat's final moments. But tears wouldn't bring him back. They'd never brought anybody back.

She covered him with an old pillowcase and rolled him up in a tattered bedsheet. She put him in a box in the back seat of her car and drove him to the vet, where he was picked up by a man who ran a pet cemetery and offered cremation of beloved pets. He had a nice selection of urns that the departed could occupy. Grace picked out a simple, inexpensive one and was assured that Wilbur's ashes would arrive in due time at Grace's house. She wrote a check for the expense, gritting her teeth as she saw the pitiful amount of money she had left after paying bills. She'd have to see if she could get a few extra hours to work this next week, at her second job, to increase her bank balance.

She'd heard at work about Garon's attendance at Jaqui Jones's party. It had wounded her, to know he hadn't spared Grace a single thought after he'd spent time with the beautiful brunette. Grace looked at her drab image in her mirror and felt hopelessly tacky. The only good dress she had was one of her granny's, the black one she'd worn to the funeral. Most of her wardrobe consisted of jeans and sweatshirts and T-shirts with pictures or writing on them. She hardly owned any makeup, and she never took any time to do her hair.

On an impulse, she took her hair down and ran a brush through it. She was amazed at the change it made in her appearance, to have that thick, silky fall of blond hair draped around her shoulders. She put on just a touch of pale mauve lipstick and traded her sweatshirt for a long-sleeved black T-shirt with Japanese writing on it.

She did have a nice figure, she thought, even if her face fell short of beauty to go with it. Her mouth was too wide, her cheekbones too high and her nose had a crook in it. She wished she was prettier. The first time in her life that she wanted to be pretty for a man, and he was infatuated with Mata Hari.

She put down the brush and walked back out onto the porch. She hadn't quite finished pruning the roses, and it was pleasant out by the steps, in the sun.

She'd no sooner started clipping when she heard a vehicle drive up. To her surprise, it was Garon, the last person she'd expected to see. She stood up with the clippers cradled in her hands while he got out of the car and came up to the steps.

He stopped short. His dark gaze slid over her face and shoulders, and down her body, with odd intensity. They began to glitter.

She opened her mouth to ask what was wrong. Before she got the words out, he had her up in his arms, and he was kissing her as if there wouldn't be a tomorrow.

8

GARON COULDN'T HELP himself. The sight of Grace's trim, pretty figure in those tight jeans and shirt, the delight of her long blor.d hair cascading down her back, robbed him of reason. He had a sudden, urgent arousal that he couldn't control. The feel of her in his arms, against his tall, powerful body, was like a potent narcotic.

"Open your mouth, Grace," he bit off against the taut line of her lips. He drew her even closer. "Come on, baby," he whispered seductively, teasing her lips with his own in a passionate whisper of touch, "do it. Do it, Grace…"

She tried to speak, and ended up doing exactly what he'd asked her to. She gasped at the rush of feeling it provoked. He knew too much. He made her hungry. She'd never in her life wanted to belong to a man, until right now. She could feel the heat and power of his muscular chest crushing against her soft breasts, she could hear his heartbeat, the rasp of his breathing. Or was it her own heartbeat?

Older, frightening memories rushed in on her as his ardor became less controlled. She pushed at his chest. He drew away from her. He looked as shocked as she did. He fought to breathe normally.

"I know," she said, holding up a hand and forcing a smile to her swollen lips. "It was a helpless reaction that you can't explain, but I can. I had Miss Lettie down the road make a doll of you and rub my photo over it, so now you can't resist me." She grinned.

He burst out laughing. "Damn!"

"Not that I normally resort to such measures," she added demurely. "My extreme good looks usually get me all the men I want."

He drew in a long breath. She had this uncanny way of defusing dangerous situations. He'd been in over his head, and he knew it. But she didn't seem to be angry at him, despite her past. He had to remember her background, so that he didn't frighten her. She was so very innocent, for a woman her age. Despite her bad experience, she seemed to like being in his arms. The thought excited him. "There goes my illusion of being the only man in your life."

"Your illusion left skid marks," she agreed. "Why are you here, if you don't mind saying?"

He blinked. "I don't know."

She gave him a wry look. "Short-term memory loss can't be good for your job..."

"Hell, I know what I'm doing when I'm at work!" he muttered.

"Well, that's a relief!"

"I have to drive over to Palo Verde to interview a man," he said. Marquez had located an ex-policeman from Palo Verde who remembered the cold case about the dead child from two years before. He said that a neighbor of the dead child claimed to have seen a man with the child earlier on the day she was abducted. The witness, Marquez said, had been acknowledged by police at the time, but the witness had been out of town when the detectives went back to speak to him. Apparently he'd gotten lost in the shuffle when publicity brought in hundreds of tips that had to be checked out. Garon wanted to see the witness, if he still lived in Palo Verde. Perhaps he might have remembered something else in the years since the crime occurred. He might be just the break they needed to find a suspect in two child murders. Like Marquez, Garon was certain they were dealing with a serial killer. The cases were much too similar to be coincidences.

"You working today?" he asked Grace.

"I only worked this morning. I get off this noon on Saturday," she said.

"I wish I did," he signed. "Want to come with me?"

Her whole face radiated the delight the invitation caused. He wasn't infatuated with the Jaqui woman. He couldn't be, if he was taking Grace out for the day!

"I'll just change into something better," she began, worried that she didn't have many clothes to choose from.

"What's wrong with what you've got on?" he asked. "You might have noticed that I'm not wearing a suit."

She did notice. He was in tan slacks that emphasized the powerful muscles in his long legs, and a pale lemon designer shirt that outlined the muscles in his chest and arms. He was wearing a lightweight jacket with it. He looked very handsome.

"Don't you usually wear a suit?" she wondered.

"Only when I plan to arrest someone and the media might show up," he said amusedly. "The Bureau likes us to look professional at such times."

"Well!"

"But since I don't plan to arrest this man, I can be casual."

"In that case, I'll get my purse and a sweater."

He waited for her by the car, looking around curiously. "Where's the cat?" he asked when she rejoined him.

She bit her lower lip. "He got out of the house while I was gone. I found him…" She swallowed. "I buried him."

"I'm sorry," he said, and meant it. He knew she was fond of the old cat. "Our white cat had kittens. She lives in the barn, keeps down the rat population. When the kittens are old enough, you can come over and pick out one."

She blinked away tears. "That would be nice."

"For us, too. One less mouth to feed."

"How's Miss Turner?"

"She had to drive to Austin to see about her father," he said. "He had a heart attack."

"Poor thing! Her father is the only family she has left. Has she called to tell you how he's doing?"

"Not yet. But she will, I'm sure."

"What do you have to interview this witness about?" she asked, changing the subject.

"We think he might have seen the perpetrator in a cold case murder," he told her. "If he did, and he can remember anything about the abductor, that might give us a head start on a suspect for our current case, which has similar features. If he didn't, we're back to forensics evidence to search for a killer."

"That cold case—it's about that little girl who was killed there, isn't it?"

"You're sharp," he murmured.

"Palo Verde isn't big enough to get in the news unless there's something terrible going on," she said. "I thought when you mentioned this latest case that it was very similar to what they said happened to the girl up at Palo Verde."

"Marquez made the connection."

"You said you'd be looking for evidence at the autopsy. Did you find any?" she asked with deliberate carelessness.

"Plenty," he said flatly. "Including DNA evidence. If we can find the man who did it, we can hang him."

"If only it wasn't such a big state," she said quietly.

"Oh, we'll get lucky eventually." He glanced at her. "Have you ever heard of the Locard Exchange Principle?"

She frowned. "No."

"It's a theory of evidence that forms the basis of modern forensic investigation," he said. "Dr. Edmond Locard was a French policeman who noticed that criminals leave trace evidence behind them, and pick up trace evidence from any location they visit. It's an exchange of fibers, hair and other materials. Analyzing this evidence can place the criminal at the scene of a crime, without any other proof of involvement."

"I love to watch those television shows about cold cases," she said. "It's fascinating to see how the smallest things can connect the dots in crimes."

He smiled. "I watch them, too." He glanced at her. "But a large part of police work is surveillance and interviewing witnesses or family members of victims. Boring stuff."

"To someone who works part-time jobs for a living," she pointed out, "it's not all that boring," She glanced at him. "How long have you been an FBI agent?"

"Since I was twenty-three," he said.

"And you're eighty now…" she began mischievously.

"I'm thirty-six," he reminded her.

"Did you always work murders?"

He shook his head. "I've only been assigned to one serial murder case, back east. But I've worked violent crime for most of my career. I worked on the Hostage Rescue Team for six years, and on the FBI SWAT team in D.C. for four more. After that I worked out of Austin. Now I'm in the San Antonio Field Office. I head a squad that covers violent crime."

"Those first two things—that's dangerous work. I've seen movies that show how those teams operate."

His hand tightened on the steering wheel. "Yes. Very dangerous."

She frowned. "You chose that sort of work. Something happened to you, too," she guessed. "Something traumatic."

His jaw tautened. "Something," he said. He glanced in her direction. "I don't talk about it."

"I wasn't prying," she said, turning her purse over in her lap. "But you asked me if I talked to anyone about what happened to me."

"So you did."

"So turnabout is fair play."

He didn't answer. He was silent for a time, caught up in the past, in the anguish of those years. The pain was harsh.

She realized she'd stepped on broken glass and she searched for some way to lighten the tension. "Do you believe in werewolves?" she asked.

The car swerved faintly. "Excuse me?" he asked in disbelief.

"I saw this movie. It was very realistic," she told him. "I'm sure that I know at least one person who's never seen during full moons. You have to use silver bullets on them, you know, regular lead ones won't work."

"I don't have a silver bullet to my name," he pointed out.

"We're in trouble if we run into one," she remarked dryly.

"Tell you what. If you see a werewolf, you tell me, and I'll rush home and melt down some of the silver service and start making bullets right away."

"Deal," she said smugly.

He felt his heart lighten. She was good company, for a shy and damaged spinster. She made him forget the past. He liked being with her.

She was feeling something similar, especially after the way he'd kissed her earlier, with such need and pleasure. She tingled all over remembering how it had felt. Maybe he had a hard time with relationships, and that was why he wasn't married.

THEY STOPPED at the police department in Palo Verde to talk with its police chief, Gil Mendosa. He was sheepish and embarrassed when Garon told him about their current murder investigation and Marquez's efforts to find out about his department's cold case from him through e-mail that was ignored.

"We had these e-mails that embarrassed Miss Tibbs," he explained. "She's seventy, and handles the phone and the mail for us. Well, ever since, if the heading doesn't have something specific about a case in it, she just deletes it unread, like we told her to. Tell Marquez I'm sorry."

"I will. What we want to know is if you're keeping back any information about the little girl's murder—something you want to keep out of the news."

The chief glanced at Grace uneasily.

"She's a clam," Garon told him easily. "It's all right."

"Okay, then. Yes, there was one other thing. The man tied a ribbon around her neck and strangled her to death with it. A red ribbon."

"HERE, SIT DOWN for God's sake!" Garon growled. He'd caught Grace just as she folded. "What's the matter?"

She fought for every breath. She couldn't give herself away. She couldn't!

"It's that twenty-four-hour stomach virus that's been going around," she said with a weak laugh. "I had it yesterday and it's knocked me to my knees. Drastic way to lose weight, you know."

"Would you like something to drink?" the chief asked gently.

"How about a martini, shaken, not stirred," she began, with twinkling gray eyes.

"You can have a Diet Coke," Garon returned, moving to the drinks machine in the department's canteen with a handful of change, "if I can find the right change."

"Don't feed it a dollar bill," the chief cautioned. "It eats them."

She gave him a hard look. "You're a policeman and you let a machine rob customers right in your own office?" she exclaimed.

"A man we arrested last month got hold of a gun and shot the last machine we had in here," he replied. "Two months before that, one of our own officers accidentally hit the machine it replaced with a baseball bat. Don't wonder out loud," he advised when she started to ask how someone could accidentally smash a machine with a bat. "So, you see, we can't ask the machine people to give us a third one. They'd never understand."

"I see your point," Grace agreed.

Garon handed her an icy cold soft drink. She popped the lid and drank thirstily. "Oh, that's so good," she said, sighing. "Thanks."

"You should have told me you weren't feeling well," he said.

She smiled at him. "You wouldn't have let me come with you."

He pursed his lips and his dark eyes twinkled. Grace blushed.

Garon forced his attention back to Mendosa, and told him about the witness Marquez had unearthed in San Antonio.

"His name is Sheldon," Garon said. "He apparently lived two doors down from the murder victim. Some homicide detectives from San Antonio talked to him. Marquez and I followed up, and he recalled seeing the suspect."

Mendosa grimaced. "We had an apparent eyewitness ourselves, a man named Homer Rich. But our former chief said the guy was loopy and he wouldn't let us go talk to him. The witness lived right next door to the child." He frowned. "But he doesn't live here now. He moved out of town not long after the murder."

Garon frowned. "Was he a suspect?"

"No," Mendosa said. "The guy was handsome, he made a good living, although I never knew exactly how he made his money. He had a fiancée somewhere. Nobody local ever saw her. He wasn't a suspect. In fact, he joined the search when her family knew she was missing. He even printed up some flyers at his own expense."

Garon didn't say a word. He took notes. But he knew very well that sometimes murder suspects joined in the search and even spoke to the police about the progress of the investigation. He wasn't telling Mendosa. It would only make the man feel bad. He was operating on a shoestring as it was.

"Know where Rich moved to?" he asked.

Mendosa shook his head. "He kept to himself, mostly. You might ask Ed Reems, he rented the house to Rich." He gave Garon the address, which he jotted down. "Ed loves to talk. If he knows anything, he'll tell you."

"Thanks," Garon said warmly.

"You're welcome. If you need help, let me know. We're all on the same team, when it comes to murder. I'd love to heat up that cold case and solve it. It haunts me. There's just me and one other part-time officer to handle things here. We have to call in the county sheriff's department for assistance if anything major breaks. We just don't have the resources to commit to a decent investigation. I hope you catch this guy."

"You and me and half the FBI," Garon replied. "Child killers evoke sympathy from nobody, especially if they get sent to prison."

"Amen. If you need help, just call."

Garon smiled. "I will. Thanks."

GRACE FINISHED her soft drink just as they pulled up at a dingy single-wide trailer on a quiet street just outside the Palo Verde city limits.

"Stay put," he told her. "I won't be long."

He got out and walked up the steps to the front porch. The door opened. He displayed his credentials. A minute later, he went inside the house.

Grace wondered what he was going to find out. The mention of the red ribbon had made her sick. Garon would be suspicious. She didn't want him to know why it had upset her. It was too soon. Far too soon.

Less than five minutes passed before he came back out, frowning. He got into the car beside her.

"Wasn't he home?"

He drew in a long breath. "He was home," he said, staring at the house. "He said that Rich didn't leave a forwarding address. What's more, he left the furniture in the house, along with appliances he'd bought. He must have been in a hell of a hurry to get out of town."

Grace bit her lower lip and mentioned what they were both thinking. "What if he wasn't a witness? What if he did it?"

"That's exactly what I was thinking." He started the car and put it in gear. "I'll leave you at the chief's office. I need to do some door-to-door investigating."

"Couldn't I help?"

He smiled gently. "Not without credentials," he said. "I'll get Mendosa to help me. If we're lucky, we may turn up something."

But four hours later, they hadn't turned up one single witness who'd seen anything connected with the crime.

"Look," Garon told Mendosa, "it's a real long shot, but I'd like to send a forensic team down here to scour the house where Rich lived. We might get lucky and turn up something. We can find traces of blood even after houses are wiped clean with disinfectant and bleach."

"I'll arrange it with the landlord and his tenants," Mendosa promised. "How about next Monday, first thing?"

Garon shook his hand. "That's fine. I appreciate the help."

Mendosa grinned. "So do I. Nobody likes to see a murderer walk."

"You can say that again."

GRACE WAS FASCINATED with the idea that bloodstains couldn't be totally eradicated by murderers.

All the way back to Jacobsville, she pumped him for information on blood spatter patterns, crime scene protocol and what the FBI lab could do with a single human hair.

"It's like something out of Star Trek," she exclaimed.

He chuckled. "Yes, it is. Our high tech tools give us a real edge in solving crimes."

"If it weren't for the gory stuff, I think I'd like law enforcement work," she murmured.

He couldn't picture Grace at a crime scene. On the other hand, she'd chased a coyote right out of her yard with nothing more menacing than a tree limb. She had grit. He admired a woman with staying power. But she kept secrets, Grace did. He wondered what they were.

"THANKS FOR TAKING ME with you," she said when he stopped at her house. "I really enjoyed it."

"So did I," he had to admit. He walked her up onto the porch. "You're good company."

"You'll have to go and make your own supper, because Miss Turner's gone," she said suddenly. She looked up at him. "I could make supper. I've got some fresh cube steak and potatoes I could fix."

He hesitated. He was hungry, and he didn't fancy trying to cook. "You must be tired," he began, feeling guilty.

She shook her head. "I like to cook."

He smiled. "Okay. What time?"

"Seven?"

"I'll be here."

He drove off and Grace ran inside to start things in the kitchen. She felt like a child with a treat in store. She'd never enjoyed a man's company so much in her whole life. It was a beginning.

THEY SAT IN THE KITCHEN for a long time after they'd finished eating, just talking about the state of the world. They agreed on a lot of issues. In fact, they thought alike on politics and religion, which were said to be the two most controversial subjects on earth.

"You make good coffee," he remarked, finishing his second cup.

"It's decaf," she confessed. "Caffeine bothers me."

"It's good, regardless."

He checked his watch. "I hate to go, but I have to pick up a visiting agent at the airport tomorrow morning, early. He's going to be in our office for a couple of days, doing an inspection."

"Inspection?"

He grinned. "It's a way to make sure we're efficient."

"I could write a testimonial for you," she offered lightly.

"It will take more than that, I'm afraid." He walked to the front porch and out into the yard, his eyes on the sky. "There's a halo around the moon. We're going to get some rain, I guess."

"How would a city fellow like you know that?" she asked, impressed.

He turned, smiling. "I grew up on a ranch in west Texas," he replied. "We had an old cowboy—he looked eighty—who used to work with the Texas Rangers. He could smell rain a mile away, predict weather, make poultices. I used to sit and listen to him by the hour when he talked about catching bank robbers. I suppose that's why I became a lawman. He made it sound like a holy cause. In some ways, I guess it is. We speak for victims who can no longer speak for themselves."

"Will you catch that killer, do you think?" she asked quietly.

"I hope we will," he said, moving closer to her. "This man is no amateur. He's smart. But he did leave trace evidence that will convict him, if we ever get lucky enough to take him into custody."

"My grandfather used to say that most criminals are stupid," she recalled. "He said one man he arrested had killed a man and then left his business card in the man's pocket. And there was a thief who robbed a bank and went out the wrong door, tripped over somebody's dog that was waiting there and actually knocked himself out on the pavement."

He chuckled. "We've had our share of those, too," he assured her. "But some aren't as easily caught."

"You'll get him," she said with utter confidence, as she smiled up at him.

He moved still closer and took her by the arms, holding her lightly against his tall, powerful body. "You're good for my ego, Grace," he murmured. "But I don't think I'm good for you."

She traced a button on his jacket, without looking at him. "You mean that you don't want anything permanent. That's okay. I don't, either."

"You'll want children one day," he began.

She took a long, shuddering breath. "I…can't have a child."

"What?"

It hurt to say that, but they were almost friends now, and he needed to know. Just in case they became more involved. She forced herself to look up at him in the light from the windows. "I was in an…an accident, when I was twelve," she said. "A bad accident. I got cut up, especially my stomach. So I can't have children."

Something inside him mourned for her. He knew without asking that she would have wanted a family if she married. He felt an emptiness in himself at the thought, and he couldn't decide why.

"I'm sorry," he said.

"I'm sorry, too," she said somberly. "I love children." She searched his eyes. "But you could have them, if you married someday."

His face closed up. "I don't want to get married."

He said it so deliberately that she knew there was something in his past, something devastating, that he never discussed. He kept secrets, too, she knew, like she did. But her secrets had to be more life-shattering than his were.

"I'll remember that," she promised him, and her eyes began to twinkle. "But you're way down on my list of prospective grooms, you know. Almost at the bottom!"

His eyebrows arched. "Well, I like that!" he exclaimed.

"I can get any man I want," she informed him. "I learned about it on television. There's this new perfume that causes men to parachute out of planes with bouquets of roses and big diamond rings. All I need is a dab of it behind each ear."

"What if you catch the wrong man?"

"That won't happen. The guy in the commercial is a knockout."

"They won't give you the guy in the commercial," he pointed out.

"How do you know? They might run a contest and give him away as the prize," she chuckled. "Aren't you disappointed?"

He shook his head. "I don't need a man with roses and diamonds."

She laughed. "I meant, that you aren't on the top of my list!"

He pursed his lips and moved closer. "Honey, if I wanted to be on the top of your list," he murmured deeply, bending, "I wouldn't need roses to get there." His hand went behind her head and brought her mouth close, close to his. "I'd only need this," he whispered as his lips crushed down over hers.

9

GRACE MELTED into his tall body with a faint, shaky sigh. The feel of him, the taste of him, was becoming familiar. He wasn't at all threatening this way. Not anymore. She loved being close to him.

That was obvious, but it made him wary. She wasn't worldly, and he was. He could take a woman in his stride and never look back. There were plenty of women the same way. No ties, no complications. But Grace would expect marriage.

The word felt bitter. He lifted his head.

She radiated joy. Her eyes were brilliant with it. Her swollen mouth was smiling. He felt like a heel. He shouldn't have touched her. But she was appealing in her innocence, as so many experienced women weren't.

He touched her cheek with his fingertips. "The inspector's going to have everybody doing handstands Monday, so I'm taking the afternoon off, to get my supplies at the feed store. Want to come along?"

"Yes!"

He chuckled at her enthusiasm. What the hell. He was enjoying her company. He didn't need to start worrying about the future. It could take care of itself.

He bent and kissed her again, very softly. "Then I'll see you Monday. Good night."

"Good night. I really had a good time."

He smiled. "So did I."

She walked into the house on a cloud. Life was sweet.

EARLY MONDAY morning, she drove into town to shop for some clothes that weren't as old as she was. She had a little cash in her checking account that wasn't necessary for bills. She wanted something pretty to wear for Garon. She stopped by Barbara's to ask her advice.

Barbara directed her to the little strip mall in front of the community college, where there was a thrift shop. There were some beautiful things there, used but like new, and they didn't cost much. Grace walked out with two bags full of nice things, and with a cashmere coat with a fur collar over one arm. She felt like flying.

"Grace," Barbara said gently, "you know I'm happy for you. But don't walk into a relationship blind. That man isn't the marrying sort. And whether he knows it or not, he's not small town material, either."

"That's what they said about his brother," Grace pointed out, smiling, "and look at him!"

Barbara didn't return the smile. "Just...go slow. Okay?"

"Worrywart," she chided, and hugged her friend. "I'm happier than I've ever been in my life," she whispered. "I'm so happy!"

Barbara gnawed her lower lip as she hugged Grace back. "Be happy, then. But if he hurts you, I'll make him sorry. I swear I will."

"Stop that. I'm a grown woman."

"I know," Barbara agreed. But she didn't smile. Garon Grier was a mature, worldly man, and Grace was a card-carrying innocent. She'd suffered enough already at the hands of one man. She didn't need Garon to put nails in her coffin. But Barbara knew she couldn't stop this train wreck of a relationship from happening. She could only be there for Grace when the bottom fell out of her world.

GRACE HAD BOUGHT a pair of embroidered jeans and a matching long-sleeved white shirt and a denim jacket to go with them. She left her hair around her shoulders, because Garon liked long hair. She studied herself in the mirror and felt really good about the way she looked.

Remembering how tender he'd been with her, she was walking on clouds. She was falling in love. Surely, he must be, too. A feeling so deep and wondrous had to be shared.

He pulled up in her driveway at one o'clock sharp, and she ran outside to meet him, radiant with joy. He was driving one of the ranch pickup trucks, a black one with lots of chrome trim. His Expedition was still with Miss Turner in Austin.

He got out of the truck and didn't even try to resist the urge to open his arms for her. She made him feel young again, full of hope and optimism. She made him feel like the man he had been, before tragedy had turned his world black.

She hugged him, feeling closer to him than she ever had to anyone else. It was like a miracle, that she could enjoy letting a man touch her, hold her, kiss her. She lifted her face to tell him, but his mouth was already burrowing tenderly into her lips. She opened them for him and held on tight. It was like flying. Joy overflowed like a dammed river suddenly free.

After a minute, he had to put her away from him. He was almost shaking with the need to carry her inside to the nearest bed. He couldn't do that. It was too soon.

"Ready to go?" he asked, smiling.

"I'll just lock the door," she replied breathlessly, her gray eyes shimmering with happiness.

He watched her go up the steps. Odd, she'd come down them running, but now it seemed like an effort to go back up them. She took longer than necessary to lock the door, too. He wondered why.

She could feel the question on his face before she read it. Her heart was cutting cartwheels, and she couldn't let him see. She forced a smile. "See what you do to me?" she asked pertly. "You take my breath away."

The suspicious look was replaced by an arrogant one. He actually grinned.

SHE WALKED into the feed store beside him, smiling and happy. Old Jack Hadley, who'd owned this feed store, one of two in Jacobsville, since Grace's grandfather was a young man, smiled benevolently at Grace.

"Nice to see you out and about, Miss Grace," he said. "And in good company, too." He smiled at Garon and winked.

Garon shifted, as if the teasing look made him uncomfortable. "I've got a list," he said, handing it to the manager.

He pursed his lips. "Well, this seed is a special order. Will next week be soon enough?"

"Yes," Garon replied.

"But the rest is in stock. Jake!" he yelled, and his teenaged assistant came running from the back of the store. "Get this feed for Mr. Grier and carry it out to his truck, will you?"

"Sure thing!" the boy agreed. He smiled at Grace. "You look nice today," he said, blushing as he made the bold remark.

"Thanks, Jake," she said, but her smile was impersonal and faint.

Garon moved to her side, glowering at the boy, who took off like a human rocket.

Grace was confounded at the look on Garon's face. And when he noticed, his dark eyes began to burn in an odd, intimate way as he held her gaze until she flushed and dropped her eyes.

His big hand slid over her small one and held it tightly, as if to emphasize what his eyes were telling her. She could barely breathe for the stab of joy right through her body. She returned the pressure, and felt his fingers ease slowly, sensuously, between hers.

She bit her lower lip, hard, to keep from moaning.

"Don't forget the fertilizer, Jake," Mr. Hadley called after the boy.

His voice broke the spell, and Grace stepped back, laughing nervously at the tension that still held them both in its grip.

Garon didn't say a word. But what he felt was hard to conceal. She was getting right under his skin. Now he was jealous of high school kids. He wondered what in hell was happening to him!

THE NEXT FEW DAYS passed with Garon making casual visits to Grace's house, first for an occasional meal, and then in the evening to watch movies he'd rented. Miss Turner's father had rallied, and she'd called to say she'd be back within a week.

Garon and Grace were watching a new murder mystery he'd

rented, but his mind wasn't on the film. He kept noticing Grace's body in the demure rounded neckline of her blue blouse. She was wearing a skirt for a change, a long denim one. Her hair was around her shoulders and she smelled just faintly of roses.

"You'll lose the connection," she warned, looking up at him with a breathless smile.

He turned toward her on the sofa and tugged at her arm until she got the message and slid close to him. He was wearing a long-sleeved chambray shirt with jeans. His boots were lying on the floor with her shoes. He drew her across his lap and let her head slide down into the crook of his arm.

"Relationships don't stagnate, Grace," he said quietly, searching her wide, gray eyes. "We either go forward, or we stop seeing each other. I'm too old to settle for a platonic relationship."

Her heart jumped. She'd been right. He was interested in a long-term relationship. He wanted her for keeps!

Her fingers went up to his hard mouth and traced it slowly. "I don't want to stop seeing you," she whispered, just to make it clear. She was nervous about what he might be asking of her, but she loved him. She was curious about the feelings he evoked from her, when he kissed her and held her close. She wanted to know all of it. She wanted to erase the nightmarish memories from her mind, to over-lay them with loving caresses from a man to whom she could entrust her innocence. She smiled.

He drew in a long breath. "At last," he whispered, bending. "I thought I was going to go mad before we got to this point!"

She wanted to ask what he meant, but he was kissing her. This wasn't like the other times, when he'd been hesitant and slow. He was hungry. He was ravenous. At first his ardor was frightening and she stiffened.

He drew back at once to search her eyes. "I will never hurt you," he said in a gruff whisper. "Not in any way."

She began to relax again. "I know. It's just…"

He remembered. She'd had a bad experience as a child. He smiled slowly and traced her mouth with the tip of his finger. "Everything's going to be all right. Trust me. I can give you pleasure—as much as you can handle."

As he spoke, he bent again. This time the kiss was longer, sensual, deliberately arousing. His hands slid up and down her sides until he was teasing just at the edges of her breasts. Something was happening to her, something unexpected. She felt her body swell and burn, as if he'd kindled a fever in it. She seemed to have no control over it anymore. It wanted his touch, his tenderness. She wanted him.

He took her face between his hands and searched her wide, gray eyes for a long time. He felt the look all the way to his toes. She made him ache all over. He wondered if she knew it, and reasoned that she probably didn't. With her history, sexual attraction to a man was going to be something of an ordeal. His eyes narrowed as he considered how some men would take advantage of her interest, rush her, hurt her because they didn't understand what she'd been through in her childhood. He hated the thought of some careless man using her for his own pleasure, and leaving her even more damaged.

"What are you thinking?" she asked curiously.

"How lovely you are," he replied.

She laughed self-consciously. "Me?"

"Yes," he said, and he didn't smile. "You."

He bent and kissed the smile, very slowly, in a way that he hadn't during their short relationship. He drew her gently against him as his mouth worked its way against her lips until she opened her own mouth, to let him inside. He felt a flash of pure animal desire at the shy action. It tested his control. But he managed to keep things tender, even so, determined not to frighten her.

As the kiss grew in length and intensity, he felt her stiffen just at first, and then slowly relax into the hard contours of his body. His hand dropped slowly to her back and slid down, moving her gently against him until his ardor became tangible against her belly.

He lifted his head to look into her wide, fascinated eyes. "Not afraid?" he asked quietly.

She couldn't manage words, but she shook her head. She felt boneless. She ached all over. Something began to throb deep in her body.

He felt those reactions. She wasn't protesting. If anything, she moved closer to him, gasping faintly at the heat and power of his aroused body.

It was like falling into fire, he thought as he bent again to her mouth and slowly invaded it, first with his lips, then with his tongue. The first silken thrust of it inside hers caused her to grip his arms so tightly that her short nails dug into the flesh even through his shirt. Then as he moved his tongue sensually against hers, she moaned audibly.

If he had any thought of pulling away, it was gone in a flash. It had been too long since he'd had a woman. He was dying for her. He couldn't stop.

He got to his feet and then bent, lifting her clear of the sofa in his arms while his mouth still covered her own. He carried her down the hall, glancing into a lit room with a double bed. He went into it, kicking the door shut behind him, and laid her out on the bed. His eyes were almost black with desire as he looked down at her, hesitating.

But she was as far gone as he was. She loved what he could make her feel. She was almost twenty-five years old and she'd never had a lover. She wanted him. She wanted to be a woman, a whole woman, with this man whom she loved with all her heart. And it wasn't as if he just needed a woman, she told herself. He wanted a relationship. That had to mean marriage! Her arms opened.

He felt her submission without a word being spoken. His blood was on fire. He sat down beside her, but she put a hand against his chest. She looked uneasy.

"The light," she whispered, biting her lower lip.

He frowned. Then he remembered the accident she'd had as a child. "I don't mind scars, Grace," he said softly. "I have a few of my own."

She bit her lip harder. She didn't know how to explain it to him. "Please?" she asked.

He sighed, but not angrily. He'd wanted to look at her. But her innocence was going to be his biggest problem. He only smiled. His hand reached for the lamp. He turned it off, and bent down to gather her against him.

It was, she thought feverishly, a banquet of the senses. She hadn't known her own body had so many sensitive areas that a man's mouth and hands could lift into realms of ecstasy. She moaned helplessly as he kissed her taut breasts. She moved her legs to admit the weight of him between them. She marveled at how easily they seemed to go together with all the clothes out of the way. His body was warm and hard and sensual against hers on the crisp sheets, and she shivered again and again with the growing, gnawing pleasure of his touch.

When he touched her with sudden intimacy she hesitated, her mind going back to horror and pain, he hesitated. "Did I hurt you?" he asked softly.

She forced her mind to shut out the unpleasant images. That was yesterday. This was today. "No," she whispered, drawn back to the present. "Of course you aren't hurting me. Don't stop!"

He laughed softly and moved down against her once more. "I won't," he whispered against her throat. "Move with me, Grace," he added huskily. "Move with me. That's it. Harder…!"

She felt his hand exploring, and then it was something…else, something hard and warm…!

She gasped and arched right off the bed as the intimate contact produced a wave of pleasure so overwhelming that she thought she might faint. She cried out, pulling him down to her, shivering.

"You like that, do you?" he murmured drowsily against her mouth. "Let's try this…"

She shuddered, again and again, as the pleasure began to spiral up. She made a strange, husky noise deep in her throat and moved her legs as far apart as she could get them, her nails digging into his hips. "Please," she choked, gasping.

He nibbled at her mouth as his hips began to move down in a quick, hard rhythm. "Like that?"

"Yes!"

One hand went under her hair to hold her head firmly while his mouth crushed down on her parted lips. The other went under her hips, lifting her fiercely up to the hard downward thrust of his body.

"I'll…die!" she choked against his devouring mouth.

"Of pleasure…maybe," he managed in a harsh whisper. "God!

Grace! Grace! Lift up! Lift up, hard!" He shuddered, gasping, as the rhythm became furious, insanely pleasurable. "Now, baby," he choked. "Now, now, now…!"

She moved with him, held him tight, shivered helplessly as the pleasure built to such a degree that she thought she might lose consciousness. And then, when it was so hot and sweet that it had to be the end, the spiral went even higher and hotter. She couldn't see, hear, think, even breathe as the rhythm quickened. He whispered something, but she was beyond understanding. Her body was on a journey of its own, carrying her along to a volcanic climax that sent her arching up into him with a quick, sharp little cry of absolute delight.

He gathered her hips up and riveted them to his as he felt, too, the sudden release of tension. "Grace," he moaned, his voice deep and husky, as his hips moved helplessly against her in one last, hard thrust that sent him right over the edge.

They lay together, bathed in sweat, clinging to each other in the darkness. They shivered, speechless, in mutual satiation.

Endless seconds later, he eased away from her and slid his hand from her neck over her full breasts, down to her flat stomach. His fingers traced the small scars that rose above the smooth flesh.

"I have a lot of scars," she whispered unsteadily.

"So do I. They don't matter." He brushed his mouth softly over her lips. "I've never had it this good," he whispered. He wrapped her up in his arms. "Grace, you were a virgin, weren't you?" he asked after a minute.

She stopped breathing. She hesitated. "Well, yes," she managed to say. Technically it was the truth.

"I'm sorry. I shouldn't have lost control like this."

"I lost control, too," she said.

"It isn't the same thing. It was like shooting ducks in a barrel." He moved away from her with a long, harsh sigh. "Damn!"

"You...you didn't like it?" she asked with dawning worry.

He turned and looked down at her in the darkness. "That isn't what I meant, Grace," he said. "I took advantage of you."

"No!"

He put his hand gently on her belly. "Are you sure you can't get pregnant?" he asked, and sounded concerned.

"I'm sure." The doctors had all agreed about that.

He didn't answer. So he didn't have to worry about the complication of a baby. But he felt guilty just the same.

"I'm glad it was with you," she said when the silence became frightening.

That didn't make him feel any better. At least he hadn't hurt her, he consoled himself. On the other hand, he'd taken something she might have wanted to save for marriage. She was very traditional.

"It wasn't because you were thinking about her?" she asked with sudden horror.

For an instant, he thought she was referring to the past. Then he realized she knew nothing about his past. "About Jaqui?" he exclaimed. "Heavens, no!"

She relaxed. "Okay."

He drew in a long breath. "I have to go."

"Now?" she asked, sounding alarmed.

He bent over and kissed her tenderly on the forehead. "As you keep reminding me, this is a small town. I don't want people seeing my car in your driveway all night and gossiping about it."

She smiled. "That's nice of you."

He didn't answer her. He dressed in the dark, feeling like a heel. She'd been generous, and warm, and loving. Her headlong delight made him feel even guiltier. He had nothing to offer her.

"Grace, you do understand that I'm not in the market for a wife?" he asked quietly.

She felt sick all over. She was shocked and trying not to let it show. "Yes," she said after a minute, and her voice didn't give anything away. Her world was crashing around her, but she couldn't let it show. "I understand."

He grimaced. He could hear the hurt in her voice. He was just making things worse. "I'll come over tomorrow after I get off from work," he said. "We'll talk it out."

"All right."

"Good night."

"Good night."

She sounded resigned to his leaving. He wanted to stay, to talk, to explain. He couldn't manage it, though. He was afraid of relationships. He never should have started this!

He left without another word. But all day, the memory of the pleasure they shared haunted him. He'd started something he couldn't finish. He thought of Grace while he was working. She came between him and paperwork, shimmering like foxfire in his memory. He ached every time he thought of her.

GRACE TURNED HER FACE into the pillow when he left and cried as if her heart was broken. She'd been such a fool. He didn't want to marry her. He just needed a woman, and here she was, waiting eagerly for him. She groaned aloud. She'd given him all she had. It wasn't enough.

She felt like an idiot. He was used to women who gave out and got out, not retiring little spinsters like Grace who never dated. He was an experienced lover, and he'd lived in big cities for years, where sex was casual. Grace, on the other hand, lived a sheltered life because of her past. She knew very little about adult intimacy. Of course he didn't want to marry her! Why marry a woman, when she was willing to give you anything you wanted without benefit of a ring? She cursed her own weakness for him. If she hadn't given in so easily, if she'd made him wait a little while, he might have fallen in love, too. But now she'd ruined everything. He'd think she was just like all his other women, the ones he took in his stride and cast aside. She was just like that Jaqui woman, who'd made fun of Grace and said Garon would never see her as a real woman.

She pulled herself out of bed and went to bathe away the scent of him. If there was anything positive about this experience, it had shown her that she could be a whole woman, that she hadn't been totally destroyed by her past. Perhaps if she looked at it that way, in a mature fashion, she could forget that the man she loved with all her heart was only looking for momentary relief. Perhaps.

GARON DROVE UP in her yard just after seven o'clock that evening. Despite her resolve not to speak to him again, she went running to open the door. She looked as if she hadn't slept. He knew how she felt. He hadn't slept, either. He'd gone through the day in a daze.

She opened the door wider, like a sleepwalker. He came in and locked it. Without missing a beat, he lifted her in his arms, and kissed her as if he hadn't seen her in a year. Moaning, helpless, she yielded at once. He turned and carried her down the hall to the bedroom.

It was better this time. It was more intense than the first time. He kissed her from her eyelids all the way to her calves, in broad daylight, whispering to her the whole time, exciting and sensual things that made her blush.

When he had her at fever pitch, he pushed her right over the edge into ecstasy and fell with her through waves and waves of throbbing, blinding heat. She cried out endlessly as the waves tore through her body, leaving her shaking in the warm aftermath. He held her close against him while he fought to breathe normally again.

"I was going to ask you out to eat," he said on a breathless laugh.

She smiled and kissed his muscular shoulder. Her own heart was doing uncomfortable things. She hoped he didn't notice. "It gets better and better," she whispered.

He held her closer. "I couldn't work today for thinking how it was last night," he confessed after a minute. "I didn't think it could be as good as I remembered it. But it was." He lifted away from her, to look down with possessive dark eyes at her swollen breasts, their pink crowns soft and relaxed now. He touched them gently, aware of faint scars around the nipples. His hand moved down to her flat stomach and he frowned. The scars were oddly uniform. He'd seen accident victims, so he knew what glass did to human flesh. But it didn't look like this.

"I know they're ugly," she began, misunderstanding his scrutiny.

His eyes lifted back to hers, shocked. "That wasn't what I was thinking at all," he said. "Were you in the hospital a long time?"

She nodded. "Two weeks," she said.

He brought her hand to his chest where the rib cage began, and pressed it into the thick hair that covered the warm muscles. "Feel."

There was a ridge there.

"Feel it?" he asked, smiling. "I took a hit with a machete when we stormed a hostage situation several years ago. Not in this country," he added with a husky laugh when he saw her expression. "I spent several days in hospital myself. So we both have scars."

She smiled back, much less self-conscious. She reached up to touch his face, explore it, caress it. This was like a day out of time, when she could love and be loved, when she could feel as a normal woman did. She felt the return of hope. He was helpless against the attraction she held for him. That had to mean something.

He felt that look all the way inside. He shouldn't encourage her to care about him. It would lead to disaster. But he loved the way she looked at him, the shy tenderness in her fingers when she touched him. He loved her fierce response when passion locked them together. For a woman with a traumatic past, she'd moved easily into intimacy. He liked to think it was because of his own skill in bed. He knew how to give her pleasure, and he could see the remnants of it in her smile.

"Suppose we go out to eat tomorrow?" he suggested.

"Lunch?"

He nodded. "I have to stop by a couple of stores afterward. The inspector gave us a great score, so the SAC said I could have the day off."

She smiled. "I'd enjoy that."

"So would I." He bent and kissed her and then rolled over and got to his feet to dress. She watched him, her eyes soft with appreciation of the hard muscles of his body as he slid back into his clothes. Belatedly she got up and dressed, too.

"Would you like me to cook something?" she asked.

He shook his head, smiling. "I have phone calls to make and re-ports to go over," he said. "But I'll phone you in the morning."

"Okay." She wasn't going to fuss or demand that he stay with her. She felt loved. It was enough. She saw him to the door and then fixed herself a bowl of soup, humming as if she'd won the lottery.

HE HELD HER HAND as they went into Barbara's Café to get lunch. Other patrons who knew Grace smiled benevolently at her, noting the man she was going around with. He was the police chief's brother, so he must be a good sort, they were saying. Garon noticed the smiles and felt uneasy, but they were seated and the spectators found other things to talk about.

Grace was so happy that she radiated it. Even Garon couldn't help but notice what a picture she made when she smiled at him.

She was proud of her enlarged wardrobe that Barbara had helped her buy at the college thrift shop. She was wearing a soft blue wool dress today that came from the shop. It was beautifully cut, fit nicely and emphasized the tiny blue flecks in her gray eyes. She'd gone to pains with her hair as well, putting it up in a becoming style. Garon had noticed, complimenting her on her taste.

They held hands again on the way to the office supply store. Grace, beaming, smiled at passersby who knew her. Garon was still uncom-fortable with their scrutiny, and getting cold feet. Colder by the min-ute, especially when they walked into the office supply store and the manager teased Grace about her companion. It was only small town banter, but Garon obviously didn't like it, and when they left the store, he didn't hold hands with her again. The teasing was getting on his nerves. He loved Grace in bed, but he wasn't going to marry her because of it.

By the end of the day, he'd made a decision he hated having to make. He wasn't going to see Grace alone again. She was seeing him as a prospective husband, but he didn't want her for keeps. He'd dug his own grave, continuing to see her when he knew how she felt about him. He had nothing to offer her. He couldn't marry her. But when he saw the beaming look on her face as he left her at her front door, he couldn't manage the words to tell her he was breaking it off, either. He made an offhand remark about being especially busy in the next two weeks, but that he'd call her. It was the first lie he'd told her.

10

GRACE WENT TO HER regular jobs for the next two weeks. She didn't phone Garon, and he didn't call her. She was still glowing with the memory of the physical delight he'd shown her. She ached for him in the darkness. His ardor had taught her that there was more to sex than pain and fear. She'd loved what he did to her. He was accomplished and thorough. Every time she thought about the passion they'd shared, she almost moaned aloud with the need to experience it again. But days went by and then weeks went by. She heard through the grapevine that the team he led was sent out of state to an emergency, and he was gone a long time. She rarely saw his car at his house when she drove to work. And still he didn't call.

Miss Turner had obviously come back home long ago, but she hadn't phoned Grace, either. Grace didn't know that Garon had told her not to, that he and Grace had had a parting of the ways and she wasn't to communicate with her until things calmed down. It would have killed her.

But worse than Garon's absence was the kindly meant teasing around town. People had been delighted to see Grace finally with a fellow of her own, holding hands in public and radiating happiness. Some of the older people remembered what had happened to her. Nobody talked about it, of course, but it was a good reason for them to wish her well in Garon's company.

Except that she wasn't in his company, and she hadn't seen him. So every time someone asked why he wasn't taking her to community events, she had to make an excuse that he was working hard on a case. Maybe he was. But she didn't know.

GARON REALLY was working on a case. The same case, the child murders. He was bad-tempered and impatient since he'd stopped seeing Grace, because he knew it was going to hurt her when she realized that he was ending their brief relationship. The odd thing was, she didn't seem to know it. He'd heard from his brother, Cash, that she'd said he was working hard and that's why they weren't being seen together in town.

She hadn't gotten the message, he realized. He was going to have to do something drastic to make her understand. Something painful.

If only she'd taken the hint and gone about her own business. He grimaced inwardly as he realized that he'd given her every indication that he wanted her in his life. She was an innocent, and he'd seduced her. He'd looked forward to their meetings. Even now, the memory of Grace in his arms was powerful enough to disturb him.

But even more powerful than his hunger for her was his memory of what it was like to lose a loved one. It had been ten years and still the anguish of that time in his life was vivid. He couldn't bear to go through it again. Better to live in the past than risk his heart a second time. Grace was a sweet woman. He liked her. But she wasn't the sort of woman who normally appealed to him. He liked aggressive, confident, powerful women; women like Jaqui. A quiet, clinging woman who couldn't relate to him intellectually wasn't going to fit into his world.

He'd let Grace sidetrack him, but now he had to put a stop to her fantasies. He had to make her understand that he didn't want her in his life. He hated having to hurt her, but she should have realized he wasn't interested in marriage. He was thirty-six and single. Surely she knew that men who were still unmarried at that age were confirmed bachelors?

"Is something wrong?" one of his colleagues asked curiously.

He forced a smile. "No. I was just thinking about this case."

"Have any luck over in Palo Verde?" he asked.

That brought back the memory of Grace with him, and it stung. "Not much," he replied. "But their police chief's been doing some interviews in the case. Maybe he'll turn up that witness."

"Maybe so."

Garon went back to work, mentally promising himself that he was going to have it out with Grace this weekend and show her, once and for all, that he wasn't interested in her.

GRACE WAS CONFUSED by Garon's avoidance of her. He'd seemed as involved as she was, especially when they became intimate. She knew that he'd enjoyed her. But then he'd taken off and hadn't even bothered to call. No man was that busy. No, he wasn't overwhelmed with work. He was trying to get rid of Grace without confrontations.

She should have realized that a man like him wouldn't be interested seriously in some small town spinster who didn't even have a college degree. If he'd wanted Grace for keeps, he certainly wouldn't have gone to that party at Jaqui's aunt's house. He was attracted to the woman. She was like him—sophisticated and career-minded. And she certainly wouldn't be interested in settling down with him. She probably wouldn't even want children....

Children! She placed her hands on her flat stomach and felt sick all over. She'd told him she couldn't have a child. Was that why he'd stopped seeing her? Before she told him that, he'd been very interested in her.

She bit her lower lip and tears stung her eyes. That explained it. He was feeling his years, maybe, and he was thinking about a family. But Grace was out of the running because she couldn't give him a child. That was why he was avoiding her. He didn't want to hurt her, but she was barren. Yes, she had to admit, that was surely the reason he'd stopped calling her.

She sat down in her easy chair and let the tears roll down her cheeks. Life had cheated her. From her nightmarish childhood to the final indignity of being left only half a woman, life had failed her entirely. She might as well get used to being alone, because it was all she would ever be able to expect. No man wanted a wife who couldn't bear children. She should have realized it!

Finally she got up, wiped her eyes and went to make herself a pot of coffee. Her sewing project was nearing completion. She had to concentrate on that, and stop trying to build castles in the air. She would get over Garon. She could get over anything. She'd proved her ability to survive tragedy. She just had to get in a better frame of mind and stop crying over spilled milk.

THERE WAS AN ARTICLE in the San Antonio paper about the little girl who was killed recently. Grace read it with a sinking feeling in her stomach. The child was only ten. She had long blond hair and light eyes. When she'd been a child, Grace's hair had been long. And her own eyes were light. She felt cold all over. Someone had mentioned that the child who died in Palo Verde was also blond.

The killer had struck three times in Texas, as far as law enforcement people could reckon: in Palo Verde, in Del Rio and now in the outskirts of San Antonio. He chose his victims carefully. He left no clues at the crime scene. He was methodical and intelligent. The article in the paper mentioned that he'd just sent a note to the local paper claiming twelve kills, in three states, and daring the police to find him. He knew that FBI behavioral specialists had been involved, to do a profile of the unknown killer. It would do them no good, he said in a typed letter. He was smarter than they were. There would, he promised, be more victims. Many more.

Grace put down the paper and came to a decision that was painful to make. She wasn't sure that Garon realized the killer targeted a certain type of child. Or that there was something about the killer that was completely unknown. He needed to know. And there was a case she remembered, that nobody knew about except a handful of people in Jacobsville. What she could tell him might help him find the killer. She'd been hiding in the shadows for too long already. She couldn't let another small life be lost.

She tried the phone, but his answering machine picked it up. So she drove over to Garon's house. It was only seven in the evening, and his car was in the driveway, so he must be home.

She went up the steps slowly, and rang the door bell.

There was a pause, then the sound of big, booted feet. There was a muffled curse before the door opened.

It was Garon, but not the man who'd become so passionate with her. This was a cold, indifferent stranger who glared down at her with eyes that seemed to hate her.

"I'm sorry to barge in," she began, "but I need to talk to you."

"You don't take hints, do you, Grace?" he asked coldly. "I tried to do it the easy way, but you're persistent. So let's get it straight. I don't want to see you again. I don't want to hear from you. Don't call, and don't come here again."

Her eyes widened. She felt the words hit her like a blow. "Ex...excuse me?" she stammered, shocked.

"You're looking for something permanent. I'm not. I don't want a long-term relationship of any kind, especially not with someone like you."

"What do you mean, someone like me?" she asked, astonished.

"You're a small town spinster, Grace, with few talents and minimum education," he said firmly, hating the words even as he forced them out. "We don't have anything in common except physical attraction, and it doesn't last. You need some steady cowboy who wants a domesticated little woman to keep house for him."

Her face flushed. "I see."

He felt like a dog, so he was more antagonistic than he would have been normally. "You needed help, and I did what I could for you. But

I'd have done it for anyone. You expected more than I could give you. I'm tired of having people gossip about us. That's over. I don't want you, Grace. Go home."

She couldn't even manage a comeback. Her heart was breaking inside her. She knew that her face had gone deathly pale. She turned away, went back down the steps, got into her car and drove away.

Garon cursed until he ran out of breath. He'd made her leave. Now he had to find a way to live with the guilt he felt about the way he'd treated her.

GRACE WENT THROUGH the motions of living during the next week, but she didn't feel much of anything. She went to her jobs and was glad that Garon didn't come into either of the businesses. She didn't want to see him ever again.

But suddenly, he was everywhere. She went to the bank the following Friday, and there he was, standing in the next line. He looked at her and glared, as if he thought she'd followed him there. She ignored him.

The next day, the local fish pond opened for business—a stocked pond with bass and bream, where customers could rent tackle and catch all they liked, paying for the fish by the pound.

Grace was excited, because she usually entered the local fish rodeos in the summer. She grabbed her pole and bait and minnow bucket and drove to the pond. It was crowded, which was nothing unusual for the time of year. It was almost spring, after all, and this day it was unusually warm. She was wearing jeans and a tank top with a big gray plaid flannel overshirt. She and her grandfather had been fishing buddies. He'd taught her all she knew about the sport.

She'd hoped to take her mind off Garon, because it was painful to remember the things he'd said to her. But she stopped dead when she was almost at the pond, because there was Garon, also in jeans and a chambray shirt, with a spinning reel, standing on the bank.

He turned and saw her standing behind him and his eyes flashed with fury. He threw down the reel and strode to her. She backed up a step, intimidated by the look on his lean face.

"I told you I wasn't interested, Grace," he said through his teeth. "Following me around isn't going to get you anything! Didn't you get it? I don't want you!"

His voice carried. At least one of the fishermen was a regular patron at Barbara's Café. He stared at Garon with surprise, and then at Grace, who was flushed and sick, with pity.

She turned on her heel and marched right back out the gate, her heart shaking her with its wild, helpless throb. The animal! How could he have embarrassed her so? What did he think, that she had so little pride, she couldn't help but stalk him like a predator? She cursed under her breath as she made it back to her car. She threw her paraphernalia into the back seat, started the car and drove herself home.

It was the weekend, so she didn't have to go to work. Instead she finished her small sewing project and mailed off a package that carried all her hopes for the future. She finished pruning her roses, planted two new ones she'd ordered through the mail, and cleaned the house from top to bottom. She slept very well from the exhaustion. She dreamed of Garon, though, and the dreams taunted her with what she would never have with him.

Monday morning, she went back to work at Judy's florist shop and spent the day working on arrangements for two funerals of local people. At least when she was working, it was possible to forget Garon for a few minutes at a stretch. If only she could forget him for good!

GARON HAD LONG SINCE contacted headquarters to do a profile on the child killer for Marquez, to help narrow down the list of possible suspects. Anyone who'd ever done time for crimes against children was immediately on the list. Detectives were going door to door again in the neighborhood where the child had lived, to ask about suspicious activity around the time of the child's abduction. Garon hadn't worked out of the San Antonio office long enough to develop a good network of informants, but one of his colleagues had. He went out and put his snitches to work, listening for word on the street of the child killer.

So far, there were no suspects who matched the DNA found under the child's fingernails. They were checking long lists of sexual predators who were out on bond or parole, but nothing had surfaced so far. Nor was the canvassing of the dead child's neighborhood doing much good.

"You'd think with houses that close together, somebody would have noticed a stranger skulking around in the dark," Marquez told Garon irritably.

"Someone did," he reminded the other man. "Sheldon. But he couldn't give us a good description. An older, bald man with a limp. I've seen six people who fit that description today."

Marquez perched on the edge of Garon's desk. "I've had one of my patrol officers talk to a couple of his informants," he said. "One of them did time for child rape. It's possible the perp bragged about his crime."

Garon's dark eyes flashed. "I want to catch this guy."

"So do I," Marquez agreed. "But he's been at it apparently for twelve years, if that note he sent the newspaper isn't just exaggeration."

"One child a year," Garon said aloud. "And never any witnesses who could give a positive description. There was stranger DNA in at least one case, this last one, but no match when we ran it through VICAP. And the trace evidence from the Del Rio killing was likely stolen."

"Maybe the perp has never done time," the younger man mused. "He's smart, and he knows it. He wants us to look like fools."

"Or maybe he's in a written report from some other law enforcement agency that never made it into the database. We need more information about this child," he said after a minute. "We need to know how she would have reacted to an intruder."

"You mean, was she the sort of child who'd fight and scream, or was she a placid child who did what she was told?"

"Exactly. And we need to work those similar cases, and find out about the other children who were abducted and murdered. We need to know how he's choosing them. The task force has worked hard, but we all have other duties as well. Everybody's working overtime, and we're going backward. We need more information."

Marquez's eyes narrowed. "Well, all the children were female," he said suddenly. "And none was older than twelve."

"Very good," Garon replied. "He also had to have a way to study the children before he abducted them. That means he probably had access to them in one way or another. Maybe he works with children."

"Maybe he was a teacher or volunteered in after-school activities," Marquez murmured.

"Or at church," Garon added reluctantly.

Marquez nodded. "Or took photographs of children for yearbooks."

"He's an organized killer. He took the instrument of death, in this case the red ribbon, with him to the crime scene. He was careful not to leave anything at the crime scene that might implicate him."

"Except for the evidence under the last child's fingernails."

"He must have missed that."

"Probably he's so confident now that he's getting sloppy," Garon returned. "He thinks we're stupid. He doesn't think we can catch him, so he's relaxing his technique a little. Pity there weren't any living witnesses," he added. "We'd be ahead of the game if we knew anything about him."

"We don't usually get breaks that good," Marquez agreed. "Although his writing to the newspaper did give us more than we had. Now we know for sure that he's killed twelve children." He hesitated. "Can I ask you something?"

"Sure. Shoot."

He studied the older man. "You aren't seeing Grace anymore."

Garon's eyes flashed. "That's personal."

"Yes, it is," he agreed. "Grace is like a little sister to me. She hasn't had an easy life."

"Grace wants a husband, but I don't want a wife," Garon said evenly, with ice dripping from his deep voice. "To keep seeing her under the circumstances would be stupid. And cruel."

Marquez nodded. "I see." He turned away. "I'll do some more research on the victims."

"Our big problem with VICAP," Garon said quietly, "is that often police departments won't take the time to send in information on unsolved murders in their jurisdiction. There could be many other cases with similar signatures—the age and coloring of the victim and the red ribbons—but we won't know about them because they aren't in the data base."

Marquez paused. "Most of these killings took place in Texas and Oklahoma. Only two similar killings were found in Louisiana. Every state has organizations for retired police officers, and Internet sites. We might put out the information and see if we get a reply. Some retired lawman might remember red ribbons in a murder case."

"Good idea. It's worth a try, at least."

Marquez nodded. "I'll get to work."

"I'll add it to the agenda and e-mail it to the rest of the task force."

Garon wondered if Grace had been crying on Marquez's shoulders. They'd known each other most of her life. Maybe Marquez had other feelings for her than he was willing to admit. Either way, Garon was growing impatient with her recent "accidental" meetings with him in town. He hoped he'd gotten the point across at the fishing pond.

But the following Friday, there was a performance by the San Antonio Symphony Orchestra at the Jacobsville High School Auditorium. Garon invited Jaqui to go with him. She dressed in a scanty little black number that emphasized her lush figure, and she clung to him like glue. He wasn't really interested in her, but he didn't want to be seen without a companion. Especially in Jacobsville.

Just as they started into the auditorium, Grace walked in, all alone, in the blue wool dress she'd worn the last time she went out with Garon.

She saw him and stopped in her tracks, looking surprised.

Garon knew damned well she wasn't. She'd tracked him here. He turned toward her with fury in his whole look.

"Again?" he asked curtly. "Why the hell can't you stop following me around?" he demanded. "What does it take to convince you that I'm not interested?!"

Grace swallowed, hard. She felt people staring at her. She'd scrimped and saved for this ticket, and now the evening was spoiled. She flushed, backing away from the hot flash of Garon's temper. He was intimidating when he looked like that.

"Stalking is against the law, Grace, in case you didn't know," he added icily. "I could have you prosecuted!"

She was too embarrassed to stay. She turned and left the auditorium. Her heart was cutting circles in her chest. When she got outside, she had to stand for a minute to get her breath. She was shaking all over, and she hadn't realized it until just now.

With tears streaming down her cheeks, she walked quickly to her car, got in, and went home. It was the longest night of her life. She didn't sleep at all.

SHE WASN'T CHASING GARON. She wished she knew how to make him understand, and stop accusing her of things she wasn't doing. But she didn't know how. Obviously she couldn't phone or write him, because then he'd really have a case against her for stalking. She just couldn't seem to win. This was just the last straw.

She grew paler and thinner. The stress of his rejection was giving her sleepless nights and causing other health problems that she kept to herself. But she didn't miss work, despite the fear that he might turn up and start trouble again.

She went to the kitchen at Barbara's Café early on the next Monday and started cleaning and preparing everything that would be on the menu.

She loved cooking. It was one of a few things she was really good at. This job had fallen into her lap. Barbara paid good wages, and even though it was a part-time position, it paid most of the bills. Along with what she made at the florists', she could live.

"I'm opening the doors," Barbara called to her. "Ready?"

"Ready!" Grace called back, smiling.

IT WAS A BUSY DAY. Superior Court was in session, and Jacobsville was the county seat of Jacobs County, so there were lots of people in town for cases on the court docket who would have to get lunch there. The café did a roaring business when court was in session. Barbara took the orders and handed them to Grace, who filled them and brought the food out. Usually there was one other girl, but she was out sick today.

There was a take-out order with no name, sandwiches and chips. She got them together and bagged them, then walked out to the counter, where Barbara was adding up bills.

"There's no name," Grace began.

"Oh, that's for Garon Grier," came the unexpected reply.

Grace felt her heart sink. Before she could speak, there he was, just coming in the front door, with Jaqui hanging languidly on his arm.

Grace started toward him with the bag, her heart shaking her.

His dark eyes seemed to explode in rage. "Good God, not again!" he raged. "Do you have radar? Every damned place I go, you turn up! How did you know I was coming here? Do you have someone spying on me, to make sure you don't waste an opportunity to ruin my day?" he demanded.

"You don't understand," Grace began slowly, trying to reason with him despite the fear he was kindling in her.

"No, you don't understand!" he snapped, moving forward. "You're thick as a plank, Grace. I don't want you in my life! How many times do I have to say it before you believe it?!"

Grace moved back, quickly, her face stiff, her hands trembling on the paper sack she was carrying. He was scary like that, all authority and rage. Violence terrified her.

Barbara was suddenly beside her. She slid an arm around Grace's shoulders. "It's all right, baby," she said gently. "I'll handle this. You go on in the back, okay?"

Grace choked, "Okay." She handed the sack to Barbara and turned toward the back of the café, tears streaming from her eyes.

"This," Barbara told Garon coldly, while all eyes in the place turned toward her, "is your take-out order. Grace was bringing it to you because that's her job. She works here! She's my cook!"

Garon felt the ground going out from under him. He hadn't known Grace was an employee, that she worked for Barbara. She'd never told him.

Barbara shoved the bag into his hands. She glared up at him. "Here. It's on the house. It's no secret around town that you've been giving Grace hell for so much as looking at you. Well, you're not picking on her in my place! I have the right to refuse service to a customer, and I'm exercising it. You are henceforth barred from this restaurant, Mr. Grier. I would like you to leave. Now!"

Customers started clapping enthusiastically. Garon looked around him and realized that there were no friendly faces in that crowd. He'd made enemies of the whole town because he wasn't willing to marry their resident spinster.

But arguing wasn't going to solve anything. He shrugged, put the carry-out order on a table, took Jaqui by the arm and left.

"It's no loss, the food here sucks anyway," Jaqui tossed over her shoulder.

"I'm sure the food isn't everything that sucks around here," Barbara told the other woman with a smug, demeaning smile.

Jaqui started to speak. Barbara slammed the door in her face. Her customers cheered. She grinned and went back to the kitchen to comfort Grace.

"Now, now," she chided softly, wiping Grace's tears on a paper towel. "He's gone. You're safe, baby. Nobody's going to hurt you here."

Grace sobbed into the comforting shoulder. For years now, Barbara had been a surrogate mother to her. Today, like a tigress defending her cub, she'd run the enemy out the door amid cheers from the audience. It was tragic, but funny, too. Grace always saw the humor in things. Involuntarily she started laughing.

"See?" Barbara asked with a smile. "It's not as bad as all that. You have to take your part, Grace. You can't let people walk all over you. Especially people like that arrogant FBI agent. You'll spend the rest of your life crying if you don't stiffen up."

Grace took the paper towel and wiped her wet eyes. "I guess so. I'm not usually such a wimp. But I've been tired lately and I haven't felt well." She touched her stomach, grimacing. "It's been a hard few weeks."

"You just need some time off. I know you've got a little money put back, Grace, and I can help if I need to," she added, serious. "You go and stay for a few days with your cousin up in Victoria. We'll all manage without you for a couple of weeks."

"That's cowardly, running from the enemy," Grace sniffed.

"Not when the enemy is stalking you all over town and accusing you of doing it," she replied, nodding when Grace looked shocked. "We all know everything in Jacobsville. He's given you hell for weeks now. He's going to stop. He just doesn't know it yet," the older woman added with a cold gleam in her eyes. "He'll wish he'd never moved here."

"His brother is very nice."

"Yes, but his brother isn't persecuting you," she reminded Grace. "I'll have Rick come up and see you."

Grace smiled. "He's nice."

"He's my baby, even if I didn't give birth to him. He likes you."

Grace didn't reply. She knew Marquez liked her. She liked him, too, but she didn't love him.

"Maybe, someday," Barbara said nebulously. "But for now, you go home and pack. Okay?"

Grace hugged her. "Okay."

11

GRACE PACKED enough clothes for a week. She'd phoned her elderly cousin the very afternoon that Garon had upset her. He'd welcomed her visit with open arms. Grace had to admit that it would be a relief to get away from her vicious neighbor for a while. She couldn't bear to even look at his house as she passed it on her way out of town. Her heart was shattered by his behavior. He'd given her every reason to hope that he cared for her as she cared for him. He knew she was an innocent, but he'd seduced her just the same, and then made it sound as if they'd only had a couple of casual dates. Obviously sex meant nothing at all to him. But it had meant everything to Grace.

She turned onto the Victoria road. Her car ran very well, thanks to Garon's mechanic. She could consider it one of the very few perks of their tragic relationship. She hoped she could freeze her heart while she was away. She never wanted another man to touch her emotions as Garon had. She should have known better than to trust a man.

GARON SAW GRACE'S CAR pull out of her driveway and continue down the road, from his front porch. He was still smarting from Barbara's defense of her employee. How the hell could he have known that Grace worked in the restaurant? She'd never really discussed her work with him. Jaqui had been incensed over the eviction. Hick towns and stupid people with little narrow minds, she'd raged. You look at someone and they expect wedding bells. She was good for ten minutes of invectives, all the way home.

Nobody seemed to realize that Grace had been stalking him. He was the victim, not their sheltered little town pet. But he did feel badly when he remembered Grace backing away from him, trembling, as he raged coldly at her in the café. It wasn't like him to hurt women. He couldn't remember ever treating one as he'd treated Grace. It had seemed warranted at the time. But now...

He'd sent one of the hands into Jacobsville to the feed store to get supplies, only to be told that they weren't carrying his brand anymore. They suggested he get his feed and ranch supplies in San Antonio. It didn't end there, either. When he contacted the Ballengers about feeding out some of his stock, they were full up. They recommended a feedlot in another county. He sent a man with some business documents to be notarized, and nobody in attorney Blake Kemp's office would even look at them.

"Will you tell me why in hell I'm suddenly poison to everybody in town?" Garon asked Miss Turner with acid tones.

She gave him an unsympathetic stare. "You really don't know, do you?"

"Apparently Grace has a fan club, and it's labeled me Enemy Number One because I don't want to rush her to the altar," he said with cold sarcasm.

Her eyes narrowed. "You aren't from around here, so you couldn't possibly know what Grace's life was like when she was a child. We all watched her grow up. Grace was always the single girl at any party. She never went to dances. She sat out the prom. At graduation, she was all alone. Her grandmother couldn't be bothered to go see her graduate, and her cousin in Victoria was in the hospital at the time. Grace never had a single date, not even a dutch treat one," she added, while he scowled as if this was unthinkable. "And here she is, holding hands with a bachelor who seems to really care about her. Of course people noticed. They knew about her past, and they were happy for her."

"I know that she had a bad experience with a man when she was a child," he said impatiently. "She told me."

She hesitated. "A bad experience?"

"Yes. Inappropriate touching, I believe? I'm investigating a case of child rape and murder," he added indignantly. "Hardly the same sort of thing. I can understand how the incident would affect Grace, but she got off easy compared to the child who was butchered and then thrown away like a used shoe."

She looked at him as if he were demented, but she didn't reply for several seconds. "I suppose you had to live here to understand. Don't worry. Nobody will pair you off with Grace ever again." She turned back toward the kitchen, her back as rigid as a ruler.

His next shock was when he met with the task force. Marquez sat several chairs away from him and didn't greet him or even look in his direction while they went over their files and threw out suggestions for furthering the murder investigation. Marquez suggested they go public and set up a tip line, asking the public's help. That sounded like a good idea, and it was approved.

When the meeting was over, Marquez started out the door without a word to Garon.

Garon followed him to the parking lot. "Have you got a problem?" he asked.

Marquez turned. His eyes were black as lightning, cold as ice. "No," he replied. "I have other investigations pending, in addition to this one. I'll be in touch if I can add anything to the body of evidence."

Garon's eyes narrowed. Of course, Marquez was Barbara's adopted son. He liked Grace. He must have heard about what happened.

"You don't understand," he began.

Marquez walked right up to him. They were almost equal in height, but Marquez was a good eight years younger and less controlled. "After everything Grace has been through in her life, she didn't deserve being persecuted by you," he said flatly.

"She was stalking me," Garon returned hotly.

"Like hell she was," he fired back angrily. "Grace is the least intrusive person I know. She's the exact opposite of that city streetwalker you go around with now," he added, meaning Jaqui. "Grace has had to leave town, did you know that?"

"What?"

"She was so upset that Mama had to drive her home Monday," he continued in the same controlled tone. "Shaking all over, sick as a dog. You didn't have to make your contempt for her public. You could have told her in private without making her the subject of gossip all over again!"

He scowled. "She turned up everywhere I went, after I told her flatly that I didn't want to take her out again."

Marquez just glared. "In a town of two thousand people, it isn't that easy to avoid a neighbor," he said. "Although I think you'll find that most people will avoid you in the future. And that goes double for me."

"You're in love with her," Garon accused, thinking out loud.

Marquez actually flushed. "Half my life," he agreed, nodding. "I'd marry her in a minute if she'd have me. She's sweet and thoughtful and kind. She has a sort of empathy that makes total strangers cry on her shoulder. She's always the first one to offer comfort when someone dies, to bring food, to share what little she has…" He stopped, his lips compressing. "Why the hell am I telling you anything? Lucky Grace, to be run out of your life before it was too late. Nothing she's ever done was bad enough to deserve you!"

He turned and stalked off to his car without another word.

GRACE LIKED HER COUSIN very much. She kept him company and stayed busy baking sweets for him in the kitchen while his housekeeper enjoyed the holiday from the stove. Grace planted flowers for him, read to him and spent lazy days enjoying the diversion from her troubles.

What she knew about the child murders dwelled on her mind. She hadn't been able to tell Garon what she thought about the similarity of the victims. But she needed to tell somebody in law enforcement. This was information that might save a life. So she phoned Marquez.

He showed up one evening in jeans and a sweatshirt, taut and somber, but pleasant just the same.

"Let's sit on the porch and talk," she invited, after they'd had sandwiches and coffee, and her cousin had excused himself to go to bed.

They sat together in the old swing, listening to the sound of crickets and dogs barking in the distance. It was a cool night, but comfortable, and the stars were out in a glorious display.

"I love spring nights," she mused. "It's so peaceful here."

"I'm sorry you can't enjoy it at home," he returned.

She glanced at him, feeling his indignation. "Barbara told you."

"Yes," he said. "I wanted to deck him."

"I felt the same, but it wouldn't accomplish anything," she said with resignation. "He's one of those people who doesn't need anybody. I should have realized it, and not gone gooey over him."

"Don't beat yourself up," he said. "He's not the person I thought he was, either."

She fingered the cold chain that supported the swing. "I suppose it did look as if I were following him around. I couldn't make him understand that those were normal activities for me."

"It's water under the bridge. Why did you want me to come up?" He grinned. "Have you finally discovered a raging passion for me, and you want to give me a diamond ring?"

She gaped at him and then burst out laughing. "You idiot!"

"It was worth a try. Come on, come on, I've got a drug dealer on a back burner and I need to take him off pretty soon. I can't stay long."

She smiled, remembering him as a sort of juvenile delinquent who was always in trouble at school. Nothing serious, usually, but he couldn't manage to be placid.

She sobered then. "It's about the child who was killed."

He was still. "Yes?"

"I remembered something," she said. "I meant to tell Garon, but he thought I went to his house because he hadn't called me."

"So I heard."

She drew in a breath of cool air. "All the children had long blond hair," she said.

He frowned. "Well...yes, they did!"

"And light eyes."

He nodded.

"And red...ribbons."

He was suddenly very quiet.

She stared down at her hands in her lap. "Rick, you were away when it happened," she said. "But someone, Barbara maybe, must have told you something about it."

"Very little," he replied. "Except that you were traumatized by a sexual predator." He hesitated. "I didn't feel comfortable asking you about it."

She looked up at him and smiled gently. "Thanks."

He shrugged. "I'm a private person myself. I understand."

She curled her fingers around the swing chain. "Only a few people ever knew the truth. There was a cover-up," she said. "My grandmother was beside herself. Mama had heard about it from Granny, and that very night, she committed suicide."

"Your mother?" he exclaimed. "But why?"

"Who knows? Granny said Mama felt responsible, because she'd thrown me out of her life and left me at the mercy of a bitter old woman who drank alcohol to excess almost every night."

"I didn't realize that old Mrs. Collier ever had a sip of anything alcoholic," he admitted, surprised.

"She sobered up when she had to come and see me in the hospital. I was...I was a mess," she bit off. She shifted in the swing. "If you saw the body of the latest murdered child, maybe you can imagine what I looked like."

"Dear God!" he burst out.

"I was lucky," she continued. It felt good to talk about it, after so many years of stoic silence. "He panicked. He couldn't quite figure out how to strangle me to death. He was clumsy with the red ribbon, and then the police sirens started wailing. He stabbed me with just a pocketknife, over and over again. I was in terrible pain, but even at the age of twelve, I knew that if I didn't play dead, I'd *be* dead. I held my breath and prayed and prayed. And he ran. Someone had tipped off the police when they saw him carrying me across a field in the moonlight. I never knew who, but it saved my life." She looked at him, aware of his tense, smoldering anger. "Apparently it isn't that easy to choke someone to death, even a child."

"No, it isn't," he confirmed tautly. "It takes several minutes of concentrated pressure. A noose with a stick twisting it is easier than using your hands, but it still takes more than a minute or two to kill a person."

"I remember his hands most of all," she said uncomfortably. "They were bony and pale, weak-looking. I got a glimpse of them, under my blindfold. I think one had deep cuts on it. They were nothing like my grandpa's, who was a deputy sheriff and worked with horses. He had lean, strong, tanned hands. Good hands."

"They took you to a doctor," he prompted, because she'd gone silent.

She drew in a steadying breath. "Dr. Coltrain had just gotten his license. I was one of his first patients," she added with a smile. "I learned some new bad words listening to him when he examined me. He was eloquent."

"He still is," Marquez said.

"Anyway, it took some minor surgery and a lot of stitches. I lost an ovary and my spleen and even my appendix," she added. "They said it would take a miracle for me to ever have a child. As if I'd want to get married and give a man power over me, after that," she said sadly, and tried not to remember how comforting Garon's strong arms had been in the darkness. He'd walked away from her so quickly when he knew she couldn't have a child. It was just as well, though, that she was barren, after the way he'd treated her.

"A reporter heard something on his police scanner. Not enough to tell him the truth, but enough to make him curious. He came over here snooping around. My grandmother called Chet Blake. Chet told him I was attacked by a crazed man and that I had amnesia, that I couldn't remember anything about it. That seemed to satisfy the reporter, because he left and nobody saw him again. But after he left, Granny was afraid the man who abducted me might come back and finish the job if the true story got out. Even though I was blindfolded the whole time, he might think I could still identify him. So our police chief, Chet Blake, hid the file, and talked to the local media. He said I had been slightly injured by a mental patient, that I had amnesia and couldn't even remember how I got hurt. Everybody around me swore it was the truth. The paper ran a story saying a juvenile had been injured by an escaped mental patient and I couldn't remember anything that happened. The mental patient, they said, was taken back to the institution he came from, and I was fine. It was too small a story to make the big city papers, so that was the end of it. If the man was checking about what I told the police, and he read our local paper, he'd have felt safe." She glanced at him. "I was so afraid that he'd do it again, to some other little child. And he is, isn't he, Rick? He's still out there, but now he's killing children. I didn't want to be protected at the cost of someone else's life, but nobody would listen to me. I was just a kid myself. I've had to live with that ever since."

"Damn!"

She sighed heavily. The memories were stifling, frightening. Her hands gripped each other. "I feel guilty because I didn't come forward and tell the truth."

"You were a child, Grace. You had no say in what was done."

"But I'm not a child now," she said earnestly. "I couldn't pick him out of a lineup, Rick, but I'd remember his voice. At least you could look at the file and see what evidence they saved. I know they had swabs, and they took my underclothes," she choked, swallowing hard. She didn't want to remember the rest. "There might be something else that would help with the investigation."

"Yes, but, Grace, if Chet hid the file, how will we find it?"

"You can find out. I know you can. I want you to go to El Paso and talk to Chief Blake. I want you to tell him that we have to give that information to the task force. I'll try very hard to remember what he talked about, anything that might help identify him. I was in that place for three days."

He didn't speak for several seconds. "Grace, what purpose would it serve to open the file twelve years after the fact?" he argued. "We've got DNA evidence from the latest victim. We've got leads. If they open that file, someone's going to let the cat out of the bag.

Any gossip about the case would put you in danger. He might come back and kill you, to silence you."

"I know that," she replied. "But he's killed a lot of little girls," she said sadly. "Maybe I could have saved some of them if..."

"Stop right there," he said firmly, catching her cold fingers in his own. "Child predators are everywhere. You couldn't prevent a kidnapping if you were living in the same town as the perpetrator right now! There's been plenty of press coverage about this predator. Parents know to watch out for their children, but this guy is very smart. Warning people won't stop him."

She shifted. "Maybe not. I do think I might have been his first victim," she continued. "He was nervous the last day he kept me. He used a pocketknife, but I'd gained a lot of weight that year. I had a fat stomach and it saved my life. He left me for dead, panicked and ran. I managed to scream. Someone heard me and I was found in time." She stared into the darkness. "He took me right out of my own bed, in the middle of the night, with my grandmother sleeping in the room beside mine. If she hadn't been drinking, she might have heard him. She hated me for the rest of her life, because everybody knew she'd been too drunk to lock up properly. She pretended to be such a moral pillar of society. Then I got abducted and she was exposed."

"She should have been charged with criminal negligence," he snapped.

"She's dead. Everybody's dead but me, Rick," she said sadly. "It doesn't matter anymore. Catching this lunatic does. You have to make Chief Blake tell you where that file is. There may be something in it that will give you a clue leading to the killer, especially if I really was his first victim. He might have made one mistake that he's too savvy to make now. And that one mistake might help you catch him."

He smiled gently. "You're quite a lady."

She leaned against his shoulder. It was the first time she'd ever touched him voluntarily. He was a sweet man. "I wish I could be what you want me to be, Rick," she said honestly. "You're the nicest man I know."

His heart ached. Having her curled up beside him so trusting, made him feel humble. He wanted to wrap her up against him and kiss her until she moaned, and make her love him. But it was never going to happen. He loved. She didn't. She was only his friend. But even that was better than nothing.

His arm slid around her hesitantly, resting there when she didn't protest. His heart hammered at his ribs, but he drew her close in a comforting, platonic way. "You're the nicest woman I know," he replied.

He heard her soft sigh as she relaxed against his shoulder. It was sweeter than honey, this interlude. At least she liked him. She trusted him. Who could say that one day she wouldn't realize what a good catch he was. He just had to be patient and not rush his fences.

He rocked the swing back into motion. Around them, the night was peaceful and quiet.

In the days that followed, Garon went to work trying not to think about Grace. He turned out with everyone else to respond to a new bank robbery. It was the same crew, with automatic weapons. This time they wounded a guard and a customer. He gave his squad a pep talk and had four of them staking out banks. In the meantime, he coordinated with the serial killer task force, organized his cases and doled assignments out to his squad, escorted visiting dignitaries around town, caught up some of his paperwork. But his conscience still hurt about Grace. He could have been less cruel. She was like a child, in so many ways. She wasn't used to people deliberately hurting her. Maybe it was like Marquez said, it was a coincidence that she'd been at the same places he was.

Two weeks after she left town, his brother Cash called him one afternoon and invited him over to the police station.

"Why here and not at home?" he asked his brother with a smile when he walked into the office.

Cash didn't smile back. He was somber. He closed his office door and sat down behind his desk.

"Marquez flew to El Paso and talked to our cousin Chet Blake," Cash said. He had his hands folded over a manila file folder. "There was an attempted child murder here in Jacobsville twelve years ago. It's identical to the case you and Marquez are working. The file was sealed and hidden, because Chet was afraid the man would come back and finish off the child if he knew she survived."

Garon frowned. "The child lived? There's a witness?"

"Yes," Cash replied. "It's a tragic case. She was abducted out of her own bed and carried to an abandoned cabin just outside town. She was held there for three days," he said with tight lips. "Nobody knows what he did to her. She never spoke of it to anyone. Her injuries were life-threatening. She spent weeks in the hospital. There was a search for the perpetrator, but they never found him. He just vanished."

"The child was a girl?" he asked.

"Yes. She was twelve at the time. Like your other victims, she had long blond hair and light colored eyes."

"Why in God's name didn't they share that information with the Bureau?" Garon demanded hotly. "It might have saved lives! Especially with a living witness who could identify him!"

"She was blindfolded," Cash said. "The whole time. She heard his voice. That's all."

"But to cover it up...!"

"Jacobsville is a small town, and her people were powerful," he said. "You know Chet. He doesn't like confrontations. He was told what to do, and he did it. Against his better judgment, I might add."

Garon let out a rough sigh. "Well, what's in the file? Is there anything about a red ribbon?"

"Yes." Cash slid the file folder across the desk. He was watching Garon with an odd expression.

Garon couldn't decide why until he opened the file folder and saw the first of the photographs that were taken at the scene of the crime, and of the child at the time of her rescue.

The little girl was pudgy, as children sometimes are when they reach the outer edge of adolescence. She was covered with blood. Her long blond hair was matted with it. Her tank top was shredded, like her cotton shorts. There was dirt on her legs and her bare feet. The next series of photos were taken in the hospital, without her clothing. Her stomach showed multiple stab wounds. There were bruises all over her arms and legs. She had a black eye, and her mouth was bloody. There was blood around the tiny, pink buds of her breasts.

The damage matched that of the dead child Garon had seen at the autopsy, except that this poor victim had lived. He studied the photos and then turned to lift the police report, which gave the child's name.

Garon's breath exploded in the silence of the office. His heart seemed to stop beating. The child's name was Grace. Grace Carver.

Memories flashed in front of his eyes. Grace, shy and afraid of him.

Grace, letting him pick her up with wide, frightened eyes. Grace, clinging to him. Grace, in his arms, in his bed, loving him. Grace holding his hand and radiating joy. Grace, cringing from him in Barbara's Café…!

The puzzle fell into place. Grace was innocent because she'd been abducted, assaulted and very nearly killed by a homicidal maniac. And he'd made light of her experience. Worse, he'd seduced her and then pushed her out of his life, like a man discarding a used towel.

He put his face in his hands and tried to justify what he'd done to that poor, tortured soul out of his own fear that she was getting too close to him. God in heaven, he thought poignantly, what have I done!

Cash wasn't blind. He'd heard the gossip about Garon and Grace, especially in the past couple of weeks since she'd been forced to leave town to stop the whispers. He and Garon weren't close, so he hadn't asked any questions. But the man across from him didn't seem very arrogant now.

Garon leaned back in his chair. His eyes were blank. He'd lost color in his lean face. The shock was all too apparent.

He was trying to come to grips with his own actions. No wonder he'd been an outcast after his treatment of Grace. The important people in this town knew the truth of what had happened to her. They were delighted that she'd found someone who could heal her emotional wounds, give her a little happiness. It hadn't been malicious gossip about the two of them, or an attempt to marry them off. It had been happiness that, after all Grace had endured, she might have a loving future to comfort the pain of her past.

Instead she'd been kicked in the teeth one more time by fate. By Garon.

Garon let out a slow breath.

"Marquez wanted to tell you himself," Cash remarked after a minute. "But I didn't trust him that close to you, once he knew the facts of the case."

Garon looked at his brother blankly. "He didn't know?"

Cash shook his head. "Grace told no one. Chet gave him the details, along with this file. To date, not one person knows what that animal did to her in the three days he kept her a prisoner."

He was remembering the dead child, the horrible mutilation of her young body. That could have been Grace. She could have been dead, instead of emotionally and sexually crippled and left for dead. It was like a nightmare. He'd never thought of himself as a monster. Before.

"Was there any trace evidence?" he asked, forcing his numb brain to work.

"Yes. I'd bet my baton that the DNA will match what you found on the latest victim."

"DNA." He stared at Cash while the truth drilled a hole in his heart. "DNA." His teeth ground together. The son of a bitch had raped Grace…!

He got up from the chair in one powerful movement, almost shaking with rage and self-loathing.

Cash got in front of him before he could start for the door. "Sit down."

"Like hell I will!"

"I said, sit down!"

Cash pushed him back into the chair and stood over him, powerful and immovable. "Remember who and what you are," he said forcefully, his dark eyes even and steady on his brother's. "You can't go raging out of here like a mad dog, chasing shadows. You don't even have a suspect. What are you going to do, run cheek swabs on every male in Jacobs and Tarrant Counties?"

Said like that, it sounded absurd. But Garon wasn't thinking straight. He was furious. He wanted to hurt someone. He wanted to find the sexual predator and strangle him slowly with his own hands. He couldn't remember feeling such mindless rage. At least not since he'd lost his own love, so long ago…

But he'd lived in the past too long already. He'd used it to ward off any emotional ties, to keep himself safe from another relationship. He was alone, by choice. But Grace had paid the price for his escape. He'd savaged her to save himself. She would never forgive him…

He stared up at Cash with dawning realization. Grace had come out of the dark nightmare that was her life to reach out toward Garon with hope and breathless anticipation. He'd knocked her back, savaged her verbally and emotionally. He'd frightened her so badly in the café that she'd backed away from him, shaking like a leaf. He'd done that to her, when her only crime was that she wanted to love him.

His eyes closed on a wave of pain. Grace had sent Marquez to El Paso to dig up the most horrible chapter in her life. She'd done it not for herself, but to try to save some other child from what she'd endured. She was willing to take the risk that reopening the case might bring the killer back to finish the job he'd started.

In a flash he saw what he'd missed from the minute Cash gave him the file folder. Grace was the only person alive who could identify the child killer. And sharing the case with police might get her killed, as well.

12

IT WAS A LONG DRIVE to Victoria. Saturdays in early spring brought all the weekend adventurers out on the highway. Usually Garon didn't mind bottlenecks, but he was anxious to get to his destination. He wasn't sure how he was going to manage it, but he had to coax Grace into coming home.

He'd phoned Marquez's cell phone, but he hadn't gotten an answer. Probably the younger man was still furious and unwilling to talk to him. He couldn't blame him. The detective loved Grace. It wouldn't sit well with him that Garon had caused her so much pain.

He was wearing a lightweight jacket, which he probably wasn't going to need. It was a warm, sunny day. The SUV ahead of him had a canoe lashed to its rack and fishing poles sticking out of the back window. Fishing. He grimaced, recalling how he'd overreacted when he found Grace at the local fishing pond.

Her cousin lived back off the road in a grove of pecan trees. There was a dirt driveway that led up to the house. It was an old house, simple white clapboard, one story, with two chimneys and a long front porch that contained rocking chairs, a settee and a swing, all painted green. Off to the side was a large pond with a pier. He glanced toward it and blinked. Grace was out there, dressed in knee-high cutoffs and a red T-shirt, bending over what looked like a minnow bucket.

He got out of the SUV and walked down to the pond, sunglasses hiding the apprehension in his dark eyes. The sunglasses were an individual thing now. But when he was in the elite Hostage Rescue Team, everyone copied the team leader's sunglasses. Those had been good days, working tight with an expert group of men. His job now, even heading a crime unit squad, was less exciting. It was less stressful as well. Maybe that would seem like a benefit, one day.

Grace saw him coming and straightened. Her chin came up. She was barefoot and wore no makeup at all. Her long hair was in a braid that reached between her shoulder blades. She wasn't wearing sunglasses and she wasn't smiling. In one hand, she held a long cane pole with a cork, sinkers and a hook on the fishing line.

The memory of their last meeting, when he'd humiliated her in Barbara's crowded café, was still fresh in her mind. "Well, well, if it isn't the Prince of Darkness," she said coldly, and her gray eyes reflected the pain, indignation and outrage of the past few weeks. "I can't think of a way you could cause me any more embarrassment on this planet. So, have you come for my soul?"

He stopped just in front of her. If he'd hoped for a truce, he was disappointed. He stuck his hands in his pockets, eyeing the plain, old-fashioned fishing pole. "If you plan to catch anything, you'd have better luck with a spinning reel," he advised.

She moved to the side of the pier, bent and pulled up a string of bass. They were five to six pounds, each, and she had four of them. His surprise was visible.

She held the string of fish at her side, and she was glaring. "I won the Jacobsville Bass Rodeo two summers in a row," she informed him. "Which is why I spend every free minute at Jake's Fish Pond in Jacobsville in early spring. Practicing. Sadly I've had to forego practice since you decided that I was chasing after you!"

He felt the hot color flow into the skin over his high cheekbones. He'd accused her of following him to the fishing pond. She hadn't been chasing him at all. At least, not that time.

"Why are you here?" she asked, not moving.

He stuck his hands in the pockets of his slacks and searched for inspiration. He hoped he didn't look as uncomfortable as he felt.

But he did. She cocked her head and studied him for a minute. "Oh. I see. Someone told you the truth about my past, is that it?" she asked with icy poise.

The muscles in his jaw tautened. "Something like that."

She averted her eyes and moved to the foam cooler she'd brought to store her fish in. She opened the top and put the fish on top of the layer of ice inside. She closed it back, all without giving him a second glance.

"You sent Marquez to El Paso," he said without preamble.

She looked at him. "I know things about the killer that you don't. I tried to tell you, but you decided that I'd come to your house for, shall we say, other purposes, before I could get the words out."

His lips compressed tightly. "Listen," he began.

"No, *you* listen!" she shot back, eyes flashing like silver lightning in a face livid with bad temper. "I've spent my entire adult life backing away from men. I've never chased anyone in my life, and that goes double for you. Do you really think I have so little pride and self-respect that I'd go running wildly after a man who'd just told me he didn't want anything else to do with me?"

Now that he thought about it, no, he didn't. But it was too late for that belated inspiration to save him. Grace was furious, and he was already on the defensive and not liking it.

He drew in a short, angry breath. He rammed his hands deeper into his slacks pockets and scowled down at her. "What do you know about the killer that we don't?" he asked.

"For one thing, that he likes little girls with long blond hair and light-colored eyes," she said, trying to sound calmer than she felt. "He also said that he'd been watching me at school. He knew that I lived with my grandmother and that she drank herself to sleep. It amused him to take me right out of her house and through the window in the middle of the night. He said that he'd dreamed of collecting blond girls just my age, with long hair, and that he would tie us up with red ribbons so that everyone would know we belonged to him. I believe that's what your organization calls a killer's 'signature'?"

"My degree is in criminal justice," he countered. "I don't do profiling. That's up to the Behavioral Science Unit at Quantico."

She gave him a smoldering look. "If there's a dead child in San Antonio, and there were also dead children in Del Rio and Palo Verde," she pointed out, "with a year or so in between, similar coloring and a similar killing style, then you're looking for a serial killer."

"Perhaps you'd like to put that in writing and send it to Marquez's lieutenant," he suggested. "He still doesn't consider it a serial crime."

"Or maybe he just doesn't like the FBI," she returned sweetly, "and is trying to keep you from taking over his case."

"Criminal cases aren't property. Nobody owns them."

She picked up the cooler and her fishing pole. "Whatever you say." She was walking away.

"I saw the file," he bit off. "And the photos."

She stopped in her tracks. Her spine stiffened. But she didn't turn around.

He moved to her side, turned and looked down at her pale, strained face. "You told me the scars were from an automobile accident."

She wouldn't meet his gaze. "That's what my grandmother taught me to say," she replied simply. "I thought she was being evasive and old-fashioned. Then, when I was sixteen, one of the new boys at my high school asked me out on a date and I told him just a little of what happened to me." She didn't look at him as she drew the memory out of the past. "We went to a fast food place. I noticed that he was looking at me in a really strange way. I asked why. He wanted to know exactly what the man who abducted me did to me, how it felt and if I enjoyed it."

His indrawn breath was eloquent.

"That's right," she said when she saw his face. "All the warped people aren't in jail or seeing psychiatrists. I got sick. I wouldn't even let him take me home. I phoned Barbara and she sent Rick to pick me up. He was all for laying my date out on the floor, but I thought it wouldn't look good on his record."

So that was why Marquez was so protective of her. They had a history. It bothered him.

"After that," she continued, "I stopped going out at all. Unless you can call helping Barbara and Rick can vegetables every summer after harvest a social life. What do you want to know about it?" she asked bluntly.

"Anything you remember," he said, averting his face.

"I don't like remembering," she said with quiet honesty, putting the ice chest down. "I still have nightmares."

He recalled the one she'd had at his house. It made him feel even more guilty, now that he knew the truth. "Cash said Chet told him that your abductor had you for three days, and that you've never talked about it."

"He's right. I've never told a soul. Not even Chet Blake, right after it happened." Her face closed up tight. "If you're hoping to have me identify a subject in a lineup or in mug shots, you're out of luck. He kept me blindfolded the whole time."

"He talked to you."

She swallowed. Nausea rose in her throat. "Yes." She sounded as if the word choked her.

"You can remember his voice."

She chewed on her lower lip. "He said I looked like his stepmother. He had a picture of her as a child."

"What?"

"He said he wet the bed and she made him wear dresses and a red ribbon in his hair. He said she sent him to school like that when he started, and the teacher sent him home again. Everybody laughed. He tied my hair up with the ribbon, but later, just after he tried to strangle me, and he couldn't, he tied it around my neck." She swallowed down nausea. It was hard to remember this. "The ribbon wasn't long enough. He had white hands, very white, and he couldn't pull the ribbon tight enough to kill me. He said it was her fault his hands didn't work right. He was furious. He pulled out his pocketknife and stabbed me, over and over..."

"It's all right," he said, his voice quiet, reassuring. "Don't force it."

She was shaking. She had to fight for control over herself.

Garon watched her, concerned. He didn't touch her. He knew that if he did, she'd connect it with what was done to her. He let her fight her demons.

He pulled out his BlackBerry and his stylus, and started keying in notes. Suddenly he remembered how she'd almost collapsed at the police station in Palo Verde when the chief there had mentioned red ribbon.

"The child in Palo Verde was strangled with a red ribbon," he murmured.

"Yes," she said after a minute. "That was when I started to suspect that it was the same man, when the police chief said he used a red ribbon." She looked up at him, her face pale. "I never read anything about red ribbons in the other child murders."

"We always hold something back," he reminded her, "to make sure we've got the killer and not some lunatic looking for dark fame. You said he mentioned his stepmother. Was that all?"

"Yes," she replied, looking up. "He was using a computer, though. I heard his fingers on the keyboard. He used it a lot."

That might be helpful. He noted it with the stylus. If the man still used computers, it might be a way to track him. If he was a pedophile, he must have access to the pornography Web sites. The FBI had cyber detectives who tracked down child pornographers and locked them up.

"He said that he loved little children." She said the words as if they were some huge, cosmic joke.

"Three dead children in three years," he was saying to himself. "Maybe as many as eleven, one a year since you were abducted. But you lived. Why did you live?"

Her slender shoulders rose and fell. "The police came sooner than he expected. He taped my wrists and my ankles together with duct tape. Then he carried me out to a field somewhere and tried to choke me, but he couldn't do it with his hands. He couldn't do it with the ribbon, either. He had thin fingers, white fingers, and they were limp and cold. So he wrapped duct tape around my mouth and nose. Then he opened his pocketknife and started stabbing me. It hurt so much, and blood went everywhere... I tried to scream, but all I could do was mumble. I started kicking at him. That spooked him and he stopped. But I knew he'd finish me off if I kept struggling. So I kept very still, held my breath and played dead. The sirens came closer. He hesitated for just a minute, as if he wanted to make sure I was gone, but there wasn't time. He took off running. With the duct tape over my nose and mouth, if the police hadn't spotted me when they did, I wouldn't have been able to tell them anything. I'll never forget how good it felt when they took the duct tape off and I could get air in my lungs at last. But it really hurt. One of the knife wounds punctured my lung."

He was listening, forcing himself to concentrate on the details, not on the terror Grace must have felt. "Duct tape. He couldn't strangle you, so he tried to smother you. He hadn't killed before," he said absently. "He didn't realize how hard it is to strangle someone with bare hands."

"That's what I thought," she replied. "My grandmother talked Chief Blake into suppressing the story, so the newspapers wouldn't get hold of it. Well, they did get hold of it," she admitted, "but they printed that a mental patient hurt me, not seriously, and that I had amnesia and couldn't remember a thing. They said my doctor said I'd never regain my memory. If the killer read the paper at all, he knew that I wasn't a threat. But I was afraid he'd do it again, to some other child. I couldn't make my grandmother understand that. She refused to ever let me talk about it again. I've lived with that, all these years. If they'd pursued him, maybe all those other little children would still be alive, too."

"It took a task force over twenty years to catch the Green River Killer in Washington State," he reminded her. "They had clues and at least one living witness, too. It didn't help them catch him. Ted Bundy killed college girls for years, and they couldn't catch him, either. Even if you'd told the police everything you knew, chances are your attacker would still be killing. Serial killers, especially organized ones, are intelligent and cagey. They're hard to find, even with all our modern tools."

"Maybe so."

"You should come home."

Home. She remembered all over again how he'd embarrassed her there. She glared at him. "My cousin Bob has offered me his guest room for as long as I want to stay with him. When my grandmother's will is through probate, I can put the house on the market."

He hadn't counted on that response. He felt terrible. "You have friends there who would miss you."

"Victoria isn't that far to drive. They can come up here and visit."

"Then let me put it another way," he persisted somberly. "No killer forgets his first victim. He knows who you are, and he can find out where you are. If for some reason your name is connected with the killer, and he starts worrying that your memory might have come back, he might decide to stack the odds in his favor. We found DNA on his last victim, but we didn't publicize that. For all he knows, you're the only living human being who might be able to identify him. He might decide to come full circle."

"He might come after me and kill me, you mean," she said very calmly.

His jaw tautened. "Yes."

Her lips curled down. "There's an optimistic thought."

"Stop that. Life has its benefits. You might marry," he added.

Her gray eyes met his dark ones. "What would be the point?" she asked. "I can't have a child."

He felt as if she'd hit him in the stomach. "Plenty of marriages succeed without children."

She laughed coldly. "Really? You were attracted to me at first," she recalled. "You liked being with me, and taking me places. Then when you knew I couldn't bear children, all of a sudden I became a one-night stand with disposability potential."

He was shocked at her perception of why he'd broken it off with her. "That's not true," he ground out.

"Sure it isn't." She turned and picked up the ice chest again. She felt sick at her stomach and weak as a kitten. It must be the lost hours of sleep ruining her health. "If you're through asking questions, could you leave?" she asked pleasantly. "I have a busy day ahead of me. Cousin Bob wants me to brush his cat."

The sarcasm brought a twinkle into his eyes that he tried not to let her see. "At least, think about what I've said." He strained his mind for inspiration. He pursed his lips. "Your roses are starting to bud out. They'll be eaten alive by bugs if they're not sprayed, and without fertilizer you may not have one decent stem."

She glared at him. "I can transplant them up here."

"They won't like it here."

"How would you know?" she asked indignantly. "Do you talk to roses?"

His dark eyes actually twinkled. "Not when I think anyone might overhear me. I work for the FBI. Talking to roses might get me transferred to the Antarctic."

"The FBI doesn't have an office there," she returned.

He shrugged. "They have offices all over the world," he corrected. "They might decide to open one in a far away cold place if they catch me talking to a bush."

She rubbed at a spot of red mud on her cutoffs. "Actually scientific studies have been done on plants using audio pulses, such as classical and rock music. They actually react favorably. They do feel sensation. It's not even surprising when you consider the structure of a single leaf," she added absently, scrubbing at the red spot. "There are guard cells that protect the leaf from invasion by parasites..."

His eyebrows arched. "I thought your education ended at high school," he remarked, surprised by her knowledge of botany.

She gave him a cool look. "I thought you knew better than to take anyone at face value."

His eyes narrowed. "Come home."

"No!"

"Give me one good reason why you won't."

"Because *you* live next door to me!" she said with pure venom.

"I'll have a fence put up so you can't see me," he promised.

Involuntarily, a laugh tried to get out of her throat. She smothered it.

"Your cousin is old and infirm, isn't he?"

"Well, yes," she replied.

"So what if this animal comes looking for you up here?"

She drew in a small, quick breath. "I don't know."

"I have a big gun," he pointed out, pulling back his jacket to display it. "If he comes looking for you at home, I'll shoot him with it."

She wanted to go home, but she had cold feet. She couldn't bear to look at him, because it hurt too much. She'd gone headfirst into dreams of a shared future, and he'd encouraged her, only to shove her right out of his life in the cruelest way possible. People would pity her, all over again. She'd have to work at convincing the town that his lack of interest didn't bother her. She'd have to see him with that Jaqui woman.

He could almost see the pain and the apprehension on her face. He remembered too well the amount of damage he'd done to her. He knew he couldn't make up for it all at once, but he could protect her, and he would. It was naïve to believe that the killer wouldn't be curious about the child who lived. Especially since apparently he'd killed children all around Texas in the past three years. Garon felt that Grace was in danger.

She knew she was walking a thin line. Enough people in Jacobsville knew something about her ordeal in the past. Nobody knew who the killer was. He could walk into town and order coffee at Barbara's Café and just listen to people around him. Evidently he could blend right in. She recalled his voice. It was faintly cultured and he sounded to her like an educated man, not some backwoods idiot. His hands hadn't been those of a laborer, either. They'd been scarred. He kept them covered with thin leather gloves most of the time he'd had her in his power.

"His hands," she murmured aloud. "They were scarred…"

He put that down on his PDA. "You may not realize it, but even these small details you remember might be enough to help us catch him," Garon added after a minute. "You're the only witness, Grace. You might save lives."

She nodded solemnly. "I suppose so."

"Miss Turner has missed you."

"Has she?"

"I'm sure she'd enjoy having you back."

"I guess so."

"If rosebushes have feelings, yours are probably grieving already," he added solemnly. "I imagine they're brokenhearted. They'll cry and some passerby will hear them and check himself into the hospital for a CAT scan."

This time the laugh did escape, even though she stifled it immediately.

He smiled. "I'll even loan you a truck and a man to drive it, so you can get fertilizer and pesticides to use on your roses."

"Barbara has a truck," she said, avoiding the offer.

Which Marquez would be happy to drive for Grace, on his day off, Garon realized with a twinge of something unfamiliar.

"Well?" he persisted.

She finished rubbing the spot. It was still there. It probably wouldn't come out, anyway. Red mud was usually permanent. She glanced at him. "If you'll promise to give me a schedule of your daily routine so I won't risk appearing in the same place you do, I'll come home."

"Cut it out," he muttered. "I'm convinced that it was coincidence. I overreacted."

"Gee, was that an apology?" she asked with mock surprise.

"I don't make apologies unless the director phones me personally and orders me to."

"I figured that out for myself."

"When?"

She frowned. "When, what?"

"When are you coming back?"

She nibbled her lower lip. "Tomorrow, I guess."

"Good. I'll stop by your house and tell the roses on my way home."

"Nice of you," she said.

"I have lots of good qualities," he assured her.

"You keep them well-hidden, of course," she returned with a mocking smile.

"No use wasting them on a woman who'd enjoy putting out a contract on me," he told her.

"Unfortunately I can't afford a hit man, on my salary," she said.

"Why don't you go to college and get a degree? You could earn more."

"Why don't you go home and stop trying to run my life?" she asked him. "I don't need career counseling."

"You drive a car that is an accident about to happen, and you dress out of thrift shops," he muttered.

She flushed. "How do you know where I get my clothes?"

His teeth clenched. He shouldn't have said that.

"Spill it!" she demanded, hands on her hips.

"You wear that damned blue wool dress everywhere. Otherwise, you wear the same pair of jeans with assorted sweatshirts. It doesn't take rocket science to figure it out."

"I can't see why it should bother you how I dress," she said sweetly. "You can rest assured that you won't ever have to be seen in public with me again."

"That's comforting."

"I'm sure your friend Jaqui can afford to shop at Saks or Neiman Marcus. No cut-rate wardrobe for her!"

He bit back a hot reply. He'd done enough damage to her ego already. "She doesn't hide her assets," he admitted. "She likes having men around her."

She gave him a cold smile. "Lucky girl, not to have my history."

His high cheekbones went ruddy with color. He turned. "I'll see you."

"Not if I see you first," she replied tersely. "And that's a promise."

She went back into the house to put away her fish and to pack, after his car had roared off down the driveway. She was probably nuts to let him talk her into it, but he was right about her cousin being in the line of fire. If the killer did come after her, she didn't want any innocent people getting hurt. And she did have knowledge that might help put the perpetrator behind bars.

THE HOUSE WAS EMPTY and cold. She'd left the pilot light on the furnace, though, so she had heat. She needed it, too. The weather had turned cold unexpectedly. She went through the house, making sure everything was where it should be. Then she went out into the backyard, to check the rosebushes Garon had been so concerned about.

There were young buds among the leaves on the rosebushes. There were new leaves on the trees, too, in so many shades of green that she couldn't count them. The sun was shining down through them and there was a crisp, invigorating breeze. Impulsively she lifted her arms and danced around in a circle, laughing at the pleasure it gave her to be back on her own property again. *Her own property.* She'd never owned anything except the clothes on her back. Now, at least, she had a place to live. All she had to do was manage an income that would take care of the utilities and an occasional new dress. But there was time. There was plenty of time.

Garon had walked over to see her and make sure that the house was secure. He heard laughter from the back yard and turned the corner. And there was Grace, her long blond hair down around her shoulders, almost to her waist in back. She was spinning around like a happy child, dancing in the wind with her eyes closed and her face lifted to the sun.

Something hit him right in the chest as he stared at her. She was lovely. She was sweet and kind and loving. She'd been his for two heady days, when pleasure took on an aura of magic, like nothing he'd known before. But he'd wounded Grace. He'd thrown her away like a used cup, devalued her, demeaned her. She would never open her arms to him again and hold him in the darkness. She would never trust him again.

It was one of the most painful revelations he could remember. And until this very minute, when he looked at her unawares and knew how blessed he'd been to have her in his life, he hadn't known what he felt for her. It was bad timing. Damned bad timing.

Instead of making his presence known, he turned and went back the way he'd come. He knew that if she'd seen him, all the joy would drain out of her like water through a sieve. He couldn't bear to see that. She'd been through so much in her young life. He was sorry he'd made things hard for her. Perhaps, if he worked at it, he could earn her forgiveness. It was better than nothing.

GRACE WENT BACK to work the very next day, first at the florists' and then at the café. People seemed generally delighted to have her home. They also mentioned what a rough time Garon had been treated to after her departure. He'd had to do his shopping in San Antonio, because local doors were shut to him after his treatment of Grace. She couldn't say he hadn't deserved it, but she felt sorry for him. He wasn't a man who made friends easily, or seemed to fit in anywhere. Maybe he really had felt guilty enough to coax her back home. Or, she mused, maybe he just wanted to be able to buy his cattle feed in Jacobsville instead of having to drive a half hour to get it somewhere else.

She'd felt full of energy when she got home, but as the days passed, she began to feel an acceleration of the uncomfortable nausea and weakness that had been a hallmark of her life since she left Jacobsville. Surely it was just a virus, she told herself. She was never ill. Even if she was, where would she get the money for a doctor? She only carried a small insurance policy, which covered major medical but not routine office visits or prescription drugs. No, she'd just have to wear it out. These things usually went away in a short time. She'd get better.

But she didn't. Late one afternoon, when she was putting mulch around her roses, the world started spinning. She felt nausea rise up in her throat just as a strange weakness overcame her. With a shocked little cry, she fell to the ground. Her last sight was of the sky going from blue to black....

13

GARON WAS HOME by early afternoon. He'd been working a bank robbery with most of the agents at his office. Everyone turned out in a case like this, where the crew they'd been hunting appeared at one of the banks Garon's squad had staked out. The four men were dressed in camouflage carrying assault weapons. They held up a bank and bullets flew at civilians as well as law enforcement personnel in their desperation to get away. Two people were wounded. The robbers ran out of the bank and took off in an old car, but then they roared off and lost their pursuers in traffic. Minutes later, they wheeled into the parking lot of a nearby restaurant to trade the car for a parked SUV.

An off-duty cop had seen some men jump out of a car carrying weapons and money bags, cursing loudly as they fumbled with a key that apparently didn't fit the ignition. They hot-wired the SUV and took off. Dispatch sent out a text message to Garon's squad, giving the name and location of the off-duty policeman who reported armed men stealing a vehicle at a local restaurant. Because the parking lot contained several children with their parents, the off-duty officer felt it would have been too dangerous to open fire and invite return fire in such a crowded venue.

But his quick report sent lawmen rushing to the restaurant parking lot, where they discovered a parked SUV almost identical to the one the officer had seen the armed men hijack. Amazingly its tag was registered to a convicted bank robber who'd been paroled just weeks earlier. In their haste to get away, the robbers had mistaken another SUV for the one they'd apparently parked earlier next to the restaurant. But their escape vehicle was left behind, with the tag in the robber's own name. When he arrived home, FBI agents were waiting at his house. They arrested him, and he confessed and named his partners to shave some time off his sentence.

The Bureau took priority in federal crimes like bank robbing. But even in some other felony cases, local police were glad to hand criminals over to the Bureau because the federal charges were more severe and a suspect, if convicted, would serve a longer sentence.

Garon felt good about the quick resolution to the situation, and the fact that nobody had been seriously wounded despite the flying bullets at the scene of the robbery. Thanks to some good police work and an off-duty cop's sharp eyes, the felons were apprehended within two hours of the robbery, and all the stolen money from the latest robbery was recovered. It felt good to have the case solved. The robbers had been experienced and dangerous. Now they were off the street for years.

Garon had gone by the crime lab to drop off some evidence in the case. It was technically a little before regular quitting time, but since there was nothing pressing, the SAC told him to go home. It was Saturday, after all. He could always find something to keep him busy at the ranch.

He was driving by Grace's house when he happened to look toward her front porch and saw what looked like a bundle of clothes strewn across the ground near the steps. It was so odd that he turned into her driveway to check it out.

When he got closer, he realized that what he'd seen wasn't clothes. It was Grace, lying on the ground, unconscious.

He was out of the car and running in a matter of seconds. He dropped down beside her and felt for a pulse. Her heart was beating with an odd rhythm, but she was already stirring. Her eyes opened. She swallowed, hard, her face almost white, her stomach churning.

"What happened?" he asked at once, concerned.

"I don't know," she said huskily, swallowing again to keep the nausea from rising. "I was walking toward the house, and the next thing I knew, everything went black. I never faint," she added indignantly. "It isn't even hot. It couldn't be heat stroke…"

"The Coltrains have a clinic on Saturday evening, don't they?" he asked.

"Yes, but I don't need a doctor," she began weakly. "It's just a virus or something."

He didn't believe it. And before she could argue, he picked her up and carried her to his car. Odd, he thought, she felt heavier than she had the last time he'd carried her.

"I don't want to go to the doctor," she protested.

He balanced her on his hip while he opened the door, then he slid her in onto the passenger seat. "Sit still," he said firmly, while he reached for her shoulder belt. As he drew it across her body, his hand slid gently across her stomach…and stopped dead.

He looked down at her, frowning, as his big, lean hand settled curiously, gently, over the hardness of her swollen belly.

"What are you doing?" she asked, still dazed from the giddiness. "It isn't appendicitis. I don't have an appendix. When I was stabbed, the knife severed my appendix and one of my ovaries…"

The look on his face was inexplicable. She saw his eyes glitter and his face go almost as pale as her own was.

"You're scaring me," she protested. "What's the matter?"

His hand pressed tenderly against her stomach for an instant before he finished fastening the shoulder harness and closed her door. His face was hard and unreadable. He didn't say a word. He couldn't. He was shaken to his very soul.

"I need my purse," she protested. "It's sitting on the hall table. The key's in the door. You need to lock it if you're determined to make me see the doctor."

He was too dazed to argue. He went inside, picked up her purse, locked the door, dropped the key in and passed it to her before he climbed behind the wheel.

He drove like a man sleepwalking. He knew his heart must be turning flips. Could she really be that naïve that she didn't realize what had happened to her? He glanced at her curiously as he pulled out into the road.

"Are you eating anything at all lately?" he asked in an odd tone.

She shifted restlessly and looked out the window. "Whatever I've got keeps my stomach upset," she said heavily. "Mostly I get milkshakes and drink them."

She really didn't know! He felt his breath catch as the possibilities rushed in like mosquitoes circling his head. He'd been like half a man during the past few years. He'd avoided women, and entanglements, and hardly dated at all. Now fate had delivered him up whole to this unexpected complication, and he felt as if he'd just won the lottery. But he didn't know how to handle it.

He glanced at Grace's averted profile. She wasn't pretty, but she had a warmth and empathy that made him hungry. It had been so long since he'd had a reason to live. Now he had something to make life worthwhile. He had hope again.

"You're acting very strangely," she observed as they neared the Coltrains' office building, which they shared with their colleague, Dr. Drew Morris.

"Am I?"

"And we'll never get in," she added, noting the cars parked outside the building. "I'll bet half of Jacobs County is sitting in the waiting room. Why don't you take me home, and I'll see Dr. Coltrain next week?"

"Not on your life." He parked the car and pulled out his cell phone.

She tried to protest what he was saying to the receptionist, but he held up a hand and cut her off.

"The side door?" he added. "Right. I see it. We'll be right there."

He drove to the side of the building and parked, got out and lifted Grace, carrying her toward the building.

"But I'm not dangerously ill," she protested, flushing.

"I never said you were."

"You told her I was unconscious!"

"A tiny white lie," he said as he reached the building. "Better close your eyes unless you want to be here until midnight."

She really wanted to argue, but the side door was opening. She didn't want to spend the night in the waiting room. She closed her eyes.

"Bring her right in here," the nurse instructed.

Grace felt herself being placed gently on an examination table.

"Doctor will be right here," the nurse said, exiting the room.

Before Garon could get a word out, Dr. Coltrain walked in, a stethoscope draped around the collar of his white lab jacket. He looked uneasy as he took it off, stuck the earpieces in his ears, and bent to listen to Grace's chest.

"I just fainted, that's all," Grace whispered.

He frowned, because her heartbeat worried him. He listened, had her cough, listened again and took off the stethoscope. "What were you doing, just before you fainted?"

"I was just walking..."

Without a word, Garon caught the redheaded doctor's hand and placed it flat on Grace's belly, with a meaningful look.

Taken aback, Coltrain's hand smoothed over the hardness of her slightly swollen belly. He caught his breath.

"Labwork?" Garon suggested solemnly.

Coltrain stared at him with growing comprehension. Grace was the only one who didn't understand what was going on.

Coltrain went into the hall and called his nurse. He spoke to her under his breath.

"Yes, Doctor, right away," she said and walked back down the hall.

He took a phone call while she came back and drew blood from Grace's arm.

"It isn't an ulcer," Grace protested when the nurse had gone out of the room, closing the door behind her. "I don't have stomach problems. Don't you tell Coltrain that I do, either," she instructed hotly, "because I know what an upper G.I. series is like, and he's not doing one on me!"

Garon didn't answer. He went to the window in the small room, shoved his hands in his pockets, and looked outside. His world, and Grace's, was about to change forever. He didn't know what to say, or do. Grace was going to be upset.

Coltrain was back in ten minutes, somber and taut-jawed. He closed the door, pulled out his rolling stool and sat down.

"We have some decisions to make," he told Grace.

Garon moved to join them, his eyes on Grace, who looked completely perplexed.

"Have I got cancer?" she asked, aghast.

Coltrain took one of her hands in his and held it tight. "You're pregnant, Grace."

She just stared at him. "I can't have a child," she said in a choked tone. "You said I couldn't!"

He drew in a sharp breath, aware of Garon's stillness beside him. "I said it wasn't likely, with only one ovary. I didn't say it was impossible."

Grace's hands went to her belly, feeling its firmness, feeling the thickness of her waist. She was pregnant. There was a tiny life inside her. She felt herself glow, as if she were touched, radiantly touched, by ecstasy.

"You can't have it," Coltrain said shortly. "You're barely a month pregnant, in time for a termination. I can send you up to San Antonio…"

"No!"

The word exploded from two pairs of lips at the exact same time.

Grace and Garon looked at each other, surprised, as Coltrain's eyebrows reached for the ceiling.

"Excuse me?" the doctor asked.

"You're not terminating my child," Grace told Coltrain.

"Grace, it's just too risky," he said softly. "Listen to me, Jacobsville is still a small town, with old-fashioned views on unwed mothers. Even if there was no risk, how would you feel about having a child out of wedlock?"

"She won't be," Garon said curtly. "I'll get a license first thing Monday. We can be married in the ordinary's office Thursday morning. If a blood test is still required, you've got hers, you can do me while I'm here."

Grace felt as if she were falling into an abyss. "You don't want to marry me," she said, knowing the statement was true even as it choked her pride.

Garon leaned back against the examination table and glanced from Coltrain to Grace. "This doesn't go outside this room," he said quietly. "Even my own brothers don't know." He sighed heavily. His dark eyes seemed to see into the past as he spoke. "It was two years after I graduated from the FBI Academy. I'd just been posted by the Bureau to a field office in Atlanta when I met Annalee," he began. "She was a civilian employee who had a degree in computer technology. She did background checks for us. She was a strong, independent, intelligent woman. We both knew on the first date that we'd be together forever." His jaw tautened. Beside him, Grace felt her heart sink. "We were married two months later. She got used to having me work long hours and sometimes travel out of the country on assignment. But she had her job to occupy her. We drifted along, we grew closer. We were happy. When we knew she was pregnant with our first child, we spent hours walking the malls, picking out furniture and toys..." He stopped until he could compose himself. "When she was five months pregnant, she started feeling tired all the time. We thought it was a part of the pregnancy, but she was having other symptoms as well. I took her to the gynecologist, who ran blood tests and sent us immediately to an oncologist."

Coltrain's jaw clenched.

Garon saw it. "The oncologist diagnosed it as non-Hodgkin's Lymphoma."

"One of the most aggressive cancers," Coltrain said.

"Yes. And she refused treatment. She wouldn't risk the baby, even to save her own life. But the cancer was advanced and quickly aggressive." He felt again the grief of that knowledge, the coldness in the pit of his stomach. "I lost them both," he added flatly, forcing himself not to yield to grief. "That was ten years ago. I decided that I'd never take that risk again. I'd live for my job. And I did. I volunteered for the Hostage Rescue Team. For six years, I was on the front lines of any desperate situation where lives were in danger. From there, I went to one of our SWAT units. When I started losing my edge physically, I opted for a transfer to one of the Texas field offices. I was sent to Austin, and then transferred down here, to lead a squad in the violent crime unit. But I've only been going through the motions of living," he concluded. He looked down at Grace and there was an odd light in his dark eyes. "I want this baby, Grace. You don't know how much!"

Coltrain felt himself losing ground. He looked at Grace worriedly.

"I'll be all right," she assured him. "I'm not giving up my baby. I've never had anyone of my very own, Copper," she added in a soft, husky tone. Her hands lay protectively on the small rise. She smiled with wonder. "He'll be my whole world."

Coltrain couldn't fight that look on her face. And he wasn't without sympathy for Garon, now that he understood the man a little better. It didn't take a mind reader to know that Garon was the child's father. But this was going to be more dangerous for Grace than she realized.

"I need to talk to your prospective husband," Coltrain began.

"No, you don't," Grace told him belligerently. "There is such a thing as patient-doctor privilege. You don't have my permission. That's the end of it."

Coltrain was worried. But she was right. He couldn't betray her secret. He understood why she didn't want Garon to know. That didn't make it less risky. But he couldn't force himself to go behind her back, not after all she'd been through. She obviously wanted this baby enough to fight any hint of interference. His lips compressed. "All right, I'll do the best I can."

Garon, who'd just relived the most painful episode of his life, was only half listening to a conversation he didn't understand anyway.

He looked down at Grace with an expression she couldn't decipher.

"I'm sorry about the complication," she said worriedly. "I didn't know…"

"It isn't a complication, Grace," Garon said gently. "It's a baby."

"But you don't want to marry me," she started again.

"No, I don't," he said honestly. "But it's only for eight months," he added. "After the baby comes, we'll make decisions."

Which meant he wasn't ready for any happily ever after, and

she couldn't blame him. She'd been careless, but he was going to pay the price.

At least he wanted the child and wasn't going to try to force her to get rid of it. She wasn't going to tell him anything at all that might upset him. He'd lost one child. She was going to make sure, somehow, that he didn't lose this one.

HE DROVE TO HER HOUSE, got out with her and went inside when she unlocked the door.

"Pack a bag," he said. "You're staying at the house until we get married."

"But I just got home…"

"Do I have to remind you of the risk?" he asked quietly.

For one frightening moment, she thought he meant the other risk. Then she realized, relieved, that he was talking about the killer.

"He probably still thinks I have amnesia," she said.

"He's avoided arrest for twelve years and gotten away, if he's the killer, with eleven murders. He's not a stupid man. He must have lived here at the time."

She'd never considered that possibility. She caught her breath and sat down heavily on the arm of her grandfather's old easy chair. "Do you think so?"

"Most serial killers choose their first victim within a comfortable radius of where they live," he said.

She bit her lip, thinking back. "We had two renters down the road," she recalled. "One was married, but his wife was visiting family back east. The other was elderly and in a wheelchair."

"He didn't necessarily live next door," he said. "He could have been involved in some program at school or church that brought him into contact with children."

"He could have been anybody," she said heavily. "All these years, I've wondered."

"We'll catch him," he said with firm confidence. "I promise you we will. But right now, I'm taking you home with me. There's no way in hell I'm leaving you here alone."

She saw that he meant it. Well, at least he was concerned for her. He did want the baby, even if he didn't want Grace. She got up and went to pack her things.

Miss Turner was fascinated, not only with the news of the wedding, at which she would be a witness, but at the prospect of a baby. She didn't even seem shocked that they'd put the cart before the horse. She was already picking out yarn and patterns for baby clothes.

Grace laid out her one decent dress, the blue wool one, on her bed the day of the wedding. Garon came into the room after a perfunctory knock, carrying a big box. He gave the blue dress a hot glare and put the box down right on top of it.

"What is this?" Grace asked.

"Open it."

She lifted the lid. Inside, there was an oyster-white suit and a small hat with a white veil. There was a silk bouquet as well. She looked at him, astonished.

"I'm not marrying you in that damned blue dress," he announced.

She touched the silk gently. She knew what it cost, because she bought it for her secret project that he still didn't know about. "It's beautiful."

"I got your measurements from Barbara," he said, and didn't add that he'd had to apologize his way into her café after his last appearance there. But once she heard that he was marrying Grace, and that a baby was on the way, she backed down just enough to go shopping with him.

"Thanks," she said in a shy, husky tone.

He shrugged. "Your friend Judy at the florists' is making you a bouquet. Barbara and Miss Turner will be witnesses."

She looked up. "Rick?"

He had to clench his teeth. "He has to work tomorrow. He couldn't get off." That wasn't exactly the truth. He refused to watch Grace ruin her life, were his exact words. The young detective was furious when he knew why Garon was marrying Grace. Garon could understand how he felt, but he couldn't jilt Grace when she was carrying his child.

"Oh," was all she said. She knew how Rick felt about her. She was sorry she couldn't feel the same about him. It was probably better that he didn't show up in the probate judge's office.

"I'm going to drive to the courthouse. Miss Turner will bring you."

"Okay."

He hadn't asked if she wanted a church wedding, or offered her an elaborate affair with bridesmaids and groomsmen. Probably he'd had that sort of wedding with his first wife. She didn't protest. He was still grieving for the woman he'd lost. It was enough that he was giving their child a name. She'd never expected him to want her permanently. Nobody ever had.

THE PROBATE JUDGE was a woman, Anna Banes, and she'd been married herself for two decades. She knew Grace, and her family, and the ordeal Grace had been through. She gave them a short but dignified and poignant service, with Barbara and Miss Turner standing to the side of them.

She didn't think Garon would buy her a wedding ring, but he had. It was a wide gold band with platinum edging and a grape leaf pattern. He didn't buy one for himself. That was hardly surprising. The judge declared them legally married, and Garon bent to brush a cool kiss against her cheek. It had been a long time, but he still remembered the joy of his first wedding. He was fond of Grace, and he wanted the child, but he couldn't separate himself from the past.

Garon treated them to lunch afterwards at Barbara's Café, and the owner herself brought out a magnificent wedding cake that she'd made for the occasion. Grace felt tears running down her cheeks at the thoughtfulness. She hugged the older woman warmly, because she was the closest thing to family that Grace had.

They were on the way home, with Miss Turner returning separately in Garon's Expedition, when Garon's pager beeped. He pulled it out, slowed to check the text message and grimaced.

"I have to go in to the office," he said, stepping on the gas. "We've got a new lead in the case."

"The killer?" she asked excitedly.

He nodded. "I'm sorry," he added. "But I don't work a nine-to-five job."

"Grandaddy was a deputy sheriff," she replied. "He had to go out at all hours of the night if there was an emergency. Granny always raised the roof," she added quietly. "I thought it was selfish of her. He saved lives."

He glanced at her with a warm smile. "That's why we're all in the business."

"I have lots to keep me busy," she said easily. "Including my jobs."

"You can quit them and stay home if you want to," he said. "I make a good salary, and the ranch is additional income."

She fiddled with the beautiful silk bouquet. She'd thrown the real one, and Barbara had caught it. "I like working," she replied. "I'm not very domesticated."

That was a surprise. She'd done nothing else, that he knew of, except look after her grandmother.

She felt his curiosity, but she didn't say anything else. He pulled up at the door of the house and went around to help her out.

Unexpectedly he swung her up into his arms and carried her up the steps. That was when she noticed the Expedition sitting beside the porch. Miss Turner had gotten home first. In fact, she was already opening the door with a big grin.

Garon laughed as he carried Grace inside and put her back on her feet. He bent to kiss her with gentle warmth. "The roses can wait. You rest," he said.

She gave him a gamine grin. "You planning to stop by and tell my roses where I am, on your way to work?"

He tapped her straight little nose with a long forefinger. "I'll be back when I can."

"Okay."

He was gone in a flash, leaving a weary Grace to be shooed down the hall to change and rest by Miss Turner.

MARQUEZ WAS SITTING in Garon's office when he walked in a few minutes later. He hesitated at the door.

The younger man gave him an impatient look. "Okay, I was way out of line, earlier," he confessed tautly. "At least you're not leaving Grace in the lurch."

Garon's eyebrows arched. "Do you know everything?"

"Pretty much. My mother and I don't keep secrets from each other." He studied his knee. "I talked to a detective in Oklahoma. There was a red ribbon involved in their child murder four years ago. They held back the information, just in case."

"It's got to be the same guy," Garon said quietly.

"Yes. I imagine he's been busy in other places in the past few years as well. We have DNA from this latest murder, but no hits when we ran it through the computer," he added. "I had hoped the perp might have a history and a rap sheet."

Garon shook his head. "He's too good."

"One of the older detectives on the Oklahoma case said they had an eyewitness who was sure he saw the killer abduct the child from her room."

Garon frowned. "We talked to Sheldon, the witness in San Antonio. And when I went to Palo Verde, the chief there said they had an eyewitness named Rich who lived right next door to the victim who said he saw the killer abduct the child. He left town just after the murder."

"That's three eyewitnesses at three crime scenes."

Garon's eyes brightened. "Yes. I think he's been trying to insert himself into the case," he said. Then he remembered something. "By God, remember Sheldon's hands were scarred and he wore gloves? Grace only saw her abductor's hands. She said they were very pale, and had scars! What if Sheldon's our man?"

"Let's go!" Marquez exclaimed.

Garon was right out the door after the younger man. For once, things were looking up!

14

GARON AND MARQUEZ rushed to Sheldon's house just inside the city limits of San Antonio. The killer just might be Sheldon, Garon thought. If they could get the man into custody, on any pretense, and question him properly, they might break the case. It would take some planning. He was intelligent. If he was the killer, he wasn't going to confess easily, not after eleven murders.

"We don't have probable cause to arrest him," Garon muttered after he'd called the office on his cell phone and had one of his men check for any criminal history on Sheldon. There was none.

"We'll think up something," Marquez said.

"With our luck, he'll have photos of the murder victims spread around, and we won't be able to touch him without a search warrant. We should have asked a judge for one before we drove up here."

"Without probable cause, we couldn't get a judge to issue a search warrant," Marquez said gruffly. "We'd have to list everything we hoped to find. Even then, if it wasn't on the warrant, we couldn't touch it."

"I know," Garon said, his eyes glittery with feeling. He was thinking about Grace and what had happened to her. He'd love nothing more that to catch her assailant and put him in the nearest prison.

"We could do a consent search," Marquez suggested, not quite jokingly, with a wry smile.

Garon gave him a wry look.

"Oh, come on! You go to the back door and I go to the front door," the younger man replied. "I yell 'knock, knock,' and you yell, 'come in.'"

"And we both end up in court," Garon reminded him.

"No guts, no glory."

They pulled into Sheldon's driveway. There was no car in the driveway and no lights on in the house.

Garon knocked loudly, announcing that he was an FBI agent. But there was no movement inside.

An elderly lady from next door saw the men on the porch and called to them, with a shovel in one hand and Dutch wooden shoes on her feet. "If you're looking for Mr. Sheldon, I'm afraid you won't find him," she said with a smile. "He moved out several days ago. Put everything he had onto a truck and drove away."

"Do you know where he was going?" Marquez asked.

"He said California," she replied.

"What sort of truck?" Garon asked.

"Just an old white pickup truck," she said. "He was such a nice man," she added. "So helpful. He'd carry my groceries in for me. If I got sick, he'd pick up my medicine at the pharmacy. Such a sweet man. I'll miss him."

Garon didn't dare tell the old woman what he suspected about her sweet neighbor. He did go with Marquez to get a search warrant for the house. A team of FBI criminologists scoured the small house for any trace evidence, just as they'd done at the house in Palo Verde where the so-called witness had lived. Neither venture gleaned any evidence. There wasn't so much as a stray hair left in either house.

Nor was there any way to trace the white pickup truck. They didn't have a tag number, and they couldn't find any information on a man named Sheldon. The day had started out full of promise. Now, like so many investigations, the trail went cold. The child's parents phoned Marquez and asked if he had any leads. He had to tell them he didn't. But he wasn't giving up, and neither was Garon. Somehow, they were going to nail the killer, whatever it took.

But weeks went by, and then months. There were no more child murders. Searches were launched for Rich and Sheldon, but no trace of either man could be found. There was no driver's license, no fingerprints, nothing that would help them to locate either man. Garon recalled the man bragging about belonging to Mensa, but the organization had no information about a man named Sheldon.

"Have you found anything that might help you locate the computer expert?" Grace asked one night at the supper table. She and Garon were having second cups of coffee. Miss Turner had already cleared the table and gone to bed.

Garon shook his head. He glanced at her on the other side of the table. She was tired a lot these days, five months into her pregnancy, and her color wasn't good. She spent a lot of time in bed. Garon worried about it. He'd phoned Coltrain, who'd come out to see Grace. He pronounced it as normal for a woman in that stage of pregnancy. But he and Grace talked behind a closed door for a long time before he left. Garon asked what they'd found to discuss. She said she was worried about labor, and she'd been asking Coltrain about it.

She did look bad. She wasn't gaining a lot of weight. She took her prenatal vitamins, but they didn't seem to help a lot.

"I wish you'd stop worrying," she muttered early one Monday morning as they ate an early breakfast. "I'm doing fine."

She wasn't. He did what he could to tempt her appetite, but all she seemed to eat were strawberry milkshakes and dry toast. She wasn't getting nearly enough protein. He hoped the prenatal vitamins were doing some good. He'd gone so far as to have gourmet meals flown in, so that she had exotic meals to eat. But she picked at her food.

"Grace, if you don't eat properly, you could hurt the baby," he said in desperation.

She felt part of herself die every time he said things like that. He had an absolute passion for their forthcoming child. He read books on childbirth and child rearing. He watched programs on the health channels about delivery. He went with her to Lamaze natural childbirth classes, and walked around the yard with her, so that she got a little exercise. He was forever watching her, making sure she took care of herself. But all of it, everything, was for the baby. She had no illusions about his feelings for her. They had separate bedrooms, separate lives. He went to work and stayed there late at night. He said he was working on the child murder case. She wondered if he wasn't really working on Jaqui Jones.

Jaqui had phoned her, unbeknownst to Garon, to remind her that as soon as the baby came, Grace was only going to be a footnote in Garon's life. Jaqui insinuated that Garon was sneaking around to see her. He wouldn't risk upsetting Grace, of course, the woman purred. But a virile, masculine man like Garon wasn't going to be happy trying to sleep with a whale in maternity clothing.

Grace put the receiver down and stopped answering the phone. She didn't tell Garon about the phone calls. She knew he wouldn't care, unless Jaqui's harassment was endangering the baby, of course.

Garon saw the lack of animation in Grace's manner, and it made him feel guilty. Was she reliving the pain he'd caused her? Was that why she winced when she looked at him? He'd been careful not to make any sort of physical demands on her during her pregnancy. She didn't feel well most of the time. Even her efforts with her rose-bushes were less than perfect. In the end, she'd asked Garon to have one of the cowboys see to fertilizing and spraying them. She did as little physical work as she could manage. Spring turned to summer, and summer to fall. Garon had cases that took him out of state, and once, out of the country. The task force met infrequently, because funding was being channeled to other areas, and the killer continued to elude discovery. One thing Grace did notice was that Garon had someone watching her all the time, just in case. He hadn't stopped worrying that the killer might come back to finish the job. She saw little of Garon otherwise.

He'd long since eased her into the guest room and kept her there, explaining that she needed her rest and he'd be coming in at all hours while working. It wasn't the truth, but he didn't think she really wanted the truth. He'd seen her face when he told her and Coltrain about Annalee and the child he'd lost along with her. He hadn't wanted to love anyone since then. Grace knew it, without being told. The light had gone out of her eyes forever during that quiet, somber explanation. It hadn't come back.

She was still working her two jobs. In the evenings, she locked herself into the sewing room she and Miss Turner had made of a third guest room. She was working on a project, she told Garon, something to do with Christmas. He didn't ask what or why. She was entitled to her secrets.

But her lack of spirit was worrying. He was concerned enough to go and talk to Barbara, who knew her possibly better than anyone else in Jacobsville.

"She won't talk to me," Garon told the café's owner. "She changes the subject or leaves the room, or finds an urgent errand to run." He looked at his hands clasped between his long legs as he sat at a table just before the café was supposed to open for lunch. "I know something's upsetting her. I can't find out what."

Men, Barbara thought, were the stupidest people on earth. Grace was in love with her husband and certain that he wanted nothing more than the child she was carrying. He'd told her they'd only be married until the baby came. He'd probably forgotten saying that, but Grace hadn't. She was just marking time, feeling like an insignificant incubator in his house.

"It might not be a bad idea to get her out of the house," she said finally. "Except to work for Judy or me, she never goes anywhere."

His chiseled lips made a thin line. "She goes to church with you and Marquez," he said.

Barbara had to restrain a smile. He sounded angry. He thought of Marquez as a rival. Certainly, Grace laughed and was natural with

Rick. With Garon, she was subdued and hardly spoke. The difference must have been noticeable.

"You don't go," she replied. "Grace takes her Sunday mornings seriously."

He traced a flat, clean fingernail with a fingertip. "I don't talk to God anymore."

"Is there a reason?"

He looked up. Didn't they say confession was good for the soul? Barbara didn't like him, or trust him. Maybe he kept too many secrets. "I was married," he said, noting her surprise. "Very much in love and looking forward to a lifetime with my wife and our children. When she was about as far along as Grace is now, they diagnosed her with a fatal cancer. I lost them both."

The tragedy of it was in his taut features, his hard eyes. Barbara softened toward him. She knew loss. Her husband had died ten years earlier in an airplane crash. She'd never thought of remarrying. She still grieved. It was obvious that the taciturn FBI man did, too. His heart was buried with the family he lost. Grace must know that. It would explain her lack of spirit.

"My husband died," she told him quietly. "In an accident. I miscarried the only child we were able to conceive. I lived in the past and hated life. And then Rick came along, and all of a sudden, my life had meaning again." She met his searching eyes. "I stopped thinking of myself and started looking around me to see who needed help."

A corner of his mouth tugged up. "Is this a story with a moral?"

"You've lived in an open grave since you lost your wife and child," she said simply. "Don't you think it's time you lived in the present?

You have another wife, and a child on the way. It isn't fair to them to make them second best after ghosts."

There was an odd flicker in his dark eyes. "That's harsh."

"That's truth," she countered. "Grace may not be a powerful, independent career woman like your friend Jaqui, but she has skills of her own."

"She can cook and sew," he said heavily. "Once upon a time, those were desired skills for women. It's a new world."

"Obviously Jaqui is the sort of woman you admire," Barbara said, her eyes growing cold. "Once the baby's born, you can get a quiet divorce and saddle up with your ideal woman. With any luck, Grace will realize that Rick is far more her style than you are. Excuse me. I have to get ready to open."

She got up and left without another word.

Garon went back home, feeling empty. There was a distance between himself and Grace that was getting harder to close. He'd had to spend a lot of time away during the summer, working on cases. When he was home, he'd had to catch up on work both at the office and on the ranch. His father and brothers had come by the house once to see Garon's new bride, but they hadn't stayed long. Grace had been shy and withdrawn, and Garon's father had remarked that it seemed an odd match. Garon hadn't answered. It was an odd match. But he got used to the smell of fresh baking bread in the kitchen, and Grace's soft laughter when he made jokes about her rosebushes. He'd gotten used to the faint smell of roses that clung to her soft skin and the sound of her footsteps muffled by carpet. The only bad thing was his unending desire for her, which he'd been reining in with difficulty. He wanted her all the time, but she was so fragile in pregnancy. She had sick spells constantly and it was difficult for her to breathe properly. She could walk only a short distance without getting winded. So he teased her gently and held hands with her when they walked. And worried. He tried not to put any pressure on her at all, so that she wouldn't be stressed and risk losing the baby. He was looking forward to the birth of his child. Just the thought of it lifted his heart, made him live again. But Grace wasn't reacting as he'd expected. He knew she loved children. But she wasn't the woman she had been.

He could see for himself that Grace was sinking deeper into depression with every passing day. That wouldn't do. He had to shake her back to life.

"Why don't you come up to the office with me?" he asked, keeping his eyes on his coffee cup. "We could have lunch and you might like to shop while I finish up some paperwork."

She hesitated. It was an olive branch. Maybe it was pity. But the thought of sharing several hours with her sexy husband made her feel warm inside.

"I'd like that," she said. But she didn't look at him.

"Why don't you wear one of the new maternity outfits?" he asked.

"I suppose I could."

"I'll wait while you change."

"Okay." She finished her decaf and went down the long hall to her bedroom. She pulled out one of the three mix and match outfits she and Miss Turner had purchased. He'd given her a credit card and had Miss Turner take her to San Antonio for shopping. She'd been afraid to spend much, frugality having been drummed into her by her late grandmother. Miss Turner had coaxed her toward sportswear, but she wouldn't even look at that section. She wasn't going to be accused of going on spending sprees with his money. If she'd had enough of her own, it would have been a different story. Her income from her two jobs was being used mostly on her project. But it was now complete and in the hands of the purchaser. It would be a big surprise for Garon when he knew about it. Meanwhile, she wasn't wasting her hard-earned money on trifles like fancy pregnant sportswear. Not when a muumuu was so cheap and cool as hot weather descended on Texas.

She put on a rose pink top and skirt, and slipped into white loafers to wear with them. She brushed her long blond hair until it fell in soft waves around her shoulders. Her heart-shaped face looked pale in the mirror. He didn't know what she was hiding. She didn't want him to know, because it would worry him. His wife had been five months pregnant when she was diagnosed with cancer. Her pregnancy must have reminded Garon of what he'd lost.

She walked back into the dining room, carrying her small purse. "I'm ready when you are," she said.

He got up and looked at her openly, smiling at the pretty picture she made in the outfit. "Not bad, Mrs. Grier," he murmured.

Her heart skipped. It was the first time he'd called her that. He didn't usually comment on her looks, either.

"Thanks," she said shyly, avoiding his eyes. Maybe he thought flattery would lift her mood and make her eat properly. He really wanted the child.

"Come on, then."

He opened the car door for her and helped her inside. It was a hot day, without a cloud in the sky. She wondered how his colleagues would react to her presence in his office. She felt uncomfortable at the thought of meeting them. Most men still made her uneasy.

THEY WALKED into the office together, but Garon was immediately hailed by one of the other agents, and pulled away into an office for an urgent meeting.

A good-looking woman paused and stared at Grace. "May I help you?" she asked.

"Uh, no, no, thanks," Grace faltered, embarrassed. "I'm just waiting for my husband."

"Is he the witness Agent Carlson is trying to interview in there?" she asked, indicating a cubicle nearby.

Before she could answer, a spate of impatient Arabic wafted from the cubicle, having a strange, foreign, almost musical tone in the quiet office.

"Oh, hell, why couldn't you get someone to come in with you and translate?" the agent asked irritably. "Joceline!" he yelled.

"Yes?" the woman replied.

A tall, blond man stuck his head out beyond the freestanding wall. "This guy doesn't speak English. Is Jon Blackhawk out there?"

"Sorry. He had to be in court this morning to testify on that murder last year."

"Well, what am I supposed to do now?" the agent grumbled. "This guy witnessed a murder. If he leaves, I may not be able to get him back!"

The man in the cubicle, clearly middle eastern, appeared in the doorway, lifted both hands and expressed his dismay that nobody in the FBI could understand him.

Grace moved toward him with a soft smile. "It's only because the agent who usually translates is in court," she said in perfect Arabic.

The foreign man smiled from ear to ear and greeted her warmly. She replied politely, and with a smile.

Joceline and the agent both gaped at her.

"You can speak Arabic?" the agent exclaimed.

"Yes. What do you want to know?" she asked.

"Come right in," the agent invited, smiling.

TWENTY MINUTES LATER, Garon came back out and started looking around for Grace. He scowled. He hadn't told her to stay in the office, but he hadn't expected her to go walking around town in this heat in her condition. He had been worried that she'd feel totally out of place in his upscale office.

He stopped by Joceline's desk. "Have you seen my wife?"

Joceline's eyes widened. "You're married? You never said you were married."

"Nobody needed to know," he returned in an icy tone. "It's a complicated story, and I'm not volunteering it."

"The maternity outfit volunteered it already," Joceline mused. "If that pregnant lady is your wife, she's right over there."

Grace had a group of agents clustered around her; all were talking and laughing.

"Is she yours?" one of the agents, Blackhawk, asked Garon.

"Mine?" He shifted. "Yes. This is my wife, Grace," he said belatedly.

"Jon Blackhawk," the newcomer introduced himself, taking Grace's small hand in his. "A pleasure."

"Same here," Agent Carlson agreed.

She smiled. "I'm glad to meet you both."

Garon caught her hand in his. "We have to go or we'll miss lunch."

"Bring her back again sometime," Carlson called to Garon.

Garon didn't answer. He tugged Grace gently out the door and put her in the car.

He turned to her before he started the car engine. "Well, it looks like you had a good time."

Her eyebrows lifted. "Yes, you can sometimes take me out in public. I can talk and walk," she replied. "Mostly you talk about your job, eat supper, watch the news, shut yourself up in your office and then go to bed. I don't suppose we've had more than an hour's conversation all told since we married."

She was right. He'd deliberately avoided being alone with her. It was all he could manage not to sweep her up, toss her into the nearest bed, and ravish her. But that was taboo right now.

"I've been busy," he acknowledged.

"Anyway," she added, fastening her seat belt, "I guess getting to know me better doesn't really concern you. Once the baby's born, I'm going home."

There was a profound silence in the car.

She glanced at him, curious about his strained expression. "That's what we agreed, when we got married. You said we'd go our separate ways once the baby came."

He had said that. He wished he hadn't.

"You're working part-time at menial labor jobs. I thought you wouldn't be able to handle a more sophisticated level," he pointed out curtly.

"I'm doing what I like," she corrected. She stared at him quietly.

"I can't handle a high-pressure, high-paying, overstressful career. That doesn't mean I have to stick my mind in a box. Although apparently that's what you thought I was doing, so much so that you thought I couldn't even get along in an office environment for half an hour without you."

"I never said you were stupid."

"You wouldn't dare," she pointed out with a smirk. "You'd never get another apple cake."

One corner of his mouth pulled up and he chuckled.

"Careful, laughter can be habit-forming," she cautioned.

He sighed deeply, watching her. "You really do look pretty, pregnant, Grace," he said abruptly.

That was below the belt. He was flattering her. He didn't love her, but he did appear fond of her. He just couldn't bear her company when they were home together.

But she didn't mind so much. She would have the baby, when he left. Her fingers touched the swell lightly. Or he would have the baby, if Coltrain's worried predictions came true. At least she could live with Garon, be near him, for as long as it lasted. She knew that she'd never love anyone else. She just had to hide her feelings. It wouldn't do to give him a guilt complex. It wasn't his fault that he still loved his late wife. Some people just couldn't love twice.

TIME PASSED, and Garon realized with a start that Grace was now almost eight months pregnant. He'd spent a large part of those months working on the task force, but the killer had left no trail that could be followed. They'd questioned witnesses over and over again, hoping for a single clue to break the case. But they never came close.

They checked out every white pickup truck in Texas eventually. None of them belonged to a man named Sheldon. It was a dead end. More and more, the investigators gained sympathy for those poor law enforcement people in Washington State who'd spent twenty years trying to catch their serial killer. Garon and the task force had Grace's memories to work with, but they hadn't given them the edge they'd hoped for. Sheldon had to be the key to solving the murders, but lead after lead vanished. They'd spent months tossing out ideas and following them through, with no visible result. There was talk of disbanding the task force. Certainly, it wasn't making progress.

Meanwhile, Garon was irritated that Marquez seemed to be taking an increasing interest in Grace. He managed to be visiting Barbara at least two days a week when Grace was cooking at the café. It was the only time she acted naturally, he thought irritably. Grace did nothing to give Garon hope. She was fond of him, but she seemed disinterested in any romantic leanings.

When they met, Marquez was courteous to Grace, but he never said anything that might disturb Garon. The one place he never trespassed was on the ranch.

Garon came home unexpectedly on a blustery cold autumn day. He couldn't find Miss Turner or Grace inside, so he changed to his ranch clothes and went out looking for them.

The Expedition was gone. At first he thought the two women had gone to town for something. But he became aware of voices in the big barn out back. He started toward it, curious about what was being said.

As he approached closer, he noticed two things. There were no cowboys around, and the man talking to Grace was the missing link in the child murders. It was Sheldon!

15

GARON COULD HAVE TRIED to bluff it out, by moving closer with a display of careless welcome. But Sheldon was too sharp for subterfuge to work on him. Instead Garon did the only thing possible in the circumstances. He drew his service weapon, snapped its sights on the visitor and called, "FBI. Keep your hands where I can see them!"

Grace caught her breath as she realized that Garon had recognized this man and considered him a threat. He'd come to the house to ask about adopting one of the kittens in the barn and Grace had gone out there with him. She remembered him from her childhood. He'd been a substitute teacher at her school. All the children had liked him.

Sheldon was moving back to Jacobsville, he'd told her, and he needed a cat to get rid of mice. Someone had mentioned that they had a new litter. Which they did. Grace always had kittens from the barn cat.

The man was intelligent and pleasant, just as she remembered him being. But there was something about him that made her uneasy.

Something… She was trying to put her finger on it when Garon appeared at the door of the barn.

It happened so fast that she didn't realize what was going on until her visitor suddenly grabbed her around the neck and held the sharp edge of a knife to her throat. She knew then why she'd been apprehensive. There was a smell to this man that was individual and chilling. She could see his wrists above the thin gloves he wore. His skin was white. She knew who he was now, and that he'd come back to make sure she couldn't identify him. Her mind went back to the past, to the things this animal had done to her. Now she was pregnant, and he seemed eager to rob her of her child, and her life.

"I didn't expect you to identify me, Grier," Sheldon called to him, laughing. "I've always kept on the move, one step ahead of the law. But everywhere I go, people are looking for me. Know why?" he asked. "Because of my damned hands. I thought wearing gloves would throw people off the track, but that description you put out on me was too good. I've been on the run since spring."

Garon's eyes didn't waver from the subject. This wasn't a new situation for him, not after six years in the Hostage Rescue Team. "What do you want? Transportation? Money?"

"I'm through running," the man replied. His arm tightened around Grace's slim neck and the knife pressed harder, cutting the skin. "But before you get me, I'm going to clear the deck. This—" he indicated Grace "—is the only one who got away. They said she had amnesia. But when you started identifying me by my hands, I knew she'd lied about forgetting. She hadn't forgotten a thing."

"She's pregnant," Garon said through his teeth.

"That's nothing to me," the man said in a monotone. "I hate children. Especially little girls. My stepmother hated me, especially when she found out she couldn't have a child. I wet the bed and she punished me by making me wear frilly dresses. She kept my hair long and tied it up with ribbons. She sent me to school like that." His face grew red with temper. "My father was afraid of her, so he never said a word. Everybody made fun of me. But I grew up. I got bigger than both of them. And I got even." He smiled coldly. "I told the cops that a strange man did it, that I ran for help when I saw what he was doing. I cried and cried. Stupid cops. They believed me."

"Is that why you wear gloves?" Garon asked, the pistol still aimed at the suspect. "Because you feel guilty?"

Sheldon moved restlessly. "When I was twelve, I started wetting the bed again. It was dark and cold and all we had was an outhouse, and I was still afraid of the dark. I held it until it was almost light, and then I couldn't hold it anymore. I covered it up and went to eat my breakfast. I hoped she wouldn't see it until I went to school. But she went to make up the bed before the bus came and saw where I'd wet it. She was starting a stew for lunch. The water was boiling on the stove. She screamed at me, that I was stupid and retarded, and that she'd make me sorry. She grabbed my arms and rammed my hands into the boiling water…"

Garon grimaced.

The suspect saw it. He hardened. "I told my dad what she'd done. He said I was a liar, because she was a good woman. He said she'd never hurt me. He took me to the doctor and told him that I stuck my hands in boiling water so I could blame my stepmother for it." His voice trailed away. "The pain was awful. They gave me an aspirin and put some purple cream on my burned skin. When they healed, the scars covered them. I had to learn to do everything with gloves on, so nobody would make fun of me."

"You killed little girls who'd done nothing to you," Grace choked.

"You looked like her," he spat. "All of you looked like her! Like my stepmother. I was twelve when she ruined me for life. So I killed twelve girls who looked like her. One for each year. Except you lived," he muttered into Grace's hair. "I can't let you live. You'll break the chain."

"Let her go," Garon told him.

"It's your kid she's carrying, isn't it, Grier?" he asked, tightening his arm around her neck so that she gasped. "Too bad she won't live to give birth to it." He shifted his weight.

Garon had never felt such anguish. The man wasn't bluffing. His fantasy was linked to killing the girls who looked like his stepmother, and this was the end of it. There was no time to call in negotiators, to ask for backup. There was no time to do anything except react. In split seconds, he'd slit Grace's carotid artery, and no power on earth would stop her life from bleeding out into the soil at her feet. He pictured those beautiful gray eyes closed forever, and his very soul ached.

He had to act. Now. "Grace," he called quietly, his face like stone. "Do you remember the day I found you in your front yard, the day we went to see Copper?"

"Yes," she whispered.

"Do you trust me, baby?" he asked in a voice like soft velvet.

She managed a taut smile through the terror. "With my very life."

"Okay, then."

She knew what he was asking and she saw in his eyes that he knew it could go either way. She had a chance to live, a slim one. Everything depended on timing. She looked at her husband, shivered, and let the man behind her take her whole weight as her eyes closed and she slumped with a soft groan.

The tiny diversion was enough. Garon never missed. He snapped off just one shot and watched it penetrate as Sheldon turned his head a fraction to look down at Grace.

Grace felt the body behind her jump even as she felt the warm wetness of blood down her cheek. At the same time, the knife at her throat dropped to the ground and the kidnapper and murderer of children fell dead at her feet.

She slumped to the ground, shaking, gasping for breath. The wetness she felt was her own blood, where Sheldon had cut her just as the bullet got him. It was running out quickly. For a few seconds she was terrified that her artery had been nicked. But as she felt for the cut, and realized it wasn't the artery, her heart jerked in a shaky, unnatural rhythm and she gasped like a fish out of water. She knew what was happening. She was terrified. Not now, she prayed silently. Not now. It's too soon! The baby's not ready...

She fell onto her side, still trying to hold the skin together to halt the flow of blood. She was aware of voices around her, followed by sirens. But she didn't understand much. She felt her life draining away. She was weightless, buoyant, merging with the air, the clouds, the sky.

Garon ran to her, kneeling, curling her head into his chest. "Oh God, that was close! Are you all right, Grace? Baby, are you all right?" he repeated, kissing her hair, her cheek feverishly. He was vibrating with the aftereffects of the terror. If he'd missed...!

"I'm...okay," she whispered. She wasn't. But he looked shaken enough. She kissed his cheek. "You saved me," she managed to say weakly. "Thank you."

His fingers in her hair were insistent as he pressed a quick, hard kiss against her lips. "My sweet girl," he said with breathless tenderness.

Two police cars roared down to the barn and stopped, along with an ambulance from Jacobsville General. Copper Coltrain jumped out of the ambulance and ran to Grace's side, motioning furiously for the paramedics.

"It's just a nick," Garon said in a forcibly controlled tone. He pushed back her sweaty hair. "Coltrain will look after you, sweetheart," he said softly. "You'll be fine. I have to give a statement about what happened. I won't be long." He squeezed her hand warmly. "Good girl," he added gently. "You were very brave."

She couldn't answer him. It didn't matter. He was walking away, assured that she wasn't badly injured. But Copper Coltrain knew otherwise.

He threw out orders to the paramedics as they loaded Grace on a gurney and put her into the back of the ambulance.

Cash Grier had just pulled up. He glanced toward the fallen man and the people standing over him, and he started toward them. Coltrain stepped in front of him.

"Get your brother and bring him to the hospital as fast as you can," he told Cash. "I'm going to call the life-flight helicopter and have her transferred immediately to Houston. I have a friend in the cardiology unit, the best surgeon they've got. I'll have him meet her in the emergency room there."

Cash was reeling. "But it's just a cut," he protested, looking at Grace.

"No." Coltrain took a deep breath, and told him the truth.

Cash's face tautened. "Good God!" he whispered. "I'll get him to the hospital," he promised and went toward the crime scene.

Local police were on the scene, along with one of Cash's detectives, who was taking Garon's statement about what happened.

Cash took Garon by the arm just as Miss Turner came rushing out to see what all the commotion was about.

"You have to come with me to the hospital," Cash told his brother grimly. "Right now."

"I know she's frightened. It was an ordeal for her. But I have to wrap this up and call my office—"

"Coltrain's calling in a helicopter to fly her to Houston," Cash interrupted.

"For a cut on her neck?" Garon exclaimed, certain now that Coltrain had lost his mind.

Cash took a deep breath. He remembered another night of terror with Christabel Gaines, now married to Judd Dunn. He remembered a rush to the hospital and endless hours in the waiting room while doctors fought to save her life. "Garon," he said gently, "Grace has a bad heart valve. It's gone critical. If they don't operate very soon, she won't make it."

Garon heard the words, but they didn't make sense. He stared at his brother blankly.

"She has to have open heart surgery," Cash added.

That was when the terror hit. He remembered Grace's bad color and her lack of energy, Coltrain's eternal cosseting, the townspeople protecting her. Now, when it was too late, it made sense.

He felt the blood drain out of his face. "Houston," he said unsteadily. "They're taking her to Houston?"

"Yes."

"I have to go with her," Garon said through his teeth. "Can you call the ASAC and tell him where I've gone and why?"

"I'll have one of my men do that," came the reply. "I'm going with you to Houston."

"Thanks."

"Not necessary. Come on."

CASH RACED to the hospital with lights and sirens blaring. Garon sat quietly in his seat, remembering another pregnant woman who'd died. He might lose Grace. He closed his eyes on a shudder. She'd been in his house for months now, making him apple cakes, laughing with Miss Turner, making pillows for the living room, smiling at him across the dinner table. She'd never complained about his absences, or started arguments or done anything to make him feel guilty. She had to live. Nothing else mattered.

He told that to Coltrain. It was the first thing he said when he met the redheaded doctor in the emergency room.

Coltrain didn't make sarcastic remarks. He just nodded. "I'm going to Houston with you," he added. "Just in case."

Garon couldn't manage a reply. He nodded.

Grace was white as a sheet. He could see the cover over her jerking with the odd, unstable rhythm of her heartbeat as he and Coltrain shared the helicopter with the pilot and the EMT. Cash was driving to Houston—most likely with sirens and lights going full tilt, Garon thought.

He held Grace's hand while Coltrain monitored her progress, an IV drip going into her other arm, an oxygen mask over her nose.

He remembered painfully an episode just a month ago. She'd been too sick to go with him to a cattlemen's association meeting and dinner. For some reason, Jaqui Jones had been there, sitting next to Garon. A photographer for the local paper had snapped a shot, showing Garon smiling, leaning toward Jaqui.

Miss Turner had hidden the paper from Grace, but she was too sharp not to realize the effort to protect her. She'd found the newspaper and just stared at it, Miss Turner told him. She hadn't said a word. She'd dropped it in the trash and gone on about her business.

Garon had been out with the men, moving the bulls out of summer pasture. It was a blazing hot day. He'd come inside stripping off his shirt, his hair damp with sweat. And there stood Grace, in the hall, her hands folded at her waist.

"Are you having an affair with Jaqui?" she'd asked bluntly.

He'd laughed. It was unforgivable, but it was a ridiculous question. Here he was with a very pregnant new wife, living in a town of two thousand benevolent gossips.

"Are you nuts?" he'd asked, grinning at the picture she made in a jade-green maternity blouse with white maternity slacks. "Barbara would skewer me and serve me to you on a hot bun!"

She'd looked sheepish then, and her eyes had dropped helplessly to his broad, hair-roughened chest, at the play of muscles. Her thoughts had been as plain as a statement of desire on her lovely face.

With a wicked smile, he'd tossed his shirt onto the hall table, swept her up in his arms and kissed her with such passion that she moaned and clung to him.

Just as he entertained forbidden thoughts of easing her down on the floor and doing what he felt like doing to her, the phone rang. It was a call from the office about a high-profile case back east. The SAC had him slated to go help with it. He only had minutes to pack and get to the airport.

He'd glanced at Grace with a rueful smile, and she'd smiled back, dazed. But when he came back a week later, she was quiet and withdrawn. Miss Turner said she'd had a long talk with Dr. Coltrain and it had depressed her. He'd asked what about. But Miss Turner didn't know, and Grace and the redheaded doctor passed over it as if they'd just been discussing labor and Grace was nervous about it.

Now, weeks later, Garon knew what they'd talked about. Grace had risked her life to bring this child into the world. She knew how much Garon wanted a child, and how much he'd have worried if he'd known about her heart. So she'd sworn everybody around her to secrecy, and she'd carried the secret, the burden, all these months.

He drew her small hand to his mouth and kissed it hungrily. He felt the hot mist in his eyes and lowered his head to hide it. If she died...if she died, what would he do? How would he go on living without her? And he'd never even told her what he felt.

THERE WAS A TEAM waiting at the hospital when the helicopter landed. Coltrain had told Garon what would happen when they arrived. They'd examine her. They'd schedule a heart catherization to see the extent of the damage and decide on the procedure. There was a heart surgeon in Houston, Dr. Franks, who was world famous in his field. He'd already agreed to take the case. Coltrain had phoned him from Jacobsville. The surgery would take several hours.

It was a recipe for a nightmare. It got worse when the surgeon, Dr. Franks, and Coltrain told him what could go wrong. Grace's pregnancy was advanced enough that they could take the child. But a C-section or natural childbirth compounded the risk. Dr. Franks made the terse statement that she should never have been allowed to conceive knowing this condition was already working up to open-heart surgery.

Garon had been crushed when he heard that. Coltrain snapped to his defense, informing him that Grace had refused Coltrain permission to tell her husband, adding that nobody had expected that Grace could even get pregnant in the first place.

Dr. Franks apologized, but Garon was beyond guilt. If he'd only known, he kept thinking. If she'd just told him!

CASH CAME INTO the waiting room sometime later. Garon was in a seat by the window, staring out onto the hospital grounds. People walked along sidewalks, came in and out of buildings. Garon didn't see them. He was remembering his first sight of Grace, when she came to his house looking for help with her grandmother.

He felt Cash's big hand on his shoulder.

"What's happening?" Cash asked, dropping into a seat beside Garon. He was still wearing his uniform, and a family in the waiting room gave him curious looks.

"They're doing a heart catherization," Garon said dully. "They don't know which is riskier, to induce labor or do a C-section. She could die before they ever get to the valve."

Cash took a deep breath. He knew how his brother felt. He'd almost lost Tippy in the early days of their relationship. And he certainly remembered when Christabel Dunn was shot and almost killed by one of the notorious Clark brothers, before he and Tippy had become involved. He'd been crazy about Christabel. The anguish of her ordeal grew fresh in his mind as he realized the odds against Grace.

"If I lose her," Garon told his brother, "there isn't anything on earth worth staying for."

"That isn't what she'd want," Cash replied quietly. "She values life. You can see it in the way she fusses over those rose bushes."

He bit his lip. He was remembering Grace teasing him about talking to the roses for her. She did love growing things.

"Did you call the SAC, about the shooting?" Garon asked after a minute.

"Yes. He said some of the guys will be up tonight to sit with you." Garon only nodded.

Cash smiled. "I'd forgotten how close-knit you guys are," he remarked. "Most of my life, I worked alone, or with a spotter."

"That's not the case now, is it?" Garon asked.

Cash chuckled. "No. When the city fathers threatened to fire two of my officers because they arrested a drunk politician, the whole police and fire departments threatened to resign if I got the boot. It was a life-changing moment. Suddenly, I went from being an outsider in Jacobsville to being part of a big family." He shrugged. "I like it."

Garon had felt some of that closeness when he'd first become obsessed with Grace. So quickly it had ended, when he'd savaged her and pushed her aside. He was never going to get over the way he'd treated her. Especially now that he knew the whole truth.

"If they tarred and feathered family, I guess I'd qualify," he told the other man. He drew in a long, weary breath. "I didn't know she had a bad heart. I kept pushing her to go to college, to learn a trade, to live up to her potential. She told me she couldn't manage a high-stress job, and it never occurred to me that it could be because of a health problem. I just thought she needed more than high school to cope in the modern world." He glanced at Cash ruefully. "Then I took her to work with me and left her in the waiting room. When I came back, she was happily chatting away in Arabic to a Jordanian murder witness, translating for him. She speaks several languages," he added proudly.

Cash smiled. "I don't suppose she's told you that she belongs to MENSA?"

His indrawn breath was audible. "MENSA?" It was an organization whose members had extremely high intelligent quotients, far higher than the average college graduate.

He nodded. "Marquez mentioned it. He had a flaming crush on her when he was younger, but her intelligence intimidated him. She has a photographic memory. And there's this secret project she's been working on all year that just hit the big time." He glanced toward Garon, who looked as if he'd been hit in the face with a pie. "She didn't tell you?"

Garon's eyes narrowed. "Why do you know more about my wife than I do?"

"Because Barbara likes *me,*" he emphasized.

"My God. Barbara!" he groaned. "I didn't call her…!"

"Relax. I called her. She's getting together a prayer group tonight."

In years past, when he was still hating God for Annalee, Garon would have scoffed at that idea. But now, with Grace's precious life hanging by a thread, he only nodded gratefully.

Garon stood up and went to the phone. He pushed the buttons that would connect him to the chaplain's office. They'd offered help if he needed it. He did. He asked if someone could tell him how the catherization was going, and they gladly agreed to find out. In potentially fatal cases, such as Grace's, there was no agency that surpassed the chaplain's service. They provided liaison between the doctors and patients' families, as well as comfort and companionship when people faced such anguish over the lives of their loved ones.

The chaplain's office didn't call Garon back. One of the staff came to find him, a middle-aged woman with short blond hair who reminded him of Barbara. She wore the identity tag of the chaplain's service, and her name was Nan.

"They're almost finished," she said gently. "She's doing fine."

"Thank God," Garon said heavily. His eyes were tired.

"The cardiologist will be along to see you shortly," she added. "They're discussing options. The decision will depend on what they see in the catherization. Is she taking blood thinners?"

Garon's face went white. He didn't know. This was a question that might mean life and death for his wife, and he didn't even know what medications she took. He was ashamed.

Before he had to admit that he didn't know, Coltrain came down the hall with a man dressed in surgical greens.

Garon walked to meet them, with Cash beside him. His eyes asked the question.

"What are you going to do?" he added.

"This is Dr. Franks," Coltrain introduced them. "This is Garon Grier, and his brother, Cash. Garon is Grace's husband."

"Pleased to meet you. Sorry about the circumstances," Dr. Franks said as he shook hands. His expression was solemn. "Dr. Coltrain has been giving me your wife's case history. You didn't know about her heart?"

"She refused permission," Coltrain said shortly. "I couldn't tell him."

"Protecting you, was she?" Dr. Franks asked gently.

"Yes," Garon said tautly. "I lost my first wife and child to cancer, when the baby was five months along. Grace knew."

Cash gave him a wide-eyed stare. He hadn't known that. It was indicative of the distance that had existed between the brothers.

Dr. Franks grimaced. "A kindhearted young woman. But now we must decide how best to proceed. You must realize that the child complicates things...."

"Grace comes first," Garon interrupted, dark eyes narrow with feeling. "No matter what."

Dr. Franks smiled. "I'm hoping to save them both. We must decide whether it will be more stressful to induce labor than to perform a caesaerean section," he added. "I tend to...excuse me," he said, pulling out his cell phone. He spoke into it, listened, replied and closed it. "That was Dr. Morris, our cardiologist. He's looking after your wife. She's gone into labor. Please excuse me, I'm needed."

"She comes first," Garon repeated.

"Yes," the surgeon replied.

"I'll go along and do what I can to help," Coltrain told Garon with unusual kindness. He smiled at the chaplain. "You'll stay with him?"

"Of course," Nan replied, smiling back.

Cash's cell phone rang. He excused himself and went outside the building where the reception was better.

Garon watched the surgeon and the physician walk away and his heart felt like a lead weight. Everything depended on them, now, on medical science. But if Barbara was praying, and there was a chance that prayer might help...

He turned to the chaplain. "Is there a chapel?" he asked very quietly.

She nodded. "This way."

IT FELT ODD, being in a chapel after all the long years that he'd turned away from faith. After he lost Annalee, he never expected to rely on it again. He'd prayed about Annalee. It hadn't saved her.

But he was older now, less confident in science. He'd seen so much death. Today, he'd dealt it himself. He remembered the killer talking to him, remembering a childhood that must have resembled hell. He would have killed Grace. Garon had no choice but to fire and hope his bullet didn't miss.

Now, in the silence of the chapel, he felt the twin impact of Grace's desperate situation and the reality that he'd taken a human life. Despite the situation, he had killed a man. It was a struggle to try to cope with it now. There were counselors that he could ask for through his office, and there would of course be an investigation. He hadn't spoken to the SAC, but he knew that he'd be on administrative leave while the shooting was investigated by both the county sheriff—since the ranch was out of the city limits—and the FBI. He had no doubt that it would be sanctioned. But it was a complication he couldn't handle right now. All he wanted was for Grace to live. He'd pamper her. He'd spoil her rotten. He'd make up for all the missed dinners, all the thoughtless things he'd done that had given her the idea he didn't care about her. If only he had the time. If only God would spare her!

He'd been through this with victims' families. How many times had he gone to intensive care waiting rooms to talk to survivors and heard them trying to bargain for a loved one's life?

I promise never to say anything hurtful again, if you'll just let her/him live, they would say aloud. *I'll go to church every Sunday, I'll give to the poor, I'll volunteer time, I'll do charity work, I'll cut off my arm if you'll just spare her, if you'll just spare him, if you can just let this person live!*

It was anguish to hear the promises. And now here he was, doing it himself; bargaining for Grace's life. But she was important, he prayed silently. Much more than he was. She was a nurturing woman. She was always cooking things for sick or bereaved people, sitting with people in hospital rooms, going to church, sharing herself with anyone who needed her. He wasn't like that. He was introverted when he wasn't on the job. He didn't mix well. In a way, he'd resented the fact that he had to marry Grace because of the child. He hadn't said so...or had he? But as they lived together, he'd come to rely on her bright presence, her calming spirit, her laughter in the face of problems. He could talk to Grace as he'd never been able to talk to anyone else, not even his first wife. Grace didn't argue or complain or resent his job.

Annalee hadn't liked the hours he worked, or his colleagues, and she'd hardly ever stopped complaining about his absences and the time she was missing from her job because she was pregnant. Until she became pregnant, she'd been career-minded and sacrificed any free time with Garon because she wanted to get ahead. She'd even worked Saturdays and evenings. They'd been growing apart, because he was ambitious as well. They'd both assumed they had forever to make up their time together. Then she knew she had cancer, and she was terrified. Their last months together had been agony. She'd cried and apologized for being so hateful to him. And then she'd prayed, and made promises, and tried to bargain for her life. She'd been a bad wife, but she'd change, if she could just live. She'd start going to church, she'd be a better person, she'd care more for her family than her job...

And so it went. But you couldn't bargain, he thought. Not ever. You could ask. Nothing more.

He bowed his head and spoke to God. He didn't bargain. He just prayed for what was best for Grace.

16

THE CHAPLAIN SLIPPED out of the room and when she came back, Garon was coming down the aisle toward her.

"They need you," she said gently.

He followed her down the hall, past the waiting room, to the desk. An aide was signaling frantically to the chaplain.

"Just a minute," the chaplain told him, going to confer with the aide.

Garon waited, taut as steel cable. She must live. She must live! He felt panic as he watched the chaplain's face go somber.

She came back. "She's all right," she said immediately, because he looked absolutely frightened to death. "Come on. We'll go up and talk to the surgeon."

They went into the elevator, which was already packed, and up to the surgical ward.

Coltrain and Dr. Franks were waiting for them. They both looked at Nan.

"I didn't tell him," she said softly.

"You have a son," Coltrain said in the gentlest voice Garon had ever heard him use.

"What about Grace?" he asked through his teeth.

"She's holding her own," Coltrain said. "It may even have helped us. It was a quick labor, very unusual for a first child. She came through it with very little stress beyond the usual. Now they're prepping her for surgery."

"She's given us permission to operate," Dr. Franks said. "But I'd like yours as well."

"Of course," Garon said at once. "May I see her?"

"Just for a minute," Dr. Franks said. "Dr. Coltrain will take you back."

"Do your best," Garon asked the surgeon. His eyes said more than words.

Dr. Franks put a firm hand on his shoulder. "I don't lose patients," he said with a smile. "She's going to come through it. Have faith."

Garon nodded. He followed Coltrain and Nan back through the ward to the room where Grace had been given her pre op medication. She was very drowsy, but she saw Garon and her eyes brightened.

"Grace," he choked, bending to kiss her eyelids. "Oh God, Grace! Why didn't you tell me, baby?"

"I couldn't do that...to you," she whispered. Tears were pouring down her cheeks. "You were so excited about the baby. You wanted him so much. We have a little boy, did they tell you?"

"Yes," he managed to say. He was fighting the wetness in his own eyes and losing.

"Come here," she whispered, drawing his face down to hers. He came without a protest, drowning in the comfort she gave him. He felt ashamed. He should be comforting her…

She kissed his eyelids slowly, tasting the wet salty moisture on her lips. He shuddered at the tenderness, and she felt it. He was devastated. Poor, poor man, to have to go through such anguish with two pregnancies. But she didn't want to die. She was going to fight. What he was feeling, and showing, was far too deep for pity. It hurt her to see him so shattered, when his strength had carried her so far from danger. "It's all right, Garon. Everything will be all right. I promise." But she hesitated, because she was taking a step into the unknown. She was getting sleepy. "Take care of our baby, if…"

"Don't," he ground out in anguish.

"Tory," she whispered drowsily. "I want to call him Tory, for my grandfather. And his middle name should be Garon, for you. All right?"

"You can have whatever you want," he said stiffly. "Only don't…leave me, Grace. Don't leave me alone in the world." His voice was husky with feeling.

She felt beautiful. He did feel something for her. Something powerful, like what she felt for him. Her fingertips traced his mouth. She loved him so much. More than he knew. "You gave me more happiness than I've ever had," she whispered. "You saved my life. I love you."

"Grace…!"

She'd taken a quick breath and she seemed to be straining to get the next.

"We have to go," Coltrain said. "You can tell her later."

But Garon was frozen at her side, terrified, hurting, terrified that this might be the last time he saw her alive. He didn't want to leave her. "Don't you die, Grace," Garon choked as he stared down at her through a misty haze. "Don't you dare!" He took a harsh breath. "I'm not going back and telling those damned rosebushes that you aren't coming home!"

Amazingly she laughed.

The sound was like a chorus of angels to Garon. He bent and kissed her dry lips one last time. "Don't leave me," he whispered into her ear. "I can't live if you don't."

Tears stung her eyes. "My darling," she whispered as her eyes closed. The medicine was working.

"Come on." Coltrain half dragged him out of the room. Grace was already going to sleep. Garon got one last glimpse of her, blond hair curving around her shoulders, around her pale face as her gray eyes closed. Please God, he thought in panic, don't let them be closed forever! Whatever I've done, punish me, but don't take her away! Please don't!

"She's come halfway," Coltrain told him, sensing the panic in the usually rigidly controlled features. "Don't give up on her yet. Let's go down and get a cup of coffee."

COLTRAIN TOOK HIM downstairs and bought him black coffee. The man was steel right through, Garon thought as they shared a table in the commissary.

"I must have been a despot in a former life," Garon muttered, "to be condemned to go through this hell twice in one lifetime."

Coltrain understood the reference. He remembered that Garon had lost his first wife while she was pregnant.

"Grace may have a bad heart," Coltrain told him. "But she's got as tough a spirit as any human being I've ever known. She survived an ordeal that most children wouldn't have. She's a scrapper. Don't give up on her."

"I wouldn't dare," Garon replied heavily.

"Would you like to see your son?" Coltrain asked.

The child he'd wanted for so long. His child. But he shook his head. "Not yet," he said. "Not until…we know something."

"All right."

Cash had been missing for an hour. He came into the commissary, looking weary. "We had an emergency back home. I had to make half a hundred phone calls to sort it out. A bank robbery. Can you imagine? In Jacobsville. They got the guys, but I had to be available. How's Grace?"

"In surgery," Garon replied.

"He has a son," Coltrain added.

Cash glanced at his brother, who was morose. "I'm an uncle? Wow!"

Garon sipped coffee. His whole look was one of exhaustion.

"Come on," Cash said. "I want to see if your son looks like you."

Garon gave him a depressed glance. "I hope not, poor little kid."

"They'll have him ready about now," Coltrain remarked. "Well?"

Garon went with them, reluctantly. He wasn't sure it was right for him to be enthusing over a child while Grace was fighting for her life. But he knew he'd go crazy if he had to sit here thinking about it. At least, the child would be a diversion.

But when he was looking through the window at the little boy, his mindset changed. His whole attitude changed. He stood staring at the tiny thing in the blue blanket with eyes that hardly focused.

"He's so tiny," he exclaimed. "I could put him in my pocket!"

"Want to hold him?" Coltrain asked, seeing a way to erase the terror from his eyes.

Garon looked at him, surprised. "Would they let me?"

Coltrain smiled. "Come on."

THEY PUT A HOSPITAL gown on him, sat him in a rocking chair, and handed him the tiny little boy, wrapped in his blanket. A nurse showed him how to support the baby's head and back.

Garon looked down at his child with a mixture of awe and fear. He was so small. All his reading hadn't prepared him for the impact of fatherhood. He counted little fingers and toes, smoothed his hand over the baby's tiny bald head. He saw Grace in the shape of the child's eyes, and himself in the chin. His eyes grew misty as he thought of the days and weeks and months and years ahead. Please God, he thought, don't let me have to raise him alone.

The baby moved. One tiny hand grasped Garon's thumb and held on. The baby's eyes didn't open. He was curious about that, and asked. The nurse, beaming, told him that it took about three days for the baby to open his eyes and look around him. But he still wouldn't be able to see much yet. Garon didn't care. He looked down at his son with an expression that no artist in the world could have captured.

Watching through the window, Coltrain and Cash smiled indulgently at the sight.

"What a picture," Coltrain said with a grin.

"Picture!" Cash took out his cell phone, turned it, looked through the eye and snapped several pictures of Garon holding the baby. "Something to show Grace," he told Coltrain, "when she comes out of recovery."

Coltrain nodded. He hoped that prediction was correct. He knew far more than he was going to tell Garon or his brother. That could wait until there was no longer any choice about it.

FOUR HOURS LATER, Dr. Franks went looking for Garon. He looked very tired.

"She's holding her own," he told Garon. "We'll know within eight hours."

"Know?" Garon moved closer. "Know what?"

The doctor drew in a long breath. Coltrain grimaced. Dr. Franks looked at Garon and said gently, "In eight hours, either she'll wake up—or she won't."

It was the most terrifying thing anyone had ever said to him. He knew he must look like the walking dead as he gaped at the surgeon.

Coltrain laid a heavy hand on his shoulder. "Don't give up now," he said.

"I'll go mad," Garon said huskily. "Eight hours...!"

"We're going to go to the motel. I booked a room," Cash began.

"Leave the hospital, now? Are you out of your mind?" Garon raged.

"Only for a few minutes," Cash promised, exchanging a covert glance with the two doctors over Garon's shoulder. "Come on. Trust me."

"You'll call me, if there's any change?" Garon asked Coltrain unsteadily.

"I promise," the redheaded doctor agreed.

"I got you a room, too," Cash told Coltrain. He handed him a key. "Don't argue. I have friends you don't want to have to meet."

Coltrain chuckled. "Okay, then. Thanks. I'll take advantage of it, in a few hours."

"We'll be right back," Garon promised.

Cash didn't say a word.

AN HOUR LATER, Garon was passed out on the sofa in the suite Cash had registered them into. It wasn't quite fair, he knew, but his brother seemed to be on the verge of a coronary. Cash had filled him full of scotch whiskey and soda. Since Garon hardly ever took a drink, the combination of worry, exhaustion and alcohol had hit him hard. He went out like a light.

Cash wondered at the depth of the man's feelings for his young wife. He hadn't spoken a great deal about Grace in the past few months. They'd both come to the house for dinner a few times, and Tippy and Grace had become fast friends. Grace loved to hold their baby, little Tristina, whom they called "Tris," and cuddle her. Garon had watched his wife with the little girl, and an expression of pure delight had radiated his normally taciturn features. Garon didn't speak about Grace very much, but when he did, it was with pride. Perhaps he hadn't known his own feelings until this tragedy unfolded. It was impossible not to know them now.

Six hours later, Garon awoke. He blinked, looking around the room. It was a hotel room. Why was he here? There was his brother, Cash, on the phone. He didn't remember....

He sat straight up on the couch, horrified. "What time is it? Have you called the hospital? Grace...What about Grace?" he exclaimed.

Cash held up a hand, nodded, and said, "We'll be right there." He hung up, smiling. "Grace is out from under the anesthesia. She's awake."

"Awake." Garon shuddered. "She's alive!"

"Yes. She isn't responsive yet; she's still pretty much under the anesthesia. But the doctors are cautiously optimistic. The new valve is working perfectly."

Garon got to his feet and held his head. "Damn! What did you ladle into me?"

"Scotch whiskey, soda and a substance I'm not allowed to own or explain because it's classified." He grinned.

Garon couldn't help a chuckle. His brother really was a devil. But he'd become a good friend, as well. He paused by Cash and clapped him on the shoulder with rough affection. "If you ever get in trouble and need anybody arrested, you can call me."

"I'll remember that. Let's go."

GARON WAS ALLOWED in to see Grace, but only for a couple of minutes. She was white as a sheet, but her breathing was steadier and the blip on the monitor was fairly regular. He brushed back her hair, loving the softness of it, the quiet beauty of her face.

As if she sensed his presence, her gray eyes opened and she looked at him, a little blankly.

"You're going to be all right," he said softly. "Very soon, I'm going to take you home."

Her lips tugged into a faint smile before she closed her eyes and went back to sleep. Garon touched his finger to her dry lips, loving just the sight of her.

He went back out into the waiting room feeling more optimistic. The fear was still there, but he'd deal with it. He stopped when he saw six men surrounding Cash. They were colleagues from the San Antonio office, all except one—who was the former leader of their Hostage Rescue Unit. His heart felt lighter as they came to greet him, asking about Grace and offering help. He had to choke back overflowing emotion. He really did work with the best group in the world.

GRACE IMPROVED DAILY. They had her up and walking the day after surgery. It horrified Garon, but they insisted that this was what had to be done in order for her to recuperate and, more importantly, not develop a respiratory infection to go with the side effects of the surgery.

Garon walked her down to the nursery with painful slowness. He pushed the pole where her IVs hung. She held on to his arm and felt lighter than air, despite her ordeal.

They stopped at the nursery and the nurse held up little Tory for them to see. Garon didn't know it, but Cash had snapped several photos of him holding the little boy and shown them to Grace. If she had any doubts about his feelings for his son, the photos erased them. Grace was fascinated by his love for the child.

"He looks like you," Grace whispered, in tears as she saw her child for the first time. "He's beautiful."

"Like his mama," he whispered, and bent to brush his mouth over her dry lips with breathless tenderness. "Thank you for risking so much to bring our son into the world."

"You gave him to me," she replied, her eyes full of softness.

He kissed her hair. "I've given you a hard time, Grace. I'm glad I'll have the opportunity to make it up to you."

She gave him a wry look. "Penance, is it?"

He smiled. "In spades."

"That sounds interesting."

He nibbled her lower lip. "When you're back to yourself, in about two months or so, we'll explore some sensual pathways together."

His wicked tone amused her and she giggled like a girl. "You stop that," she told him firmly. "Right now it's all I can do to walk. They did split me right down the middle, you know, and I'm going to have even more scars now than I did to start with."

He grinned. "I like your scars. They're sexy."

Her eyebrows arched. "Well!"

"We've got the whole world, Grace," he added, glancing back into the window of the nursery, where their child lay sleeping. "The whole wide world."

She smiled. "Yes." And she slid her hand trustingly into his.

THEIR FIRST CHRISTMAS together was the most wondrous of Grace's entire life. Garon went out and got a tree, brought it home and had several of the wives of his ranch hands decorate it for him. The result was a delightful triangle of color and light. The baby could focus now, and he seemed to find the lights fascinating. He lay in Grace's arms, making baby sounds that fascinated both his parents.

"It's just beautiful," Grace remarked, smiling up at him. "It's the nicest tree I've ever had."

He nodded, eyeing it. "My dad wasn't keen on celebrations, but our stepmother liked to decorate them. I never took to her. After dad found her out and divorced her, our housekeeper started making Christmas special for us. I've always loved Christmas trees."

"Me, too," Grace replied. "I had to fight Granny to put one up every year, but I got my way."

They were watching television together. Garon had been hard at work, trying to nab a new drug smuggler who'd set up shop locally. He'd formed a task force, and Marquez was on this one, too. The two men had settled their differences and seemed to be getting along well. Rick came by to see the baby from time to time, but he always brought Barbara. He didn't want to alienate Garon, apparently.

The news contained a feature about a new line of dolls that had broken sales records everywhere, and Grace watched it raptly. It was about a new line of handmade cloth dolls, called "The Mouse Family." There were male and female mice, and baby mice. There was a line of clothing for them, and even a candy named after them. They were selling like hotcakes. Every child seemed to want one for Christmas. They'd sold out everywhere. Grace grinned as she watched the screen.

At the end, they mentioned that the dolls were the creation of a hometown Texas girl, Mrs. Grace Grier, of Jacobsville, Texas.

Garon had almost passed out when he finally found out what her secret project actually was. She'd sold the rights to the mouse dolls even before they married, and she'd done prototypes of all the outfits that would go with them. Nobody had expected them to sell this fast. Well, the agent for the department store that Grace had written to, enclosing a sample mouse doll, had expected it. He had great faith in Grace's sewing ability, and the dolls were really cute. He'd spent weeks lobbying for presentations, and he'd managed to convince the toy buyers for a huge department chain that they would be the newest fad and make a fortune. He'd been right. Grace was going to be very rich.

"I thought I knew you, when we married," Garon remarked with a chuckle. "I didn't have a clue what you were really like."

"I told you I wasn't domestic," she pointed out.

"That's why we have Miss Turner, baby," he said softly, smiling down at her. "You just go right ahead and make dolls."

"I only make the prototypes," she reminded him. "They have a whole department of workers making the dolls. It's getting harder, too, because they really are selling out everywhere."

"Which reminds me. Carlson would love it if you'd make a white mouse for his daughter's birthday. A special one, with big blue eyes."

She grinned. "He can certainly have one. You'll have to take care of Tory while I'm working on it."

He grinned back. "That isn't a chore."

"You've turned into a very good father," she pointed out.

"I'm not, yet. But I'm working on it."

"I have something for you, by the way, after I put Tory to sleep for the night."

"For me?" he asked, puzzled.

"Don't bother guessing. I'm not saying. Not yet, anyway."

"Does it have anything to do with roses?"

She pursed her lips. "Not quite. Help me up, would you?"

He eased her up from the sofa, with Tory in her arms. Her chest incision had healed, but it was still just a little sore. It had been impossible for her to breast feed the baby, which was a disappointment. But it also meant that Garon got to give the baby his bottle, and he loved it. She was over six weeks past her surgery and improving daily.

"I'll be back soon," she told Garon.

ACTUALLY SHE WASN'T. He got involved in a movie while Miss Turner closed up the kitchen and went to a gospel singing with Barbara. The house was quiet.

Just as grenades started blowing things up on screen, a shadow fell over the television. He looked to one side and his eyes bulged. There was Grace, her long blond hair almost to her waist now, her slender body encased in a pink satin gown that was held up by tiny spaghetti straps. She looked young and very sexy.

"What are you up to, Mrs. Grier?" he asked. She was raising his blood pressure, and the doctor hadn't said anything about letting her resume intimate activities.

She grinned. "You said you thought my scars were sexy, didn't you?"

He nodded. His heart was racing at the sight of her, because those straps let the gown sink almost to her nipples in front. She had beautiful breasts...

"If you really think the scars are sexy," she said in a husky tone, "why don't you come to bed with me, and prove it?"

HE HADN'T REALIZED he was capable of carrying a woman down the hall and putting her in bed in such a short space of seconds.

"You're sure it's all right?" he asked, but he was already stripping off the pretty gown, to reveal a body that made every muscle in him go taut.

"It's all right," she assured him.

He was out of his own clothing in a flash, and beside her on the clean white sheets. He threw the comforter off the side without even looking at where it landed. "Your chest must still be sore."

"It is," she agreed, loving the feel of his mouth on her own, on her shoulders and then, on the soft rise of her breasts. She moaned. "Be inventive," she whispered.

He eased her onto her side. His mouth found hers. His hands slid

up and down the soft skin of her hips and thighs while his lips played havoc with her senses.

It was like the first time. He didn't hurry, despite the need that made him shiver every time his skin brushed against hers. He seduced her, in the most tender way he knew, and brought her slowly to such a pitch of desire that she pushed against him with anguish.

"Easy, sweetheart," he whispered as he moved her up just enough to accommodate the slow, vibrant thrust of his body. "Yes. That's it."

They were lying side by side. She moaned, wishing that she could feel his weight.

"I want that, too, Grace," he whispered into her mouth, "but it's too soon. I don't want to hurt you."

"It isn't hurting," she whispered back. Her eyes closed as he pulled her hips roughly against his and began to fill her in a slow, deep rhythm that echoed their rapid heartbeats.

She pushed closer into her husband's arms and pleaded with him to ravish her.

She thought she heard a husky chuckle, but the spiral was already beginning. It took them both higher and higher, into a vivid red heat that stopped breath, sight, hearing, everything except the feverish union of their bodies. Seconds later, she cried out in delight and arched against him with her last bit of strength. She felt him shudder, heard him whisper her name over and over again as he, too, found completion.

A long time later, he propped himself on an elbow and looked down at Grace, who was sprawled on her back. She gave him a breathless grin.

"Now tell me you only married me because I got pregnant," she dared him, chuckling.

"Okay, you win, I married you for great sex," he agreed.

"And?" she prompted.

"And your apple cake," he added. "And to learn how you grow roses twice as big as mine. So why did you marry me?"

She tweaked his hair and smiled up into his dark, dark eyes. "I married you because I loved you," she said softly, "because you were the only man I was ever able to want."

"Thank God for that," he whispered. He kissed the tip of her nose. "I gave you a difficult time."

She put her finger over his lips. "We're happily married with a new baby," she reminded him. "All that other stuff is gone."

He sighed. "At least you won't ever have to worry about Sheldon again."

She nodded. There was a sickening feeling in the pit of her stomach, just at hearing his name. "That therapist I'm seeing is really good. She's helping me cope with the memories."

He smiled. "If today is an example, she's really helping you a lot."

Her eyes twinkled mischievously. "It wasn't that."

His eyebrows arched. "Then what was it?"

"You had your shirt off while you were watching TV," she replied, her eyes on his broad chest. "You shameless man. I really can't resist you when you're half naked."

"I feel exactly the same way about you," he agreed, and kissed her again.

She glanced at the baby monitor. Its light was on, but she only heard soft breathing. "I'm glad we got that," she pointed to it. "Otherwise, I'd never sleep."

"Neither would I." He brushed back her hair. "Are you happy?"

She smiled. "I could die of it."

He kissed her eyelids tenderly, remembering how he'd done that just before they wheeled her into surgery. "When Tory is old enough to go to school, I want you to come to work for me."

"Doing what?"

"As a translator," he said. "You might not realize it, but Arabic is one language not a lot of agents can speak. You'd be an asset."

She pursed her lips and grinned at him. "I might do that."

He rolled over onto his back and yawned. "I have to go to court tomorrow and testify against those bank robbers we caught. I'll probably be home late."

She kissed his shoulder. "I'll make a late supper."

He smiled, sliding his arm around her. "You're the nicest wife on earth. It's no wonder I love you."

Her heart skipped. It was the first time he'd said the words. "Do you, really?"

His dark eyes emphasized the feeling in the words. "With all my heart. For all my life. And I hope we have a very long time together."

She curled up against him, enveloped in happiness. All the lonely, painful years had led her down a path that ended in love and passion and a child born of that love. We earn our happiness, her grandfather had once told her, with pain and tears. She smiled drowsily, ignoring the faint twinge of her incision, and pressed a soft kiss against her husband's strong, warm shoulder.

"We're going to have years and years," she promised. "And I'll love you more with every one that passes."

He drew her closer, careful not to hurt her chest. "I'll love you the same way."

"And we can both talk to the rose bushes," she mused.

"As long as nobody hears us," he agreed. "I work for the FBI," he reminded her. "I can't be overheard talking to plants."

She kissed his shoulder again, still wrapped in the warm aftermath of belonging. "And they say that federal agents have no sense of humor," she scoffed.

He gave her a squinty look. "Listen, this businesslike expression is the reason I just got promoted to ASAC in San Antonio. Now I can give orders and go to luncheons with famous politicians. I'll even take you with me, if you promise not to wear that blue dress."

The dress was a standing joke. She'd hung it in her closet. She brought it out when she wanted to irritate him. That wasn't often, since her surgery. He'd been the most wonderful caretaker she'd ever imagined a man could be.

"I'll promise," she agreed.

"Did Barbara tell you that Jaqui left town?" he murmured.

"She did? How wonderful!"

"Stop that," he said drowsily. "She was never any competition for you. She'll go to some big city and become a tycoon."

"Like me?" she teased.

He glanced at her. "You can only be a tycoon if you don't have to travel ten months out of the year promoting your project. I don't even like having you away for a day. I have insecurities. You have to reassure me that I'm valued."

"I do?" She moved up a little and nibbled his mouth again. "How's this?"

He grinned. "Nice. Don't stop."

She kissed him again, with more fervor. "Better?"

His arms reached out for her. "Addictive," he whispered. "I want years and years of this."

She smiled against his hard mouth, tangling her fingers in his thick hair. "Me, too."

There was a sudden wail from the monitor.

THEY BOTH GOT UP at the same time, moving hastily into the next room, where their son was screaming. His tiny face was red as fire.

Garon took a whiff and swallowed hard.

Grace pursed her lips. She recognized that smell, too.

"We could draw straws," Garon suggested.

She punched him in the ribs. "Somebody who can lift him has to do this, and I can't yet."

He still hesitated.

"Listen, tough guy, you were a hostage rescuer. You were even on the SWAT team...."

"It's in the rule book that FBI agents do not have to change diapers," he informed her haughtily. "Paragraph 211, section three, page 221."

"There's no such rule," she scoffed.

"Yes, there is. I'll go right now and look it up, while you change him. You don't have to lift him," he added hopefully. "It's a very high bed."

He sounded very desperate. She had to force herself not to burst out laughing. He'd never told her himself, but she knew from Miss Turner that when he was faced with his first really dirty diaper, during her recuperation, he threw up before he could change it.

He handed her the wipes and a new disposable diaper, and his eyes spoke volumes.

She gave him a wry look.

He shrugged. "You wipe, I'll tape?"

She did laugh then. Shaking her head, she did her half of the dirty work and left him to put the fresh diaper in place.

He lifted the tiny boy to his bare chest and held him there, kissing the top of his small, soft little head.

She watched him, her eyes brimming with quick tears, at the picture it made.

He glanced down and saw the look. "What?" he asked.

She leaned against him, her fingers tracing the baby's soft cheek. "I was just counting my blessings," she said huskily. "It's impossible. I have too many."

He bent and kissed her forehead with breathless tenderness. "As many as grains of sand in the ocean," he said huskily, with profound feeling, his dark eyes glittery with it. "I'll cherish you all my life. All the way down into the dark. And the last picture I have in my mind will be your face, smiling at me."

Tears rained down her cheeks. "I love you."

"I love you, too," he whispered tenderly, kissing away her tears as the baby went to sleep in his arms. "I'll never stop!"

And he never did.

the same